TUMBLEWEED TUMBLINGS

ALSO BY MARK GREATHOUSE

The Frontier Chronicles

Perilous Trails

Wyoming Calls

Longhorns North

Warpath

Hunter Vs. Hunted

Freedom Drovers

A Poison Spreads

Darkness Looms

The Tumbleweed Sagas

Nueces Justice

Nueces Reprise

Nueces Deceit

Nueces Blood

Nueces Grit

Nueces Truth

Nueces Legend

The Tumbleweed Sagas: Junior's Story

Lone Star Vigilante

Guns on the Guadalupe

TUMBLEWEED TUMBLINGS

WESTERN TALES & VERSES

MARK GREATHOUSE

WOLFPACK PUBLISHING
— EST 2013 —

Tumbleweed Tumblings: Western Tales & Verses
Paperback Edition
Copyright © 2025 (As Revised) by Mark Greathouse

Wolfpack Publishing
1707 E. Diana Street
Tampa, Florida 33610

www.wolfpackpublishing.com

Paperback ISBN 979-8-89567-228-0
Ebook ISBN 979-8-89567-227-3

Dedicated with love to my wife, Carolyn, and to our two sons, Mike and Matt.

CONTENTS

Preface   ix

Second Chances   1
Requiem for a Texas Ranger   24
The Kin of Kildare   26
Homestead Woman   28
Bert the Buckin' Bull   44
Mindin' the Herd   46
Penateka Spirit Wolf   47
Noble Savages   66
Comanche Raid   68
A Bawdy Lady   70
Heart and Soul Are One in Texas   90
Texas on My Mind, Texas in My Blood   91
Discriminating Treachery   93
It's in Our Bones   114
Gold on the Guadalupe   116
White Slaver   118
Texas Deep Within My Soul   135
True Texans   137
Redeemed   140
The Cowboy's Possibles Bag   155
Wanna Be a Texan?   157
Hidden Revenge   159
Nicholas Dunn: A Requiem   176
Prairie Dog   179
Frontier Justice   201
Dead Men Tell No Tales   203

A Look at Nueces Justice: Life, Love, and Law on the Strip   205
Acknowledgments   207
About the Author   209

PREFACE

There's a bit of semi-rational logic here as I invite you, the reader, on this journey along the trail blazed by *Tumbleweed Tumblings: Western Tales and Verses*. The short stories and poems are embellishments, backstories, or expansions of characters from my novels and biographies. As you've read my Tumbleweed Sagas, have you wondered at the stories behind the likes of the Comanche chief Three Toes or the evil Horatio Thorpe? The stories and poems within have been written over the past half dozen years. Some of the work herein has appeared with my permission in other publications, and I've noted those. With this housekeeping out of the way, please permit me to share my purpose in writing this anthology.

I'm a fifth-generation Texan by virtue of my father having been born in Alice, Texas, a railroad town a bit west of Corpus Christi that was named after the famous rancher Richard King's daughter, Alice Kleberg. I've been blessed with literally thousands of nephews, nieces, and cousins throughout Texas thanks to five brothers emigrating from County Kildare, Ireland, between 1845 and 1867. Significant? A trio of Texas historical markers around Corpus Christi are dedicated to John Dunn—my great-great-great-grandfather, Matthew Dunn, and Patrick Dunn for their contributions to the settling of the Texas frontier. Humbly, I've only met close to four dozen descendants of those adventurous Irish brothers, and the ancestral tree is likely missing many recent names. I do try from the depths of my soul to reflect my western heritage in my writings, especially my poetry. I'm unable to recite some of the poetry in this collection without my heartfelt emotions creeping in. You know what I mean.

This anthology is mostly about Texas, but especially the greater West and the values that underlie America. It is like much of my authoring in that I strive to capture the essence of the freedoms, of the opportunities, of the second chances associated specifically with the American West and the hopes and dreams of those that tamed it. I'm always struck by the remorse of my ancestral cousin Patrick Dunn after having sold his ranch that covered most of North Padre Island in the early 1900s. Notably, to the end of his days, Patrick regretted selling the island. He equated the island to a sense of freedom not to be found on the mainland, much less anywhere else on Earth. I think Patrick really captured the essence of life in the Old West. It was about freedom.

Join me in pondering that essence of freedom and the conquest of the frontier. Perhaps you will be as affected as me by the words of my poet and novelist cousin, Mary Maude Dunn Wright—pseud. Lilith Lorraine, as she posed the following question in writing the preface to her father's biography—*Perilous Trails of Texas*—back in 1932: "Not in the spirit of judging their actions by artificial standards which in their day had no existence, but by asking ourselves if we were in their places, should we have acquitted ourselves as well, and by putting to ourselves the still more potent question: how well have we kept the birthright that they have given us, how well have we safeguarded the liberties that they purchased through untold privations, how courageously are we meeting the problems that confront us today. In short, when we stand before the tribunal of remote posterity, to whom shall the laurel be awarded?" Y'all might think on that.

TUMBLEWEED TUMBLINGS

SECOND CHANCES
LUKE DUNN'S JUSTICE DELIVERED

*Luke Dunn is the protagonist throughout the Tumbleweed Sagas, deliv-
ering justice and redemption across the vast prairies of the Nueces Strip as
a Texas Ranger of ever-greater repute. Dunn's character is set in the very
era that drew the hardy Irish immigrants of the author's own family that
settled South Texas in the mid-1800s.*

THE LASH CAME DOWN a second time...a third...would it
never cease? The fifteenth lash struck. The redcoat had long since
broken into a heavy sweat as beads formed along the angry creases
of his forehead and the bulging muscles of his arms. The sound?
The sound was ugly. Still, O'Connell refused to cry out. His chains
stopped rattling. The dull sound of whip cutting into bare flesh
seemed never to end.

The sergeant finally stepped up. "Enough, Will. We don't want
to kill the poor bastard...at least not yet." His evil grimace revealed
a near-toothless cavern of a mouth. "Put him in the gaol. Lock it
good. God rest his soul if he doesn't talk by morning." The redcoat
looked over at the grisly form of a body lying but a couple of yards
from the whipping post. He sneered, turning back to the bloodied
post. He wiped his nose as though to swipe away the stench of
death.

It had been but a day earlier that the local clansmen had made an
unusually successful foray against the British post near Naas in

1

County Kildare. Ah, what an incredible melee it had been. Caught the redcoats napping, they had! Irish claymores bashed heads and sliced redcoat flesh and bone. Lucas Dunn had been a dervish among those redcoats initially able to put up a defense. In his battle-driven madness, he even relieved three crimson-clad dragoons of their horses as his blood-smeared claymore did what his anger-crazed mind ordered it to do. He'd begun the day with an old flint-lock musket, but the thing soon broke in two over a redcoat's back. Through the fury of it all, two clansmen, Donnegan and O'Connell, had managed to get captured. Dunn could do naught at the time but watch them be dragged away.

Hiding behind the tree gave him time to think…too much time. The claymore in battle was like a knife; it was personal. He recalled the first time he'd struck with the claymore and felt it cut through muscle and bone. Some tried to pass it off as no different than skinning a deer, but no. The violence made it ever so distinct from cutting hide from game. The violence factor…the human factor. These were men—men with souls. It would be an act he'd never truly get used to.

Dunn had been watching for several hours now from behind the trunk of a gnarly old oak tree a couple of hundred yards from the torture. How long might he yet have to wait? A lingering mist, a couple of alders, another oak, and a hedgerow served to further shield him from direct line of sight. He was close enough to hear whether Sinead O'Connell gave away the clan's hiding place. Red Donnegan had already succumbed to the lash, as death ensured he'd keep his silence…bless his Irish soul.

Dunn was still a bit out of breath from his pursuit of O'Connell and his captors. The Irishman squatted low and peered out cautiously as he fingered the Rosary in his tunic and murmured a bit of a prayer. He had never figured himself a man of faith, but the rebellions were making him second-guess the beliefs he'd grown up with. The British called the Irish Catholics *Black Catholics*, mostly owing to what was considered a corruption of the religion by Saint Patrick in his zeal to make converts. Dunn shifted his position, sensitive to the lingering pain of the musket ball burn across the side of his left knee. The luckless shooter had aimed low and wide, and there had been no time for him to reload before tasting the Irishman's knife. Dunn's cloak and sash bearing the pattern of his clan covered his sweaty and bloodied white *léine*. He felt a heavy, damp chill despite the woolen kilt. His knife and claymore, nevertheless, lay at the ready. If the prisoners gave the hideout away, the rebels would be hard-pressed to make their escape to the coast safely. Even then, the roiling waves of the Irish Sea could play havoc with any small boat trying a crossing.

The British had considerable numerical and weapons advantages, ones that Dunn's fellow clansmen were quite conscious of. The element of surprise earlier that day had quickly disappeared as the Englishmen rallied, grabbing swords and muskets and not even bothering to don their claret red coats, powdered wigs, and black boots.

Dunn, a strapping red-haired young lad of some twenty years and tall as Irish men went, had rightly assessed the situation and signaled the retreat. A dozen of the hated redcoats lay dead or dying. While it had been a great day for the Irish clansmen, this battle was far from over.

He was about to resolve himself to spending the night at this soggy, godforsaken oak tree post observing for signs of O'Connell cracking under the whip when he heard and then saw the redcoats gathering to form a company to pursue him and his fellow rebels. O'Connell must have finally been broken. The British would pursue at a quick march to the clan encampment. There were at least 150 well-equipped soldiers, by his estimate, and no quarter would be given. Burned into the Irish memory and lore were the massacres by the redcoats at Ballinamuck, Killala, Enniscorthy, and more. Little wonder Dunn had heard that the colonists in America called the red-coated British soldiers *bloody-backs*. The images already haunted his dreams on the nights he had a chance to sleep.

Hunkered low at first, Dunn broke into a full run as he headed to the east to warn his fellow insurgents. Brambles tore at his flesh as he plowed onward through streams, bogs, and thickets. He had but three miles to cover, yet reaching the sheltering forest near Heathfield seemed to take forever. Lingering in the inner recesses of his mind were warnings from his cousin Lawrence Dunn back in Killeigh that, with Lucas's strong sense of right and wrong and hot temper, he was not destined for a long life in Ireland under the

3

British. The atrocities committed by the British overlords, the bodies of his countrymen often found lying dead from starvation and disease along roadsides, and the weighty struggles to simply exist melded together to turn Dunn into one of the rebels most feared by the redcoats. A high price had been set on his head, and it was his head and only his that the Crown truly wanted. Capturing and hanging him would be hugely symbolic in quelling future rebellions.

With tartan flying, he burst through the pickets that had been set to warn of redcoat patrols. "Fly! We must fly!"

A burly rebel clansman suddenly blocked his path. "Stay, lad. We fight here. Got the high ground!"

Dunn looked about. Naught but a handful of Dunns, O'Byrnes, O'Connors, and O'Tooles remained. 'Twas a fearsome but nevertheless bedraggled-looking lot; loyal to the death but outnumbered three-to-one, barely half equipped with mostly unreliable muskets. The British close-ordered lines would chew the clansmen to pieces with musket and then bayonet. The ones struck down in the first wave would be pursued by the mounted dragoons upon retreat, captured, and tortured to death. "No, Patrick. 'Tis certain death! We must flee!" He flew past the clansman.

The rebel paused, hung his head in momentary dismay, and followed Dunn. They ran in different directions. No sense making pursuit easy. Luke decided to head eastward to Wicklow, thence over the Irish Sea to Liverpool, and escape…to America, as his cousin had suggested. Lives such as they'd come to know would be left behind to seek a new beginning—a second chance. The handful that might make it would be free of the British oppression, the famine, the squalor that had become life in Ireland. They rationalized it as living to fight another day.

After three days on the run, they arrived near Wicklow. Hunkering low, they snuck along the shore to where a boat had been hidden. Someone had called it a boat, but it was barely a dinghy. The tiny rowboat with its single pair of oars looked as though the first wave of any size would swamp it into the oblivion of the Irish Sea. Lucas

Dunn kneeled and offered a prayer with his two companions—the only ones left from their flight, the only ones that had thus far survived redcoat patrols, turncoat countrymen, wounds, and miserable weather. Patrick O'Toole and John O'Byrne appeared as death warmed over. O'Toole's saber wound had festered badly, and it was a miracle that he yet survived. Dunn doubted the two rebels would endure the two hundred-mile journey across the storm-roughened sea and danger-laden landfall. In truth, he was barely confident in his own success.

O'Toole finally succumbed to his wound midway across. They tossed him overboard with but fleeting ceremony. O'Byrne made it to landfall but got separated from Dunn and fell victim to a patrol of British dragoons. Upon doubling back to find his countryman, Dunn came across O'Byrne's spear-riddled body. He'd apparently put up a fight to the end. He sighed at the pity of the loss, furtively glanced around, lest the enemy be lingering about, and continued to run for his life, saddened and conflicted that he could offer naught but a brief blessing over O'Byrne's corpse.

Liverpool was abuzz with all manner of legal and illicit—but mostly illicit—activity. The docks were filled with the multimasted ships of myriad merchant seamen. Dunn's challenge would be to find one that was headed to America and upon which he could stow away. To his way of thinking, opportunity lay across the ocean. His challenge for passage was made greater, however, because he sought a ship headed to New Orleans. He'd heard stories from his cousins back in Kildare of their kinfolk finding great opportunity in a place called Texas. He was reluctantly finished with the heathers and forests of County Kildare. He sought a new life, a second chance, a place where justice and redemption would be more than the words on some meaningless document from a contemptuously uncaring monarch. Dunn sought a life of meaning, a life of purpose.

The ship, if it could truly be called such, seemed barely seaworthy. Dunn had found himself befriended by a crew member in the dank inner sanctum of a Liverpool pub. Slightly drunk, yet inclined toward sympathy for the tall Irish lad's plight, he'd pressed Dunn to help him stagger back to the boat and managed to hide him among some barrels in the hold. The hold was damp, cold and damp, with a musty odor punctuated by rum, urine, and vomit.

It served as a blessing that the craft departed the next day between rain squalls. The rocking and rolling of the ship had its effect on the lad soon enough, as he lost any nourishment still in his stomach. In desperation, he made his way to the deck where he espied Gruber, the crew member he'd helped the night before. Peeking his head out of the hatch, he caught Gruber's eye. The sailor, in turn, frantically motioned for the lad to keep down. Too late.

"What's this we have here?" boomed the first mate.

Dunn ducked lower.

The first mate swaggered over to the hatch, his hand cradling the hilt of his sword. "Who?" He peered down the hatch. "Get him up here!" he commanded.

Three sets of hands dragged the kicking and squirming stowaway to the deck. "How'd you get onboard, boy?"

Dunn glanced furtively at Gruber.

The first mate laughed. "Dammit, Gruber! You were out recruiting again!" He laughed even more heartily and turned to Dunn. "You're lucky, boy. There's but a couple of ships that wouldn't throw you to the sea monsters." He stood with hands on hips. "My name is John, and you're now a crewman on the *Western Star*. You look to be a strong one, a strapping lad. Do you have a name?"

"Dunn...Lucas Dunn."

"Ah, Irish, from your voice. And a tall one...we'll call you Long Luke." He laughed again. "Gruber! Teach this lad, and feed him. He's looking a bit green under that red hair."

Lucas Dunn didn't tarry long after the *Western Star*'s arrival in New Orleans. He bade farewell to Gruber and his shipmates and quickly found passage on a small merchant ship headed to Corpus Christi, Texas, the place mentioned in his cousins' letters that he'd read about back in Kildare. After experiencing the chill of the cold Irish Sea and the Atlantic Ocean, the Caribbean and the Gulf of Mexico offered pleasant contrasts. The pale-green, and at times. turquoise-blue warm waters of the gulf began to heal his spirits. Still, his sleep aboard the *Western Star* had been fitful at best. Despite the confines of a swaying hammock, he found himself awakened by his own thrashing about as he swung an imaginary claymore at the specters of scarlet-coated British dragoons, and nightmares of fighting the dragoons were interspersed with images of the tortures of Donnegan and O'Connell.

He'd found himself occasionally looking eastward, vainly searching the horizon for a final look at his homeland. He knew in his heart of hearts that he'd never return to the verdant heathers of County Kildare. Now, the easy gulf breezes and gentle sea swells served to ease the pain in his inner psyche, as he conjured up ever fewer phantasms of the struggles in Ireland. Yet, because of his hatred of the British and revulsion over their methods, he found his heart increasingly gripped by a burgeoning devotion to bringing justice and redemption to a world that seemed ever on the edge of the biblical end times he feared. Texas would be his second chance, a chance to make life—his and the lives of others—right.

He stepped carefully from the dinghy onto the dock so as to get his land legs beneath him. There he stood, cloak in hand, in a none-too-fashionable woolen kilt, torn shirt, and borrowed shoes. He'd likely find a cousin somewhere, but for now, any feelings of loneliness were swept aside by his wonder at the inviting appeal of his surroundings. The white-plastered buildings with sheltered verandas, broad but dusty streets, and the slow but animated movement of people around him seemed a welcoming effect. There was already a sense of warmth and friendliness that the very town seemed to exude. Corpus Christi was already capturing him.

He found himself walking from the dock and then up a street that led from it. As he approached a smithy shop that he hoped would be the place belonging to one of his cousins, a tall man with tall boots and broad-brimmed hat inadvertently bumped him slightly.

"Pardon." The man nodded and kept on walking.

Dunn blurted, "Aye, beggin' yer pardon." It all of a sudden occurred to him that he'd seen the flash of a silver star pinned to the man's shirt. As he turned to see the man walking away, he noted the gun and holster along with the large knife nearly the size of the claymore he wished he still had. He reflexively turned and called out, "Sir? Sir, do you have a moment?"

The Irish accent must have had some effect, as the man stopped and pivoted. "I did excuse myself, pardner."

"I–I'm new here. Where might a strong, honest man find labor?"

"Irish, are you?" The man pointed to the smithy shop sign hanging above them. "You might check with Peter Dunn here."

Dunn looked up. Sure enough, it was the smithy shop of his cousin from Kildare. What an incredible coincidence. He shrugged and blushed nearly as red as his hair. "Thank you. Peter is my cousin."

The tall man nodded friendly-like beneath the cowboy hat and began to turn.

Dunn continued, "Pardon, again, sir." He was encouraged by the polite friendliness of the man with the gun and star. "What of the star on your chest?"

The man smiled. "Oh, that…I'm a Texas Ranger, friend. We keep Texas safe from lawbreakers." He gave Lucas a once-over. "You interested in Rangering?"

"I believe in the law…in justice."

"Justice, hey?" The Texas Ranger gave Dunn another once-over, then smiled as if to say the Irishmen he'd met were a tough breed. He pointed to the large revolver in his holster. "Ever shoot one of these?"

Dunn shook his head. "Had a musket back in Kildare."

"I expect your cousin might give the same advice, but you ought to find your way to Colonel Henry Kinney. He runs the show here in Corpus Christi. The colonel will likely point you to Sheriff Whelan. You can learn a lot from the sheriff. That is, if you're serious." The Ranger smiled again. Experience was important; he was obviously not interested in raw recruits for his Texas Ranger Company. "Now, if you'll excuse me, I must rejoin my company. You ever get serious about Rangering and learn how to handle one of these peashooters, look me up. Name's Callahan."

Dunn watched the Texas Ranger stride away, glanced at the sign above, and entered his cousin's smithy shop. His eyes widened just a bit as he passed the open shop door and saw the myriad symbols burned into the wood. He headed toward the sound of hammer on anvil.

Visions of being a Texas Ranger were already dancing in his head. He'd learn soon enough that Callahan had earned a reputation for gallant action in the Texas Revolution, having escaped the Goliad Massacre and fought at Victoria.

★★

"It's a heavy piece, this pistol, Mr. Whelan." Lucas Dunn hefted the Colt revolver.

"Just don't go pointing at anything unless you intend to shoot it...and watch that finger. Don't be getting itchy. Keep it off the trigger except you aim to pull it."

Lucas nodded as he took care to follow the sheriff's instructions. He pointed the revolver at the target a mere fifty yards off and pulled the trigger. *Click.* Nothing happened.

Whelan chuckled. "Works best with bullets in it." He handed some to Dunn and showed him with his own gun how to load the cylinder. "Now, see if you can hit the target." He pointed to the can sitting on the fence post.

Dunn nonchalantly aimed the gun, breathed out slowly, and squeezed the trigger. The explosion in his hand was followed nearly instantly by the clank of the can as the bullet plowed through. He turned to the sheriff, smiled, and shrugged. "Lucky, I guess."

Whelan shook his head. He recognized raw talent when he saw it. "Well, it's sittin' on the ground over yonder. Can you hit it again?"

Dunn obliged, then struck the can a second and third time.

"I think you've got the hang of it, son." Whelan's eyes held wide with amazement.

"Thank you, Sheriff."

"Now, tomorrow we're going to the cock fights. The colonel has his best birds in the matches, but there are some nasty varmints that don't cotton to losing their money or their birds."

Dunn had never been to a cock fight but decided he'd have to be up to helping the sheriff. "Varmints, Sheriff?"

Whelan laughed. "These varmints are of the human variety. They can get righty nasty, but a firm hand usually is enough to cool them down. Just watch me and you'll get the hang of it."

Dunn hadn't heard such squawking since he'd run through a crowded chicken pen back in Kildare escaping from redcoats. There were at least a hundred men hanging on fighting pens, making bets, drinking, and all manner of carrying on. He gathered that the brown-skinned men were likely the Mexicans he'd heard about. He learned that some brought their fighting cocks up the Gulf Coast from as far away as a place called Monterrey. They'd certainly be likely to turn nasty at losing, he figured.

Luke followed Whelan at a distance, observing how the sheriff handled any serious and potentially serious conflicts. Now and then, he caressed the Colt revolver in the holster on his hip. He hoped he'd never have to use it. He thought on how the deadly efficiency of a bullet compared to slicing through someone or whacking off an ear—or worse—with the claymore. Likely less bloody. He gave an involuntary shudder.

Suddenly, a bystander shoved into Sheriff Whelan hard enough that the lawman's hat flew off. Whelan bent down to retrieve his hat, and as he came back up, his fist plowed deep into the attacker's crotch. The man doubled over in agonizing pain.

Dunn drew a couple of steps closer to Whelan and wrapped his hand around the grip of his revolver. He scanned the crowd for any friends of the man who now groveled at Whelan's feet. Sure enough, as Whelan dusted off his hat, a man behind him was raising the butt of his gun to hit the sheriff over the head. Dunn pulled back the hammer of his gun.

The click of a pistol hammer being cocked wasn't especially loud, but it had a rather distinct sound. In an instant, the man about to hit the sheriff paused to rethink what he was about to do. He glanced sideways toward Luke and found himself staring down the muzzle of the deputy's 1851 Colt Navy revolver that was likely to blow his brains out. He backed down, lifted his still-writhing friend, and limped away.

Whelan turned to Luke and nodded. "The Wilson boys. Bit too much to drink. They won't be any more trouble today." He smiled. "Thanks, Luke. You done good."

A few more cockfight duties and late-night patrols on the streets of Corpus Christi and Luke found himself longing for more. Longing to make a greater difference. A single month quickly became a half dozen. He'd saved enough of his wages to acquire a half-decent horse and carved out time in the evenings to ride out with his gun to his cousin's homestead and plunk at random targets. He was becoming right accurate and could yank the piece from his holster right quickly, but being a deputy sheriff wasn't measuring up to his dream of delivering justice on what he considered a meaningful scale.

This bright sunny morning, he was fixing to meet up with Sheriff Whelan to check on some cattle rustling that had been reported west of Corpus Christi. He paused at the door to his cousin's smithy shop and scanned the cattle brands burned into the wood. There in the center was the Lazy S brand of the ranch they'd be headed out to. As Luke stepped from the shop, he nearly collided with James Callahan.

"Pardon, Mr. Callahan." There was a touch of irony in Luke's respect, as he towered over his Ranger acquaintance.

"No problem, son." The Ranger paused. His eyes took Luke in, from boots to broad-brimmed hat with its cattleman's crease. His expression revealed his appreciation for the young Irishman's quite apparent transformation. "Say, you still thinking about the Texas Rangers?"

Luke nodded. "Matter of fact."

"Heard good reports about you from the colonel. We sure could use more good men. You a God-fearing man?"

By now, Luke was captured in Callahan's spell. The very idea of being a Texas Ranger had dominated his dreams since he'd first bumped into the lawman; they'd actually replaced the nightmares of the Irish rebellions for the most part. "Aye, Mr. Callahan. Do my praying to the good Lord every day."

"The Nueces Strip is vast and lonely. It's just the place for savages and desperados to avoid justice." Callahan had said the right word, the trigger word, if you will. It was about justice.

Luke's eyes drilled straight into Callahan's. "Seriously?"

"Bout as serious as can be, Mr. Dunn." He squinted at the Irishman. "You want to be a Texas Ranger." It was more statement than question, and he didn't wait for an answer. "Everyone dies, Mr. Dunn. The question is, how will you live?"

It was a heavy question, but Luke could barely contain his enthusiasm. "When can I start?"

"We're mustering in some men on Monday. Just show up at the courthouse with your outfit."

"Thank you, Mr. Callahan. I'll be there." Luke turned and walked away in a bit of a dreamy daze at the prospect of making his dreams a reality. He'd have to give Whelan the news, but felt sure that the sheriff would wish him well. Callahan's question about life wouldn't weigh on him just yet.

"Beginning Monday, you call me Captain Callahan." The Ranger paused with an eye on Luke's horse. "Just a bit of advice, Mr. Dunn, but you might give consideration to a more Texas prairie-worthy cayuse. Where we go, what you're riding is more important than your gun or knife."

Luke nodded. "I'll see what I can do."

Callahan smiled. "I saw a big gray stallion I'm partial to down at the livery. He's a sure sight, big enough to handle a rider of your size."

★★

Luke had gone straight away to the livery. The spirited big gray was there, sure enough, prancing about around the corral as though trying to find its way to freedom. Luke sensed the horse's instincts and felt an instant bond.

He hailed the stable boy. "Say, lad, what do you know about this horse? Is he for sale?"

The young boy wasn't the brightest star in the sky, and it took a few seconds for Luke's question to register. "Mr. Crane. Yep, Mr.

Crane is selling him. Says the damned hoss can't be rode. Has its own mind."

Luke was instantly taken with the size and handsomeness of the horse. "Looks fine enough. Did Mr. Crane mention a price?"

The stable boy chuckled. "Dang, but he was of a mind to give the wild thing away." The boy paused. He was slow but not stupid. "'Course, there's the fees for boarding him here."

Luke climbed up onto the corral fence, sat still, and stared into the big gray's eyes.

The stallion suddenly stopped his dancing about and stood stock-still. He sniffed the breeze as it wafted past Luke and reached the beast's gently flaring nostrils, then chortled and raised his head as though seeking assurance from the human smell reaching out to him.

Luke reached inside his shirt, and an apple seemed to magically appear in his hand. The horse needed no further persuading; the big gray snorted and eased on over to Luke. He gently plucked the tasty morsel from Luke's hand but didn't move away. He seemed to expect something more.

Luke reached out and stroked the stallion's nose. He eased himself from the fence and continued to maintain physical contact with this beautiful horse.

"Dang, Mister. He don't let no one get that close."

"Give you twenty dollars. I've got my own tack." Luke figured that Mr. Crane, likely as not, wouldn't see a penny of the twenty.

"Mr. Crane left a bill of sale, Mr...."

"Dunn. Texas Ranger Luke Dunn." He smiled as the sound rolled off his tongue. He was right certain that Captain Callahan would be pleased. He turned back to the horse. "We're going to set Texas right, big horse." The name worked its way into his conscious-ness. "That's it—I'll call you Big Horse." Luke smiled and gently stroked the big gray's muzzle.

Luke soon enough found out that being a Texas Ranger didn't differ much from his deputy sheriff job with respect to having to wait with considerable patience for missions to materialize. On the upside, he had plenty of time to keep his guns clean and Bowie knife sharp, keep his leathers sufficiently supple, and enjoy a drink or two with fellow lawmen. In a sense, it harkened back to his fellow clansmen in Ireland as they built the trust and loyalty essential to being an effective fighting force.

Luke had accompanied the Rangers on a couple of missions and was fast earning the respect of Callahan and his fellow lawmen. He'd followed them around for a couple of months while learning the ropes and was beginning to feel like a hanger-on. He chaffed for a mission he could call his own.

At the request of Sheriff Whelan, the Texas Rangers had been asked to supplement Corpus Christi law enforcement by frequenting local drinking establishments and displaying their badges. It was aimed at reminding potential lawbreakers that there were rules to be followed, and breaking them would spell trouble.

Thus, it was that one evening Luke sauntered easy-like into the Longhorn Saloon. He found himself standing at the bar beside a drunken cowboy who was well on his way to passing out. The cowpoke seemed to have some sort of problem that he was trying to numb away with the local high-test liquor. He was also letting it be known that his woman was cheating on him when somebody— Luke wasn't able to immediately figure who—hollered an insult at the cowboy. It was about this drunken man's woman, and naturally, it wasn't taken well.

The cowboy spun toward the sound of the insult, his hand grasping the grip of the Colt revolver at his hip while his index finger slipped inside the trigger guard. As he began to pull the weapon, Luke's iron grip froze the cowboy's hand in mid-draw— but it couldn't stop his finger from squeezing the trigger. An explosion rocked the saloon. A hole was blown in the floor, and a hush fell over the guests. The cowboy was strong, but he was no match for Luke's grip. The Texas Ranger wrenched the gun from the cowboy's hand, grabbed the cowpuncher by the collar, threw him kicking and hollering over his shoulder, and corralled him toward the door. Along the way, the cowboy finally passed out.

By sheer coincidence, Luke ran headlong into the sheriff. By now, the cowboy had calmed just enough for Luke to set him down.

"Sheriff, I think this fine citizen could use a bed in your establishment before he hurts himself or someone else."

Whelan laughed and quickly took charge of the now fully unconscious cowboy. "This guy's a load, Luke. Can you help me carry him to the hoosegow?"

Luke sighed. He was happy to help and pleased that no serious damage had been done inside the Longhorn, but this wasn't what he had envisioned the Texas Ranger life to be.

Finally, the opportunity for serious action emerged. Callahan had been ordered to lead his company of 130 Texas Rangers in chasing down a band of Lipan Apache prone to murderous cattle-thieving attacks in Bexar and Comal counties. Technically, the Texas Rangers had become an afterthought in some citizen's minds, given the statehood status of Texas and the so-called protection of the US Army. When that protection was not forthcoming following raids by the Apache, it had taken a concerted effort by Governor E. M. Pease to get the legislature to authorize enough money to raise the company of Rangers under Callahan.

It was now September 1855. Callahan had located the Apache, and his company crossed the Rio Grande into Mexico in pursuit. It was a flagrant violation of international law.

Luke wasn't aware of diplomatic courtesies, but he found himself itching for the action that was sure to come. About forty miles into Mexico near the Rio Escondido, the Rangers encountered the Apache reinforced with Mexican troops. Adrenaline naturally coursed through Luke's being, but something fully unexpected overwhelmed his senses as the scarlet-coated Mexican dragoons came into sight.

So far as Callahan could tell, the enemy had a slight numerical advantage, but the Rangers had greater firepower. For Luke, such calculus didn't matter in the face of the vengeful anger sweeping over him.

Callahan wheeled on his horse, waved his rifle high, and shouted, "Charge!" The words had barely escaped his mouth when Luke moved forward at a breakneck gallop toward the center of the enemy line. He hurdled past the Apache defensive positions as though they didn't exist and found himself firing his Colt with deadly accuracy at close quarters into the midst of the dragoons. The nine-foot-long dragoon lances were unwieldy when facing an opponent mere inches away, and Luke took full advantage. Anywhere he saw red, he dealt death. The dragoons broke into headlong retreat, followed by the Apache, who quickly realized they were on the losing end of the fight.

It seemed as though death had left its calling card, though, in sum, only a small number were actually killed and wounded on both sides. With the enemy on the run, Callahan took punitive action, looting and burning the nearby town of Piedras Negras before recrossing the Rio Grande into Texas. Little wonder that the Mexicans took to derogatorily calling the Texas Rangers *rinches*.

Dunn was credited with being in the thick of the battle, and Callahan and his fellow Rangers had found themselves in awe of Dunn's performance. None, including Luke, realized that it had been the deep psychological scars from his battles in Ireland that had driven him to such exceptional savagery in slaughtering the red-coated dragoons.

The Rangers were frustrated to learn upon returning to Corpus Christi with Callahan, that while public support for another expedition was favorable, the politicians were not inclined to risk another international incident. Once again, they were bivouacked with no pressing assignment.

Such was the situation when James Callahan rode easy up to the now battle-tested Irish Texas Ranger as he sat on the jailhouse steps, amusing himself by carving a whistle from a piece of live oak. "Ranger Dunn. May I have a moment of your time?" the captain requested in a slightly sarcastic tone encased in an easy smile.

Luke put his knife aside and stood. "Yessir, Captain."

Callahan had recognized Luke's impatience but didn't want to send him off before he was ready. The young Ranger had proven especially capable in the field, followed orders, and could shoot the wings off a horsefly. "We're getting ready to head to Brownsville."

He watched Luke's eyes drop with disappointment. It would be a long, boring journey across flat terrain with grasses far as the eye could see sprouting from the loamy soil. "But we've learned that an outlaw named Scose Huggins is snooping around up toward Robstown. He's reputed to have killed seven men...all from ambush. Even taken up the habit of scalping his victims. My question to you is whether you feel up to bringing him in?"

Luke felt a rush of excitement course through every part of his body. He tried his best to keep himself under control. "Er...yes– yessir, Captain." He removed his hat long enough to run his hand through his thick red hair and put off the thought of it decorating a scalper's bag.

"Dang it, Dunn. Relax! Everyone gets excited on their first solo mission." Callahan smiled warmly. "I wouldn't ask if I didn't think you were ready. Just don't disappoint me, ya hear?"

Luke was bust-a-button proud that the Ranger captain had detailed him to bring in Huggins. "I appreciate it, Captain. I won't let you down."

"Last I heard, Huggins was boasting of getting himself a Texas Ranger. 'Course, he pretty much knows where we are, but he's smart enough to know when he's outgunned. My gut tells me he'll follow the Nueces River, waiting for a bushwhacking opportunity. Maybe he'll get careless."

"Dead or alive, Captain?"

"I'm hankering to have the good citizens of Corpus Christi see him hanging from the gallows. That sort of justice discourages other folk thinking of breaking the law." Callahan's expression turned deadly serious. "Been meaning to talk with you about those dragoons you dispatched at Piedras Negras."

Dunn shifted uncomfortably.

"What drove you, Ranger? What was swirling through that mind of yours?"

Luke's eyes fixed on Callahan's for a moment as he tried to figure how to explain it. "Red, Captain."

"Red?"

"When you've been battling British redcoats at close quarters, surrounded by red, when you've watched them torture your fellow clansmen, when..." His voice trailed off. "It was red, Captain. It was the red coats of the dragoons." Luke clenched his fist against his chest. "Cannot explain it. It was personal."

Callahan sought to lighten the tension. "Well, Ranger, I'll never wear a red coat around you." He chuckled.

Luke simply shook his head. He couldn't bring himself to make light of it. "I'll get your Scose Huggins for you, Captain."

Luke right soon found himself riding the road along the south bank of the Nueces River. His big gray stallion pranced a bit, keeping with his high spirit, but they were working out their relationship. There was a strong bond building between horse and rider. Certainly, the steed had performed admirably at Rio Escondido.

The night in Nuecestown, roughly midway between Corpus Christi and Robstown, passed uneventfully. From the young man at the local stable, he'd learned that a man matching Huggins's description had passed through just the day before. Seemed that the man's horse had lost a shoe, and by that, he was able to give Luke an important clue.

"I like to sign my work, Mr. Ranger. I'm not a smithy, but I can fit a shoe pretty well. I put three notches in the front."

"Much appreciated." With that, Luke headed out on what he hoped was Huggins's trail.

Just northwest of Nuecestown, Luke found the remains of a small campfire. Was it Huggins? Hard to tell. It took a few minutes of studying the sandy soil, but Luke finally came upon hoofprints. There was the telltale print with the triple-notched horseshoe. He mounted up and cautioned himself to be extra careful, fully aware that he presented a rather large target for a bushwhacker.

Scose Huggins had followed the north bank of the Nueces River, looking for shallows that would afford him a reasonably dry crossing. He'd known that the damnable Texas Ranger had been on his tail since sunrise. By dumb luck, he'd heard the Ranger's horse neighing. Huggins had barely had time to gather his outfit, saddle up, and flee. He'd given a passing thought to bush-whacking the lawman then and there, but if he missed, he'd be in an indefensible position. Besides, the Ranger likely had already been alerted by the smoke wafting from what remained of his dying campfire.

Luke smiled knowingly. He tried to calm the big gray stallion. He and the horse were still getting acquainted, so the newly minted Ranger understood the horse's excitement. He'd yet learn to be quiet when stalking prey. Dunn figured he was no more than a quarter mile behind the fleeing outlaw. He'd been taught the importance of patience from his days stalking redcoats in Ireland. It wouldn't do to be foolhardy and ride into an ambush. After all, Huggins was wanted for bushwhacking a cowboy after having gotten the worse end of a saloon fight, among other ambushing adventures.

Huggins had his own challenges. He'd found the shallows he was looking for, but his horse was turning skittish on him. "Damn cayuse! It's just water, dammit!" The horse twisted, turned, and splashed about in the fast-moving waters.

Luke hadn't worried about a dry crossing. Holding his gun belt and rifle over his head and sitting tall in the saddle, Big Horse had easily swum across. It didn't take long to catch up with his prey.

Huggins was halfway across the river when he happened to look up and hear the signature click of a round chambered in a rifle. He found himself staring down the rather impressive muzzle of Luke Dunn's .44 caliber Model 1855 Colt revolving rifle. It might as well have been a cannon, as far as Huggins was concerned.

Luke smiled at the outlaw's predicament. "You ever gonna get that sorry cayuse across this river so I can arrest you, Huggins?"

The outlaw was half tempted to reach for his gun, but it was all he could do to hold on to the reins so as to keep his horse from dumping him into the river. "Damn you, Ranger! Damn you!" He finally managed to bring the horse onto the riverbank, but he hadn't a prayer of getting the drop on Luke.

Luke dismounted, keeping the muzzle of the rifle pointed at Huggins's belly. "Drop your rifle and that gun in your holster."

The outlaw reluctantly complied.

"Now, slide down from that saddle, and keep your hands where I can see them. You're under arrest." The Texas Ranger had the manacles at the ready.

In the brief moment that Huggins swung his leg over his horse's haunches to dismount, his hand went for a revolver hidden in the waistband under his vest. He'd barely cleared the revolver and turned it toward Luke when an ear-shattering explosion rocked the scene. A .44 caliber slug shattered Huggins' kneecap as the air was filled with the smoke and odor of burned black powder. Huggins dropped to the ground, writhing in agony.

Luke took a step toward the outlaw.

The desperado wasn't finished. He was of a mind to avoid the hangman as he lay crumpled on the ground. Huggins contorted himself enough to point his weapon in Luke's direction. He pulled the trigger. Nothing. A misfire.

Luke shouted a warning. "Damn! Don't be stupid, Huggins. Put the gun down!"

Huggins pulled the trigger again. There was an explosion, and a bullet whistled past Luke's ear.

The Texas Ranger sent his next shot plowing through Huggins's shoulder, driving the man head over heels and splashing into the muck along the river bank.

With the shoulder wound, the man's pistol had gone flying. "Damn it! Finish me, you son of a bitch!"

"You aren't dying out here, Scose Huggins. I'm bringing you in." Luke took the reins of Huggins's horse and strode over toward the wounded outlaw. "I'll patch you best I can, but you're getting in the saddle, even if I have to tie you to it."

Huggins sneered. "I got friends gonna get you fer this, Ranger. And they'll likely spring me from that excuse for a jail." Pain shot through his leg and shoulder. "I ain't hanging!"

Luke wrapped strips of cloth around Huggins's knee and shoulder as best he could to staunch the bleeding. "I'm sure they're no friends of mine, Huggins." The outlaw was an average-sized man, and Luke had little trouble hoisting him into the saddle. He attached one manacle cuff to the outlaw's wrist and the other to the saddle cinch. Luke thought back on the deadly torture he'd seen inflicted on his countrymen taken prisoner by the British. Huggins was getting off light.

Still, the Ranger couldn't totally hold back his anger. He hadn't particularly appreciated having been shot at. "What do you think, Huggins? A five-foot drop from the gallows be enough?" Luke punctuated the cruel comment with a laugh. He felt a surge of regret but wasn't about to apologize. It hadn't been all that satisfying.

The image of the scaffold and hangman caused Huggins to twist angrily in the saddle before nearly passing out from pain. He managed to blurt a threat, "My cousin Bart Strong will hunt you down, you damned son of a bitch." He gritted his teeth. "He'll make you sorry you ever got born!"

Luke moved his big stallion over beside Huggins mount and reexamined the outlaw's dressings. It was obvious that his shoulder wound was still bleeding. Luke pulled more bandage from his saddlebag and redressed the outlaw's wound, then checked to be sure the man would stay in the saddle.

Huggins winced. "You making sure I don't bleed out before getting me to jail?"

Assured that his prisoner wasn't going to fall or bleed to death, Luke shook his head. "Do I have to gag you, too? Let's have a quiet ride back to Corpus, Huggins." Luke turned the big stallion and headed them toward the ferry at Nuecestown. There was no point in risking the loss of his wounded prisoner by fording the river. Huggins let out an involuntary cry of pain at the first jostling of the horse heading up the trail. Luke couldn't suppress a smile.

The symbolic nature of Luke leading a wounded prisoner through the main street of Nuecestown wasn't lost on the little town's inhabitants. A tall, strapping, heavily armed man with a blazing-red mustache riding tall in the saddle on a handsome gray stallion stood in stark contrast to the hunched-over prisoner in manacles and bandages behind him.

Luke pulled up in front of Doc's place. He was about to dismount and knock on the door when Doc Andrews appeared with a whiskey bottle in hand.

Doc held the bottle up. Through squinted eyes, he noted Luke's badge. "Good day, Mr. Ranger." He raised the bottle. "I have the anesthesia ready." He wobbled, nearly fell over, and grasped the doorjamb to steady himself.

Luke shook his head. "I think his wounds won't kill him

between here and Corpus, Doc." From his peripheral vision, Luke saw a wagon parked in front of the general store. A young girl stood beside it, and her ice-blue eyes seemed to penetrate to his very soul. She wore a blue gingham dress and matching bonnet over long reddish-blonde locks. She was a petite thing, barely taller than the outsized wagon wheel she stood beside.

Elisa Corrigan caught her breath. God did indeed provide. She caught his eyes meeting hers and quickly turned away.

Doc was drunk, but his rheumy eyes didn't miss much. He'd seen the electricity in her look...and his. "Watch out fer that one, Ranger. Young and feisty thang named Elisa—Elisa Corrigan."

Luke turned disconcertedly back to Doc. "Gotta be heading to Corpus. Take care, Doc." Luke turned Big Horse and headed out of town, stealing a parting glance at the young woman beside the wagon.

Doc looked over at the Corrigan wagon and caught Elisa's eyes. He gave her an oversized wink. She blushed.

Ben Callahan laid a congratulatory grip on Luke's shoulder. "That was fine work with Huggins, Luke. And danged quick!" The company hadn't even yet left for Brownsville. The Texas Ranger Captain clearly held high confidence that Dunn would become an exceptional lawman.

"It's about delivering justice, Captain. I know it must sound a bit high-and-mighty, but that's what being a lawman means to me."

Callahan nodded. "I hear you." He paused. "There's a judgment side, too, Luke. Every now and again you're going to run into someone that needs arresting, but a voice inside you will tell you they're not totally lost to the lawbreaking life. You'll sense that they might be salvaged...redeemed, if you will. Don't always be set on plunking them in jail or blowing their brains out. Some folks just need a second chance. Trust me on this. When the time comes, you'll know."

Luke thoughtfully rubbed his freshly grown red mustache as he thought back on how some redemptive thinking might have served the British well. "You're saying that sometimes compassion prevails, Captain?"

"You'll learn to read it, son. There's nothing so satisfying as seeing someone given another chance and turned from a life of lawbreaking." Callahan kicked at the street dirt. "That pretty much only works for first-time offenders, Luke. It's about character, yours and theirs. But, if you're serving a warrant or there's a poster for the lawbreaker, you're obliged to bring them to jail regardless. You can forgive the crime, but not the punishment. In that case, you might say something in their favor at trial. Remember, you must always uphold the law. You've chosen this trail."

"I think I understand, Captain." It was a fine line that would only be mastered with experience. Luke smiled. "Guess I made the right choice with Scose Huggins." Luke's thoughts strayed a tad morbidly as to how he'd guessed the drop distance for the outlaw's hanging. Huggins had died nearly instantly as the noose broke his neck. Luke shook off the image. "I might have another bit of hunting ahead, Captain." He recalled Callahan's words about how he would live. Seemed this was how it would be.

"How's that, Ranger Dunn?"

"Huggins said his cousin Bart Strong would come looking for me."

"Bad Bart Strong? Hrumph! A mean one. Eluded me and a half dozen Rangers a few months back. Hated to see him get away. I'd watch your backside, Luke. Strong's a bushwhacker like Huggins." Callahan uneasily shook his head, then looked up, shrugged, and smiled. "Let's join the company to celebrate you bringing Huggins to justice."

Luke furtively glanced over his shoulder as he followed Callahan into the saloon, then glanced to his right just as he entered. For a fleeting second, he'd have sworn he saw a flash of blue gingham. He paused and looked up the street. Nothing. He entered the Longhorn with two dangers working on his mind: a vengeful outlaw...and a beautiful woman.

Little did he know that this night would be his last with Callahan.

REQUIEM FOR A TEXAS RANGER

BALLAD OF LONG LUKE DUNN

Long Luke Dunn, legend of the Nueces Strip,
Never a savage or outlaw gave him the slip;
Far and wide, the Texas prairies he'd roam,
Blue skies and starry nights his home.

Texas Rangering was the life he knew,
Delivering justice with passions true;
Sounds of stars soothed his soul,
With guile and cunning, he always met his goal.

Comanche called him Ghost Who Rides,
Knowing full well he could whip their hides;
Rustlers, killers, robbers all took Dunn on,
And one by one, they soon were gone.

Pumas, wolves, and rattlers gave wide berth,
As Luke and his stallion strode the earth;
Yet winsome Elisa knew his tender kiss,
She held him ever captive in loving bliss.

Pinned to his shirt was the Ranger's star,
And fine reputation grown both near and far;
Strong of faith and tough as they come,

Trail, motte, and arroyo were under his thumb.

When Dunn took a bead on wayward prey,
Outlaw or savage met their maker that day;
Laredo to Corpus and down to Brownsville,
South Texas made safe by this Ranger's skill.

Some men become legends long after death,
Others fall short, miss by a mere breath;
Dunn cheated the reaper, he be no easy prey,
Famous in his lifetime, Luke had final say.

This lone Texas Ranger, the vast prairies rode,
Brought justice with passion wherever he rode;
The greatest hero, you ask? I'll give you a tip,
'Twas Long Luke Dunn, legend of the Nueces Strip.

THE KIN OF KILDARE

A true tale of the five sons of Lawrence "Long Larry" Dunn, who emigrated from County Kildare, Ireland, to Corpus Christi, Texas, from 1845 to 1868. They escaped the Potato Famine and Catholic persecutions by the English redcoats to carve a new beginning in America. This is the story of my ancestors put to rhyme; it's the heritage of my sons.

'Twas the famine that drove them; thousands had died.
Their ancestral kings and chieftains had e'er long gone,
The English took their bounty, but couldn't steal their pride,
The pixies danced, hobgoblins howled, and leprechauns
    laughed,
And the pride of Ireland stood fast.
And so it was with the kin of Kildare; did ya hear?

Five brothers left County Kildare for Texas one by one,
First Mathew, then Peter, Thomas, Patrick, and John.
The sons of Long Larry Dunn sailed forth to a great
    unknown;
Lush live oak, pecan trees, and wild grapes beckoned,
Along the shores of Nueces Bay.
And so it was with these kin of Kildare; did ya hear?

They built their homes, tilled and sowed the soil,
Their acreage knew no end; their families abundant grew.
Years of starvation in Kildare replaced with bountiful toil;
Livestock bred aplenty, plus cotton, peaches, and plums,
God's bounty blessed them all.
And so it was with these kin of Kildare; did ya hear?

But the idyll succumbed to another's plan as war and sin
    crept in,
Rustlers ambushed Uncle Larry; he never had a chance.
Uncles Chris and Patrick and Joseph, the yellow fever took.
Uncle Matt murdered at his ranch by drunken bandits;
This land took as much as it gave.
And so it was with these kin of Kildare; did ya hear?

Yet, these kinfolk of County Kildare, these staunch Irishmen
    endured,
They sowed and reaped, made life anew despite the strife;
Their blood flows crimson in my children's veins.
And the green heathers of County Kildare will ever
    remember
Texans now, these sons of Long Larry Dunn.
And so it was with these kin of Kildare; now ya hear.

HOMESTEAD WOMAN
FRONTIER GRIT

Elisa Corrigan Dunn is the very embodiment of the strong frontier woman that settled America's western frontier. It took a woman with her determination and sheer grit to face the hardships of running a ranch while her man roamed the Texas Nueces Strip delivering justice. Her story offers insight into the woman who accomplished that.

SAM CORRIGAN PAUSED and swiped his sweaty brow. Trying to wipe away sweat with a grimy, soaking-wet shirt sleeve wasn't exactly destined for success. The battle had seemed to take forever, though in reality it had lasted just a few minutes. He was bleeding from a bayonet stab wound to his left thigh, but it wasn't stopping him from joining the gathering ahead. He held a bandana over his mouth to prevent himself from taking in the pungent clouds of gun smoke that yet hung over the battlefield, covering all in sight with a patina of gray. Quite a hubbub was stirring, as rumor had it that the great Santa Anna had been captured. The nondescript marshes of San Jacinto had hosted the ignominious defeat of the Mexican Army, and Corrigan had distinguished himself in the heart of the melee. It was the moment he'd relish all his life—the moment he became a Texan.

Corrigan had felt suffocated by a family life that was a tad too close-knit. His and his wife's parents had emigrated from Ireland but found that the surrounding communities springing up in the verdant fields and forests of Pennsylvania didn't exactly take kindly to assimilating the Irish. The Amish, with their Swiss cultural roots and anti-Catholicism, tended to culturally isolate. He worked hard at farming, but his heart was in getting out from under the yoke of the overly close family ties and an insulated culture. So it was that he was easily lured by Stephen Austin away from those rich northern farmlands. He and his wife had enthusiastically immigrated to Texas, setting at once to build a cabin near what would become the thriving port of Galveston.

The truth that a war was raging had been overlooked in the flyers promoting the grand opportunities in the vast region known as Texas. In fact, it was more struggle than war, as the Texas settlers seemed hopelessly under-resourced. About all they seemed to have going for them was an outsized sense of freedom and commitment to a cause. It was almost a holy war of sorts. Corrigan had to swear to the Catholic faith per the demands of the Mexican government as a precursor to being able to carve out this new life, though his Irish Catholic faith made that easy enough. The Corrigan family had barely gotten a crop in when he heard of an army being raised to defend against a Mexican government that had rejected the precepts of the 1824 Constitution, under which Austin had lured folks to Texas. Santa Anna now sought to impose stricter controls on the Anglo settlers, and thus Corrigan bade goodbye to his wife and headed south to join up with a physically imposing fellow named Sam Houston.

The new nation didn't exactly flourish in the early years of the Republic of Texas. Corrigan was not the best of farmers, but he and his wife made a life of it. A mere four years after the Texas War for Independence, the Corrigans welcomed a daughter into the world. Little Elisa was a bright-eyed bundle of energy from birth and occupied much of the Corrigan's time when they weren't out in the fields or tending to household chores. It was another four years and then two more before her brothers, Michael and Robert, were born. A family of five began to stretch the limits of their one-room cabin, and Sam Corrigan realized that decisions had to be made. He needed more land, and a bit more house. A bigger barn would also be a fine addition. He'd also received word that a couple of Corrigan cousins were seriously considering moving to Galveston, causing him to have visions of a replication of the suffocating family environment they'd escaped back in Pennsylvania.

One beautiful Sunday, Corrigan decided to load the family into their newly acquired wagon and spend the day in downtown Galveston. It figured that they'd pass the town hall, and a poster would catch Sam Corrigan's eye. It seemed that Corpus Christi founder Colonel Henry Kinney was establishing a new town and seeking homesteaders. As the driving influence for developing the region, he'd taken kindly to a location roughly thirteen miles northwest of the city to build a ferry service across the Nueces River. Originally called Motts by English and German settlers back in 1852, Kinney renamed the town Nuecestown in recognition of the myriad pecan trees along the river. The colonel required new settlers to purchase hundred-acre tracts at a dollar an acre and at least ten cows at ten dollars a head. He even saw to it that a temporary post office was established.

Sam Corrigan decided to seize the opportunity afforded by Kinney's venture. The new wagon was loaded to near overflowing with the family possessions and loaded on a schooner in Galveston for the voyage to Corpus Christi.

Kinney enthusiastically welcomed the new settlers and fell over backward to ensure their homesteading success. The land turned out to be a prime location with plenty of access to water, and the ten head of cattle were close to prime stock. The Corrigans immediately began constructing a two-room cabin with accommodations to suit the size of their family. Sam Corrigan was only able to till a small plot that first year, but it somehow produced enough to feed his family and the livestock.

Sam Corrigan stood at the entrance to the newly constructed barn and found himself absentmindedly staring at his young daughter as she sat on a bench churning butter on the gallery he'd built across the front of the house. He admired the way the sun caught the ripple of the muscles of her forearms as this wisp of femininity worked the churn. She had grown up. Perhaps he'd noticed all the more because of the way teen boys had begun to react to her when they visited Nuecestown for supplies. Elisa was unquestionably showing signs of full womanhood. He'd suggested to his wife that she have a conversation about the opposite sex with Elisa a few months back when she'd begun her monthly bleedings, but by virtue of what he'd observed of his daughter's innocently flirtatious behavior in town, the talk apparently hadn't sunk in. He decided it would be up to him as he attempted to mentally gird himself for the task.

He strode over and took a seat on the edge of the gallery. He picked up a small rock, tossing it up and catching it nonchalantly. As he couldn't help but notice the glistening sweat across her brow and upon the gentle swell of her young breasts above her bodice, his mind wandered to what the young men of Nuecestown might think.

There was an uncomfortable silence as Elisa paused her churning. The butter was nearly ready, but it was unusual for her papa to interrupt her work, much less take a seat with the obvious intent of conversing. "Plenty hot, ain't it, Papa?" She wiped her forehead.

Sam Corrigan worked up as easy a smile as he could. "Taught you better. It's 'isn't,' not 'ain't.' He shrugged. He had striven to give as much book learning to his children as he could. "Hard work, that butter churning?"

"Yes, it is, Papa." She kept churning, then paused and looked into his eyes. "You lookin' to talk, Papa?"

Her father shifted uncomfortably. "Put the churnin' aside a bit, Elisa dear. I do indeed feel a need to talk."

She offered an inquisitive expression, awaiting whatever wisdom she assumed he wished to impart.

"It's about those boys in Nuecestown."

She involuntarily giggled. "They're just that, Papa. Boys."

Corrigan sighed. This wasn't easy for him. Not easy at all. "Those boys will grow to be men. The impressions they get of you today will...well...they will also grow. When you smile at them, they see it as an invitation for...well...for a more *intimate* connection."

"I'm just being friendly, Papa. They're just boys."

Corrigan sighed again. "That's not how they think, sweetheart."

Elisa frowned. "How do they think?" She thought for a fleeting moment of having seen her brother Michael, now twelve, naked down at the swimming hole.

"Given half a chance, every one of those boys would defile you, strip you of your precious virginity without benefit of marriage."

"Papa! No! They couldn't be thinking…"

"I'm afraid so."

"Did you think that way about Mama?"

Corrigan swallowed hard. "Er…we were older, Elisa. We courted proper-like." He smiled as he reminisced. "But I sure did burn to make love to your mama."

Elisa's full lips parted as her jaw dropped just a tad. "Oh, Papa! What am I to do?"

"It's not easy, sweetheart. A frown or two at their boyish antics wouldn't hurt. You must show them that you haven't the slightest interest."

"How will I know—"

"The right man? Oh, trust me, you'll know. Your heart will seem to fall to pieces trying to keep up with its racing beat. You'll feel all sorts of sensations." Corrigan was becoming embarrassed at his own words. He shifted in his seat and looked off into the distance. "Just trust me, Elisa…you'll know."

She leaned over and kissed him on the cheek. "Thank you, Papa. I think I understand."

Elisa Corrigan's father had literally loved her mother to death. She and her two younger brothers, Rob and Mike, had been playing down by the creek when her shirtless father came staggering from the house. He sounded like a madman, crying and shouting and carrying on. Elisa ran back to the house. Sam initially tried to block her way, but she evaded her father's arms and burst through the front door of the cabin. Her mother lay exposed from the waist down with blood everywhere. She had already turned a deathly bluish sort of pale. Elisa grabbed her mother's shoulders and tried to shake life back into her. "Live, Mama. Live!" she commanded through her tears. "Live!"

Sam came back inside the cabin. He'd told Rob and Mike to stay outside. "I already tried that." He pulled on his shirt and boots. "You stay here. I'm gonna see if Doc is sober enough to see her."

"Papa, she don't need no doctor. She's past that, Papa."

He hung his head for a moment, resigned, and then turned and headed to the stable to hitch up the mules and wagon.

As Elisa went to cover her mother, she saw the tiny baby in the puddle of blood between her legs. "Oh, Mama." She felt so very helpless. She'd lost not only her mother but also a brother or sister. She couldn't bear to touch the dead baby and see what sex it was. It was so tiny, barely big enough that it might have fit in her hand. She'd heard of these sorts of things happening, but it didn't lessen the pain that shot through her. It hadn't yet struck her that she would now be the woman of the family with all the associated responsibilities.

She heard her father whip the mules as the wagon lurched down the road, but rightly figured he needn't rush. She saw it as something he felt that he needed to do.

Doc hadn't been able to help other than officially pronounce her mother dead. They buried her under the shade of a nearby live oak motte, truly a pretty spot with a right beautiful view of the surrounding grasslands. They'd given a fleeting thought to the new cemetery established in Nuecestown, but having her buried close by seemed vastly preferable.

That was more than a year ago. Now, she was experiencing awakenings within her, dreams of finding a man. Her mind drifted off to such musings as she hauled the basket of wet clothes up the path toward the cabin. It was generous to call it a cabin, but her father had done the best he could on a meager farming income. He'd done a fine job building the place, as there were no cracks where the rare winter breezes might sneak through.

In the aftermath of her mother's death, she'd been forced to take over the woman-of-the-house duties by now. She just hadn't expected to have had to learn so much so soon in her life.

Elisa had taken to what she considered "dressing down" for necessary trips to Nuecestown. She'd taken her father's words to heart and was intent on discouraging the young men. Soon enough, she got to put her lesson into practice. She'd accompanied her father on one of his necessary trips into Nuecestown. It was "necessary" because he'd taken to a bit more drinking since her mother's passing, and he needed to replenish his supply more frequently.

With Rob and Mike hanging on seemingly for dear life in the wagon bed, the rickety old rig lurched into town and pulled up in front of the general store.

"Rob, you and Mike go on down to the livery and get some axel grease. No funnin' around. I don't feel like tarrying none too much." He climbed down, giving a sideways glance toward Elisa and then nodding toward the back of the general store where ladies' niceties were sold. Corrigan went inside and assumed Elisa would follow right quick.

Elisa paused to watch her brothers run off up the dusty street toward the stable, then slipped down from the wagon seat and turned her attention to the opportunity to find new shoes or even one of those fancy parasols she'd heard about. She straightened out her loose-fitting blouse, leather vest, and ankle-length skirt. Her foot had barely hit the wooden plank sidewalk across the front of the store when she heard a whistle.

"Oh, Miss Elisa! How you doin' today, Miss Elisa?" Johnny Wastler happened to be visiting town and stood at the far end of the sidewalk, flanked by two of his friends. He whistled a second time, turning to his companions to elicit their support. "Stayin' long, Miss Elisa?"

She turned her head away as if to ignore the boys but couldn't contain a slight smile, blushing at their attention. Hormones were trumping common sense—and her father's advice. "I have business to tend to, Johnny Wastler." She took a step toward the door.

Elisa quickly found herself surrounded. Her father was busy sampling whiskeys, and she felt as though she dared not call out to him. Besides, she was coming up on sixteen and an ever-hardier frontier woman. "Be off with you, Mr. Wastler."

"Now, that's not bein' very nice, Miss Elisa." He winked at his friends. "There's a fiesta comin' up Saturday. You goin'?"

"No."

"You too good fer us local boys?"

"None of your business…and you let me pass."

Wastler made the mistake of grabbing her arm. The anger that swept across Elisa's face should have been enough of a signal for him to release his grip, but instead, he held her fast and turned for approval to his partners in crime. Turning away was a huge mistake.

The leather satchel that Elisa carried found its way to the side of his head with enough of a wallop to send him sprawling in the dirt.

"Why, you bit—" He choked on his words as she raised the satchel to hit him again.

Elisa likely would have delivered another devastating blow had it not been for her father's unexpected appearance.

He grabbed her arm and looked down menacingly at Wastler. "You boys must have better things to do."

Wastler got to his feet, rubbing the side of his head all the while. He turned his attention to Elisa. "One of these days, yer drunk pa won't be around, Elisa Corrigan."

Sam Corrigan grew deadly serious and took a couple of steps toward the boys.

"Pa…don't, Pa." She pulled on his arm. "Let's go home. I don't need anything here, Pa."

Mike and Rob appeared with the axle grease just in time for the stalemate, and they all climbed into the wagon.

Wastler licked his wounds. "Come on, boys. We'll teach her a lesson another time." He picked up his hat, dusted it off against his pants leg, and strode up the street, still rubbing the rising welt across the side of his head.

As they rode out of town, Sam Corrigan turned toward Elisa. "Wasn't very ladylike back there." He smiled. "But dang, if you didn't lay that boy out right smart-like."

"Sorry, Pa. I couldn't help it." She gave a little laugh. "Guess he was lucky I only had the satchel." She thought about the Colt revolver her father always made her carry when she went down to the creek to bathe or wash laundry.

"You understanding better now what I said about boys' intentions?"

"None of them made my heart flutter any, Pa."

Hot would have been an understatement. Elisa swiped her arm across her perspiring brow. It was a frustratingly useless act; her blouse and skirt clung to her as though they'd been coated in glue. She'd have shed her boots were it not for the rattlesnake she'd seen slither by earlier that morning. She looked over at her father as he split wood. It seemed as though he was pretty much alternating between quaffing ladles of warm water and swinging the axe.

Sam Corrigan looked over at his daughter and nodded toward the path to the swimming hole. He smiled. "You first, daughter." No point in suggesting the swimming hole to Mike or Rob as they labored cleaning the barn.

She didn't have to be asked twice. The very idea of basking in the relatively cool waters seemed to ease the heat. She put aside her work and took a step toward the trail.

"Don't forget the gun, Elisa."

She paused. He was right, of course. "Yes, Pa. I'll fetch it." Soon enough, she had piled her clothes on a rock along the stream bank and fully immersed herself in the sparkling clear waters. The water wasn't at its coolest this time of year, but at this hidden place, it eddied about before moving swiftly toward its confluence with the Nueces River.

She'd begun to relax, lying back and letting the water flow with its cooling effects over her silken white skin. Her thoughts drifted to that tall, handsome fellow on the big gray horse she'd seen in town a few weeks back. Now, *there* was a real man. She felt a tingling, an arousal of some sort, course through her body. She smiled to herself as she lolled back in the waters.

"Well, I'll be doggoned. Lookee here, boys." An all-too-familiar voice cracked the tranquility of her quietude.

Elisa's eyes grew wide with surprise. She ducked under the water but had to come back up for air. She gasped and coughed.

"Go ahead, Miss Elisa. Stand up, by all means." Johnny Wastler's smile was more of a sneer as he delivered a fake laugh. "Trust us. We won't look."

Elisa's head poked above the waters of the deepest part of the pool. Her eyes darted from the three boys to her clothes with the

Colt revolver hidden beneath her blouse. "You boys are trespass-ing." She managed to speak firmly without betraying the abject fear lurking within. "Just go." The timbre of her voice bordered on pleading.

"Like we said, Miss Elisa. We promise not to peek." As if on cue, they turned their backs.

Elisa sunk down into the waters, as low as she could manage, as she made her way to the shore and her clothes. Eventually, the water grew shallower and she quickly became exposed from her waist up. Her vulnerability was rapidly turning from embarrass-ment to anger. She looked over her shoulder at the boys. They still had their eyes averted. As she reached for the revolver under her blouse, the sound of the sloshing water alerted Wastler and his friends.

The boys turned and laughed. Wastler's eyes widened. "Hot damn. Lookee there, boys!" Then, all of a sudden, his mouth gaped.

The sound of a .44 caliber Colt revolver firing in a somewhat confined space almost resembles the sound of a cannon.

"Holy...damn! My dear God, you busted my knee!"

"Barely scratched your sorry knee! My next bullet will take your head off, John Wastler!"

Wastler's friends had already dived for cover in the stream upon seeing the gun and now scrambled, soaking wet, away from the swimming hole as fast as their legs could carry them. Wastler limped off, tears streaming from his eyes and curse words turning the air around him blue.

By now, Elisa had slipped her blouse and skirt on and was pointing the Colt in the direction of the escaping trio. Her breath began to come more naturally.

"Elisa! Are you alright?" At the sound of the gun, her father had run to the top of the trail, rifle in hand. As he looked at his daughter with her clothes clinging askew to her wet body and heard the boys yelling off in the distance, it was easy to put the scene together. "You shoot one?"

Elisa's smile bordered on deviousness. "Kinda, Pa. Grazed John-ny's knee."

Her pa's mouth dropped open.

She couldn't erase her smile. "Guess I could use some more practice."

The day had begun pretty much as most swelteringly hot summer days around their homestead did. Elisa was thinking on how her father had finally stopped burying his sorrows in booze over the loss of her mother. She'd busied herself planting fresh flowers at her mother's grave and knelt quietly while saying a little prayer.

Upon standing, she noticed that the air seemed especially still. It was an eerie sort of feeling—one that sent a chill up her spine despite the heat. Unsure of the source, she shrugged and headed toward the cabin to fetch the laundry.

She hefted the basket and plopped the Colt revolver on top.

Her father nodded and smiled as she passed. He peeked into the basket to be sure the gun was there.

"I always take it with me, Pa."

"Heard there's been Comanche hunting not far off, daughter. You'll likely be just fine, but we shouldn't take chances." He pointed to the rifle leaning against the front door within easy reach of the repairs he was making to the cabin.

"I'll be careful, Pa." She headed toward the creek.

Elisa couldn't have been aware of the three sets of eyes hidden in the brush on the knoll near her mother's gravesite. Three Comanche warriors waited patiently under cover for the right opportunity.

Elisa strolled down the path, reached the swimming hole, and began her labors. She thought briefly about bathing, but her father's warning lingered in her mind. She decided to make short work of the washing.

As Elisa beat, rinsed, and beat again, slapping the trail dirt and horse dung residue from her father's shirts and pants, her mind strayed from worries about savages, and she began daydreaming about what her future might hold. She was certainly growing up, and she'd been seeing and feeling changes to her body and soul. At least once a week, she made the short trek to the swift-moving stream that ran past their property and dumped into the Nueces River. At sixteen, she was pretty much a full-grown woman. Her smooth alabaster skin was a bit prone to freckles that made her seem younger than her years, yet her long reddish-blonde locks added an allure that drove boys crazy. Her daydreams of a home and children of her own became ever more vivid. There were those boys in Nuecestown that seemed interested in sparkin' her, but she had her heart set on a man—a real man. He was out there somewhere. Besides, she had a certain independence and feistiness about her, a spirit that demanded a man capable of fully appreciating those qualities.

Elisa began to walk back from the creek after she'd finished beating her father's fresh-washed clothes on the shoreline rocks. It was a long walk uphill from the creek, and just far enough from the cabin that you had to holler loudly to be heard across the distance unless you were shooting at ill-intentioned boys. There was a slight breeze and a quietness in the air.

As she rounded the live oak motte at the head of the path, the one near where her mother was buried, she saw them. Horror of horrors, she took in the scene of a big, well-muscled Comanche who had just finished the grisly task of scalping her father. At least two arrows protruded from her father's chest, and Mike and Rob lay unmoving just a few feet from Sam. They had taken Comanche arrows as well, and it was obvious that Rob's head had also been cracked wide open with a club. The warrior paused from mutilating his victim, scalp held high, and turned his attention to Elisa. "Who was this?" must have been running through his mind. He let go of Sam's head and smiled, a cold, evil smile. His eyes narrowed. Rape would only be the beginning. A golden-red scalp would be a beautiful addition to his collection.

Elisa fought the urge to run. They—the three of them—would surely have chased her down anyway. The Comanche were a fearsome sight with black war paint across their faces. Their bodies were nearly naked. The big one that had stood over her father, brandishing his trophy scalp, took a step toward her. Shivers of fear began coursing through her frame. Cold, unfeeling, vile, savage wickedness was moving toward her.

From under the folds of her skirt she drew the heavy Walker Colt. Now, she was faced with one of the very worst threats she could imagine: Comanche. She'd heard from the ladies in Nuecestown about what barbaric evils the savages were known to inflict upon women. Rape…slavery…beatings. Mutilation would be the least of her worries. No White man would ever want her were she to fall prey to Comanche.

She pointed the muzzle toward the oncoming savage. She'd ever remember pulling back the hammer, squeezing the trigger, and seeing the gaping hole in the savage's chest. The warrior fell at her feet.

The other two Comanche reeled back in surprise upon seeing Elisa's revolver and their dead friend. They ran for their ponies. Before she could react, they were gone from sight.

Elisa slumped for a moment, then shuddered at the sudden realization as to what had just happened. The entire attack likely hadn't lasted more than ten minutes, but the outcome was inconceivably devastating. The terrible reality crashed down her that she was alone as she stood among the lifeless forms of her family. Feelings that but moments before had been life and happiness were shattered.

She stumbled over to her father and knelt beside him. She gently cradled his head, yielding to great sobs and kissing his hand before yielding to the reality that he was gone. Laying his head down, she ignored his blood, now staining the palm of her hand. Elisa stared at the arrows protruding like ghastly spikes in his chest. She struggled to stand and looked about. There was nothing to be done save hitch the team and get help from Nuecestown. Folks would need to be warned that hostiles were on the warpath. The threat to homesteaders had become all too real.

She hitched the mules, climbed aboard the wagon, and drove them up to the cabin. Taking a final sorrowful survey of the scene, she heard a weak groan. Somehow, little Mike was still alive despite the arrow in his chest and knot on his head. Elisa came to life. She sprang from her seat and half ran, half fell to Mike's side.

"Mike! Mike! Praise the Lord."

Mike opened his eyes and tried to focus to no avail. He tried to speak but only groaned with pain.

"Let's get you to Doc Andrews." She lifted his frail form, taking particular care not to touch the arrow and worsen his wound. The effort caused the youngster to pass out, but Elisa was able to hoist him into the wagon bed. She scrambled back into the wagon seat and flicked the reins. She paid no nevermind to the aftermath of the attack; her sole focus was to save her young brother.

The ten-minute wagon ride to Nuecestown seemed to take an eternity. She looked over her shoulder now and then to be sure Mike was still breathing. Finally, she brought the mule team to a halt in a cloud of dust in front of Doc's place, leaped from the wagon, and banged on his door. The racket of the door banging alone was enough to begin stirrings in the tiny community.

Doc opened the door and leaned against the jamb. Upon seeing Elisa's panicky expression, the whiskey bottle slipped from his hand and shattered on the doorstep.

"It's Mike, Doc! Indians! He's been shot with an arrow!"

It was almost too much information delivered too fast for Doc's inebriated yet lucid condition. He managed to stagger over to the wagon and peer over the side at little Mike's near-lifeless body. He turned his rheumy eyes to Elisa and mumbled, "Come now…let's get him inside."

Mike let out a cry of pain as Doc and Elisa managed to extricate him from the wagon bed and get him into the doctor's office. Doc had to sweep old liquor bottles and some dirty dishes from the examination table before they could lay the young boy on it.

"Stove over there is fired up, Elisa. Heat me some water." Doc was fast turning sober with the task at hand. He tore Mike's shirt away around the arrow.

Elisa grabbed a pot and rushed to fetch water. Once the pot was properly placed on the stove, she returned to Doc's side. "Is he going to make it, Doc?" she pleaded.

Doc sighed. "I've seen worse, but I don't think the arrow got anything vital. Good thing he's unconscious, 'cause I'm going to have to yank this goldarned thing out. Bring that water over here with a couple of those rags."

Mike's body flinched reflexively as Doc pulled the arrow from the boy's ribs. "Here, press this warm cloth tight against the wound. I'm gonna have to stitch this up a bit."

Elisa wrung the warm water from the rag and pressed it firmly against Mike's wound. She looked lovingly at her brother.

"I'm more concerned with that nasty bump on his noggin. I

expect your brother should stay here for a day or so to be sure it's not more serious." The words had no sooner left Doc's lips than he realized that Elisa's father and other brother were not with her. "Where's your pa, Elisa? And Rob?"

Elisa's mournful gaze said it all. She was unable to find the words to describe what had happened. Finally, one word escaped: "Comanche." It was enough.

By now, Bernice and Agatha, two middle-aged ladies who owned the boarding house across the street from Doc, had heard the commotion and wandered over to find out what had happened. Immediately, they asked whether they could help.

As the four of them gently placed Mike on a settee in the adjoining room, there was a commotion out in the street. A rather tall man on a big gray stallion had ridden in with his hand wrapped in a bloody bandana. He rode up to Doc's place, slipped from the saddle, and hitched his horse beside Elisa's wagon.

He glanced at the wagon before heading to the doorway. Doc was already standing there awaiting his arrival.

Doc shook his head. "Luke, what—"

Luke Dunn waved the bandana-wrapped hand before the doctor. "Caught a bushwhacker's slug, Doc. Need some sewing up." He strode past Doc and into the exam room, already beginning to strip off his shirt only to find himself facing three very worried-looking and suddenly surprised women. "Pardon, ladies."

Bernice, Agatha, and Elisa diverted their eyes at the brief view of the chiseled features and muscular chest of the visitor. Despite her distress over Mike and the attack, Elisa couldn't resist a peek. Her heart began to race.

Doc scrambled behind the tall interloper. "Let's have a look at that hand, Luke."

"I am truly sorry, ladies."

"I think you know Bernice and Agatha, Luke. Elisa Corrigan here lives up the road. She just brought her young brother in. Seems Comanche attacked their homestead."

Luke turned to her, fully taking her in for the first time. The pain in his hand suddenly disappeared, even as Doc began to clean the wound and sew it up. "Begging your pardon at your loss, Miss Corrigan. I'm Texas Ranger Luke Dunn. I'd be pleased to help."

Her heart, having succumbed to uncontrollable fluttering, Elisa could do naught but nod.

Doc interjected, "You'll be needing to take it easy with that hand, Luke. Once the wound has healed, squeeze a balled-up bandana regular-like until the strength comes back." He stepped back to admire his handiwork, then turned to Elisa. "Let's get a few folks together and head back to your place. I'm sure Bernice and Agatha will watch over Mike."

Luke offered a bashful smile as he buttoned up his shirt. He suddenly realized, with a touch of embarrassment, that he hadn't needed to strip it off for Doc to take care of a hand wound. "I won't be too much help with this bum hand, but I'll be pleased to do what I can." He tipped his hat and headed back to Big Horse.

Elisa followed Luke out the door, feeling as though she was on some sort of tether. She found herself conflicted among the feelings welling within her body—curiosity for this handsome lawman, concern for her brother, and sadness at the loss of her father and Rob. Uncertainty for the future, however, had yet to enter her consciousness.

BERT THE BUCKIN' BULL

Sixteen hundred pounds of leaping, spinning, plunging bull;
I'm a mean, nasty, kickin', slobberin', slammin' beast.
Mostly Brahma bloodline bred of Oklahoma kin,
They call me Bertrum, Bert for short. Don't you be laughin'.
They dared not name me Mr. Majestic or Bushwhacker;
Coulda called me Tornado or Outlaw or Bandit.
My corralmates, they snort and laugh when they call my
     name,
The flankmen push me into the chute, me kickin' and all.
Dude on my back, he fancies hisself a bull rider,
Got spurs an' chaps, an' he gonna need that padded vest.
Wearin' one of them sissy helmets 'stead of a hat;
Couple bucks in the chute, show the rider I'm the boss.
Got news fur ya, mister cowboy, you can't ride this bull;
Ain't nobody ever seen eight seconds on this back.
Judges, you be watchin', and you clowns step lively now;
Fools open the gate, out I come buckin' an' ragin'.
Turn left, turn left again, twist, cowboy swings his hand high;
Five seconds, six, six and a half, he's thinkin' he's won.
I turn to the right, his head goes high, an' off he come;
Seven point eight nine seconds, his ride, it don't count none.
Judges, they be shakin' their heads as they always do;
Clowns ain't laughin as I run 'em 'round an' take my bows.

TUMBLEWEED TUMBLINGS

I exit snortin', leavin' a cheerin' crowd behind;
Ain't no corralmates snortin' an' laughin' at my name.
That cowboy be limpin' home, wishin' he'd not drawn Bert;
As he sits down to dinner, he'll still be tastin' dirt.
Yep, ain't never been ridden', an' likely never will;
I'm sixteen hundred pounds of fury named Bert the Bull.

MINDIN' THE HERD

Life flows easy 'nough, like a cowboy
Mindin' the herd, kickin' a bit o' trail dust.
Prairie far as the eye can see an' then some,
Purple sage hitched with sunset gold.
Lonely but free, nary a soul to see,
Squeakin' leather an' jingle of spur.
Coyote an' longhorn serenade,
Listen real careful, you'll hear stars blink.
The cowboy hummin' to God's symphony,
Night on the range, mindin' the herd.

PENATEKA SPIRIT WOLF
DEATH STALKS THE COMANCHE MOON

The Penateka Comanche War Chief Three Toes is a key character in the Tumbleweed Sagas, as his relationship with Luke Dunn comes to represent the dilemma faced by the conflicting cultures of Red man and White man. The Comanche were the most savage of the tribes roaming the American West. Victims of the savages were advised to save a last bullet for themselves rather than endure Comanche torture. This is Three Toes' story up until the moment he meets Dunn.

SWIMMING HORSES SAT bare-chested gazing out onto the vastness of distant hills from his perch atop the very highest point of the escarpment. The sun's rays cast an ethereal glow upon his rust-colored skin, and his long black hair hung loosely over his shoulders. Buckskin leggings and moccasins were his only protections against the early morning chill. Time seemed to have flown by, especially the five years since he'd ridden as a young warrior with Buffalo Hump and a thousand fellow Comanche. They'd raided Texas towns all the way to the Great Sea, burning down the place the Whites called Linnville and sacking and burning Victoria. The great chief had looked out at what the Comanche might have wrought and had been satisfied.

Swimming Horses proudly recalled how Buffalo Hump frustrated the soldiers sent to pursue the Comanche as the great mass of warriors and their families made the slow, arduous trek back to their

47

villages. None dared call it a retreat, as they'd never been defeated. Swimming Horses' people—the Penateka, or honey eaters—were the southernmost band of Comanche, and their domain covered most of Central and Western Texas. Now, he was on a vision quest.

To the youth of the tribe, the vision quest was a rite of passage. For an experienced warrior like Swimming Horses, it was more a meditation undertaken away from the distractions of his encampment. He'd chosen an exposed place, as was the custom, and consumed neither food nor water. With his preparation complete, he awaited a creature or element of nature that would be revealed in a vision and map his future direction. What, indeed, was the future to hold for this mighty warrior who had counted many coups and hung dozens of scalps from his teepee and lance? What might the future hold for the Comanche people as more White settlers encroached on long-cherished hunting grounds? Were they to live up to the White man's translation of the Comanche name: the Ute word *kimantsi*, enemy? Three days had passed since Swimming Horses began his solemn vigil. He waited patiently for the Great Spirit to give him a sign.

His thoughts wandered to how his squaws, Bird Woman and Flower Petals, were likely concerned for him by now. Would the Great Spirit forgive his carnality? He had found himself distracted from his meditations by visions of satisfying his sexual passions with Flower Petals just before leaving on this vision quest. She was the younger of the two wives and considered strikingly beautiful among his people. He was sure that she was with child; it would be her first. Swimming Horses already had three children by Bird Woman, and he was intent on adding more warriors to the Penateka Comanche nation. He couldn't suppress a smile as he looked forward to further intimacy with Flower Petals upon his return. He caught himself once more and shook his head as if to rid his head of the thoughts of such pleasures. Sex wasn't likely a message he'd be receiving from *Manitou*, the Great Spirit.

And so, the day passed. He resisted the urge to eat. The summer sunbathed his surroundings in a seemingly endless sea of purples, magentas, and golds as it sank ever so spectacularly into the distant western hills. The moon soon found its way slowly, ever silently, into the night sky. It was huge, hovering in the early evening sky with a brightness that rivaled daylight. The White people called this the "Comanche moon," as it was often the harbinger of night raids on farms, ranches, and settlements.

Swimming Horses had no idea how long he'd slept. He'd fallen over from his sitting position and now lay on his side. The sun was just peeking above the eastern horizon as a gentle breeze brought an aroma more often feared than sought after. Swimming Horses cautiously opened his eyes. The scent wafting past his nostrils gave him pause for the realization of his worst fear. A pair of yellow eyes penetrated his own. The aroma? Well, it was from the telltale breath of the great gray wolf that now stood over him.

"*Tseena,*" he hissed through clenched teeth. His eyes opened wide and stared back intensely into those burning yellow eyes. This was what the Penateka referred to as the conversation of death. It was not words spoken aloud, but rather a hypnotic stare that the hunter leveled at its prey to communicate that certain death lurked. It was a common habit of the wolf, aimed to drive a fear of what was to come deep within the very soul of its prey.

Swimming Horses opened his eyes even wider. The wolf—was it a wolf?—had disappeared. Where had it gone? "*Tseena atsabi.* He uttered the words aloud in his Comanche tongue. Had what he'd seen indeed been the spirit wolf of legend? Had it been real, or a vision conjured by the Great Spirit?

He sat upright and looked about, then stood. The rock ledge had made for a decidedly unyielding bed. His eyes swept the ground, but the rock yielded no paw prints. His legs and back protested, belying the fact that he was yet a young warrior. Swimming Horses' bronze skin stretched tautly over his unusually well-muscled physique. His high cheekbones and aquiline nose gave him an air of nobility not uncommon to his people, but especially so with him. He'd shed the leggings and now wore only a buckskin breechcloth, leaving no other part of his body to the imagination. He stretched out his arms, tightening the skin while flexing sinewy strands of muscle.

The warrior gathered his spirit pouch and his bow and arrows. "*Tseena atsabi,*" he murmured. "*Tseena atsabi,*" he repeated in a reverent whisper. Strong medicine, indeed. For the Penateka Comanche people, the wolf symbolized loyalty, trust of heart and mind. Like the Comanche, the wolf was an apex hunter setting atop the natural food chain. Surely, the vision confirmed his destiny to be a leader of his people, a great chief. His war bonnet already featured many eagle feathers, and he owned many ponies. He was even considering taking a third wife. Swimming Horses fully expected to be elected chief at the next council. Would this vision seal that fate? The Great Spirit had spoken, so surely it would be so.

As he hiked down from the escarpment and sought his pony, he paused and watched transfixed as a *kwihnai*, an eagle, swooped from the sky and snared a rabbit in its talons. Was this also a sign from the Great Spirit? This sign, though, was a message of war. It puzzled him. The Great Spirit seemed to be besieging him this day with strong messages.

Swimming Horses' pony grazed in the nearby meadow where the warrior had let him loose three days earlier. Like his fellow Comanche, the horse had become an integral part of Swimming Horses' life. His people were known for their expert horsemanship. Regardless of which of his many horses he rode, Swimming Horses rode as one in body and spirit with his mount. At the appearance of the warrior, the horse raised his head, whinnied with a sound akin to joy, and cantered over to him. The Comanche warrior stroked the pony's nose affectionately before turning and mounting him for the ride back to the Penateka encampment.

Swimming Horses was but a half mile from the encampment when he heard a veritable cacophony of shouting and cries. Quickly, he dismounted and put his ear to the ground. Horses...many horses. He arose and leaped onto his pony's back. He hadn't ridden much further when he was able to distinguish war whoops among what was seemingly chaotic din. There was no question now that his village was under attack. He grasped his bow, nocked an arrow, and urged his pony to a gallop. There was no time for war paint, no time for ceremony. He and his pony were as one, a mobile fortress ready for battle.

In short order, he was in the midst of the attacking Kiowa.

Cooking fires had been scattered, a teepee was burning, and smoke and dust seemed everywhere.

He saw Flower Petals running for her life. A Kiowa savage on horseback pursued her with war club raised to strike. The savage warrior quickly closed the distance, raising his war club as he rode upon her and striking her a blow atop her skull, shattering the bone and spewing blood and brain. The Kiowa's momentum carried him past Flower Petals. He turned and looked wildly at his victim. A vicious, hate-filled smile spread across his face as he saw her body crumpled in the dirt. Movement caught his peripheral vision. He looked up to see Swimming Horses but a half dozen horse lengths away. The Comanche aimed well. His arrow flew true, penetrating deep into the center of the Kiowa warrior's chest. Alas, it had been too late to save his beloved Flower Petals. Anger coursed through Swimming Horses' entire being…revenge…unbridled hatred of his enemy. He let out a blood-curdling cry.

Swimming Horses rode into the heart of the battle, delivering death to two more Kiowa warriors. He rallied the Penateka warriors, transforming a perimeter of defense into a charge aimed at driving the Kiowa out. As he turned his pony to rally the Penateka defenders, a Kiowa warrior's hatchet struck a slicing blow to his foot, cutting deeply between his outermost toes. The pain would have been excruciating, but for the heat of battle, and the hatchet-wielding Kiowa quickly paid the ultimate price. The Kiowa were now getting the worst of it. They began to run off, able to steal nary a single Comanche horse.

Now, in headlong retreat, the Kiowa war chief Thunder Cloud paused at the tree line and turned back to scan the encampment. The chief had misjudged the strength of the Penateka. He locked eyes with Swimming Horses. He'd not soon forget the warrior that had rallied the Comanche warriors and repelled the attack. He raised his chin haughtily and looked down his nose at Swimming Horses as though to say they'd meet another day. He shook his war lance menacingly at the Comanche warrior, turned, and urged his pony into a gallop away from the encampment.

Swimming Horses returned the Kiowa chief's gaze with a look of triumph aimed to unnerve his foe. He watched the Kiowa chief and remaining attackers escape with utter frustration. The juices of battle still roiled within his brain. He was afoot. The Kiowa were free to flee. For now, Swimming Horses limped over to the fallen Kiowa that had slain Flower Petals and deftly lifted the dead savage's scalp. He then stood back and surveyed the scene. The Penateka had lost two warriors and two women, including Swimming Horses' wife, and several more were wounded.

It was only at this moment that the adrenaline wore off, and awareness of all that had happened took hold. He realized that he was bleeding badly. He'd lost the two outside toes of his right foot thanks to the Kiowa warrior's hatchet blow. Had his pony not been turning, the wound might have been far worse. Thus it was that Swimming Horses felt a mixture of pain from his wound and grief over the loss of his beloved Flower Petals. The blood loss was beginning to have an effect as he started to feel wooziness overtaking him. He breathed deeply and shook it off as he called upon the power of *tseena atsabi*. Amazingly, a new strength swept over him.

The urge to chase after the retreating Kiowa was held at bay only by Swimming Horses' strong sense of seeing that his family and his people were safe. His three young sons and his daughter were unscathed, and Bird Woman stood protectively over them. She held a Comanche war club that she likely would have wielded with great effect had she been called to do so. Swimming Horses limped over to his wife and stood before her with a grim half-smile of approval and unspoken relief. He turned to face the warriors gathering around. "Death stalk *tseena* moon," he growled. There was bloodlust in every face. "Tonight, we smoke pipe, dance. Two days...Kiowa die."

Over the next two days, the Penateka would perform war dances and pray for strength to spirits such as *kwihnai*, the eagle, in preparation for the battle to come. The warriors would paint their faces and bodies with symbols of their personal power. In their frenzied ritual dancing, they'd wear headdresses with feathers or buffalo horns and carry shields painted and decorated with feathers, bear claws, horse tails, and scalps. Come morning, they would be fully empowered to slay the Kiowa. The Kiowa were destined to pay for their predations.

His foot wrapped in a poultice with medicinal herbs, Swimming Horses sat astride his best pony and proudly waved his lance. The council had met and decided that he would lead the attack to teach the Kiowa a lesson. He would do it with his new name: Three Toes, given in recognition of his bravery in rallying the warriors to fend off the Kiowa attack despite his wound. It would ever be a symbol and reminder of having given a part of his physical being in defense of his Penateka Comanche people. Three Toes was now a Comanche war chief.

From what little Three Toes knew of the Kiowa band, they were part of Chief Sitting Bear's people. Sitting Bear was a renowned medicine man as well as chief and was known to hold great influence over his people. The Kiowa had recently made a fragile peace with the Cheyenne, and that apparently had empowered the band to take on the mighty Comanche. Thus, and as was their habit in such endeavors, they had undertaken a surprise attack on the Penateka village. Thunder Cloud, the impetuous young underchief that led the Kiowa attack, was not nearly so seasoned a warrior as Three Toes and had thus misjudged the Comanche strength both of numbers and fighting spirit.

Three Toes sat erect and spoke to the three dozen assembled warriors. They'd spent the night dancing and feasting in preparation for the raid on the Kiowa camp; scouts had confirmed the location of the encampment. Unless the enemy had all of a sudden broken camp and moved away out of easy reach, the Comanche estimated that the Kiowa would be little more than twenty miles west. With the moon still shedding its brightness over the landscape, the Comanche warriors would be able to move quickly and stealthily at night toward the enemy. They knew that the Kiowa would deploy sentries, but the Penateka warriors were confident they could eliminate them without alerting the camp. Three Toes also surmised that the Kiowa would set extra sentries around their horses out of fear that the Comanche vengeance would entail stealing the herd.

The Penateka Comanche band was a fearsome lot to behold. Each warrior was painted with horizontal broad black stripes that nearly covered the entire face. Three Toes, in particular, wore a bone breastplate and tan buckskin leggings with a simple colorfully beaded moccasin on his good foot. His long black hair fell in braids on either side of his head. His shield offered protection but was not large. It was of a hardness of leather such that it could stop an arrow and even deflect some bullets. More importantly, its size wouldn't hinder his shooting of arrows from horseback at a full gallop. A war club hung from his waist along with his knife, while his quiver of arrows was slung across his back. His war lance was decorated with scalps, bear claws, and eagle feathers. The crowning glory was Three Toes' war bonnet with its ornately beaded band, more than two dozen eagle feathers, and long fur side strips of fox skins. Even his black pony featured war paint designed to protect it from evil spirits. The chief was a mounted killing machine, and he would be highly visible to friend and foe alike in the heat of battle.

Bird Woman and the children proudly waved to Three Toes as he led the band from the encampment. The mourning for Flower Petals yet lingered, but Three Toes aimed to avenge her death. She had indeed been with child; thus, he'd be avenging two of his most beloved Comanche. Warrior ponies pranced as they sensed the coming battle, and the Comanche optimism extended to bringing several pack horses carrying jerky and pemmican to eat, any necessary utensils, and room for the prizes from their expected victory.

Thunder Cloud strode from the darkness of his teepee. There was an air of arrogance about him despite the raid on the Comanche encampment having gone poorly. The triumphant expression on the face of the Comanche leader had been burned into his thoughts. He knew better than to let it cloud his thinking but couldn't help himself. He breathed deeply, looking ruefully off into the distance. The landscape before him seemed fully bathed in daylight thanks to the fullness of the moon. He sniffed the air. He had a sense that something was amiss, but he couldn't quite determine what might have alerted him from his fitful slumber.

Thunder Cloud looked up at the moon. It seemed unusually large in the early evening sky. He felt a breeze coming from the west and saw a large cloud bank moving to intercept and likely cover the moon from sight. He nodded as though understanding his vulnerability. He would feel more secure in the darkness. *Where,* he thought to himself, *where could the Comanche be?*

Sentries brought the chief no news of Comanche sightings. Still, Thunder Cloud was concerned. He was determined to move their camp come first light; there was no point in further tempting fate. The Great Spirit had protected the Kiowa thus far. Of course, he found himself conflicted, as the attack on the Comanche village had yielded no horses and cost him warriors he could ill afford to lose. He was embarrassed at his failure but nevertheless wise enough to not push his luck. Better to lose face than be foolhardy. The chief needed to rebuild trust with his warriors, but he'd have to be patient. He'd head northward in the morning, where he could rejoin bands of his fellow Kiowa. Perhaps they could join together and find better fortune fighting Cheyenne or Lakota. For now, Thunder Cloud had had enough of the Comanche.

The power of *tseena* filled Three Toes with an unusual sense of awareness of his surroundings. He and his warriors knew this country far better than the Kiowa interlopers. If his scouts had been right about the location of Thunder Cloud's encampment, the Comanche leader's band would have the high ground and be at a distinct advantage. *Tseena* was renowned for his keen sense of smell, so it was of little surprise to Three Toes that he seemed to have been given the wolf's power to pick up a scent wafting from the Kiowa camp. Being downwind helped, but it soon became quite apparent that the Kiowa had employed an old trick of using buffalo dung to disguise their human odors. Three Toes shook his head and stifled a laugh at such a feeble tactic.

The Penateka had journeyed to perhaps a half mile from the Kiowa camp when one of the Comanche warriors sidled up to Three Toes and displayed a fresh scalp. A sentry had been permanently disabled. "You have done well, my brother. We are close," he offered in a hushed tone. Three Toes stretched out his arms, giving a signal to fan out as preparation for attack. Once the dead Kiowa was discovered at the changing of the sentries, the battle would be on.

Three Toes could now only patiently wait, hoping that the clouds would move quickly.

There'd be no niceties, no chance for the Kiowa to surrender. Three Toes wondered whether Thunder Cloud's wives might be in the camp but knew it was unlikely that a war party would bring wives along. Like the Comanche, Kiowa war parties counted on unencumbered mobility. Three Toes raised his hand to bring his warriors to a halt. Despite the moon's light, his warriors blended into the landscape, hidden from sight by the shadows of tall grasses, occasional mottes of live oak, and a nearby grove of cypress. Patience was key. His foot throbbed, reminding him of how close he'd come to even more serious injury. Patience. He'd wait for the clouds to fully obscure the moon.

The distant hoot of an owl broke the silence, joined by frogs at the nearby creek. A coyote added to the evening's symphony. Patience. The faintest sounds carried far in the stillness of such an evening. The Comanche ponies, as if sensing the impending battle and the need for silence, made nary a whinny or snort while they nodded their heads, flicked their tails, and anxiously shifted on their unshod hooves.

Comanche didn't measure time by minutes or hours or days. Three Toes would wait for as long as it took for the circumstances to be just right. Ever so slowly, the cloud bank began to obscure the moon. The landscape became ever darker. Their patience was being rewarded. They wouldn't be waiting for a change of sentries after all.

The time had arrived. Three Toes took a deep breath, shifting his gaze ahead. He sat proudly on his pony as it now pranced with anticipation. He raised his war lance and waved it forward toward the Kiowa camp. The warriors silently advanced as one body, urging their ponies forward at a walk and then a canter. There'd be no noise until a sentry was encountered. It didn't take long. A luckless Kiowa was yet adjusting his eyes to the darkness when a pair of Comanche warriors in full war paint appeared but a couple of horse lengths from him. One Penateka warrior urged his pony forward, tapped the surprised sentry with his lance to count coup, and then turned and drove the shaft deep into the Kiowa's heart. The sentry was barely able to emit a grunting sort of death scream as two arrows followed in rapid succession, finding their way deep into the warrior's chest and throat. The Comanche attacker dismounted, swiftly took the sentry's scalp, and remounted in one fluid motion.

"Aarrrraaaaaagh! Whoop! Whoop!" A loud guttural holler followed by war whoops. "Arrryaaaah!" Three Toes drove his heels into his war pony's flanks and led the charge forward at a full gallop into the Kiowa camp. Pandemonium instantly broke loose among Thunder Cloud's warriors. In the darkness, targets were hard to find, but the mounted Comanche warriors' eyes had adjusted to the darkness, making them exceptional at lancing and shooting the panicking shadows that were Kiowa warriors. Everywhere the Kiowa turned, the darkness delivered death. The attack was devastatingly quick and effective.

As if on cue, the cloud cover hiding the moon began to move off, bathing the Kiowa camp in the moon's light. The stench of death already permeated the air. Three Toes found himself face-to-face with a wounded Thunder Cloud. The memory of Flower Petal touched him and filled his heart with both sadness and a lust for revenge. A deeply embedded arrow protruded from the Kiowa chief's thigh as he stood defiantly facing the Comanche war chief with naught but a knife as his weapon. Three Toes drew Thunder Cloud's eyes to his with a seemingly magnetic pull. His gaze drilled with a powerful intensity into the Kiowa's eyes. Three Toes felt the strength, the power of *tseena*, surge through the very core of his being. The conversation of death had begun.

Thunder Cloud had initially shown no fear, but his defiance began to fade under the sheer weight of Three Toes' hypnotic gaze. It was as though the Comanche chief's eyes were one with *tseena*—piercing, impaling, penetrating. Bravado was rapidly being replaced by a growing realization of what was to come. Several Comanche warriors rode up beside Three Toes, transfixed. Most of the Kiowa braves had been killed, some mortally wounded, and the rest run off. Fresh scalps already dangled from Comanche waistbands.

Three Toes raised his arm and slipped from his pony's back. In this moment, he felt no pain from his wounded foot. His gaze bore into the Kiowa chief relentlessly with the power of *tseena*, and Thunder Cloud felt the overwhelming power of this conversation of death. In a final attempt at defiance, he raised his chin and growled a challenge. He strove to break the force of *tseena*. He slammed his fist against his chest. "Thunder Cloud, chief of Kiowa!" With that, he took a painful step toward Three Toes while flailing out with his knife.

The Comanche chief easily sidestepped the blade and touched his lance tip to the Kiowa's shoulder. He'd counted coup; the Kiowa's fate was sealed. Thunder Cloud felt a sharp spasm of intense pain from his wounded leg and found himself momentarily off-balance. As the Kiowa caught himself, Three Toes deftly pivoted, plunging his lance deep into Thunder Cloud's chest. The Kiowa flailed out again with his knife but sliced naught but thin night air. Three Toes' eyes were riveted on the Kiowa's now pleadingly desperate expression. The Comanche chief's words would haunt Thunder Cloud forever in the afterlife. "Three Toes...chief of Comanche...*tseena atsabi*!" His knife swiftly deprived the dying Kiowa of his scalp.

Three Toes stood over the body of Thunder Cloud, raised the bloody scalp high, and let out a blood-curdling war cry. The attack on their encampment had been avenged. The deaths of Flower Petals and their unborn child had been avenged. The Kiowa would think long and hard before returning to the lands of the Penateka Comanche.

The Comanche gathered the many horses left behind by the retreating Kiowa. Three Toes and his Penateka warriors would celebrate by morning's light in their own Comanche encampment and be ever grateful to the Great Spirit and *tseena atsabi*.

The sun rose over the hills before them as the Penateka Comanche war party rode into their home encampment. The women and children were overjoyed that the entire war party had returned intact. Fresh scalps hung from lances, and Three Toes couldn't suppress a triumphant grin. It had been serious business, but his having led a successful attack would speak volumes to his growing reputation. He could now properly tend to grieving the loss of Flower Petals and her unborn child, as well as allow his foot to heal. He embraced Bird Woman and each of his sons. His daughter earned merely a smile. Such was the Comanche way.

It seemed that Three Toes had drawn great power from his vision quest. *Tseena* had delivered victory. The chief would have time while healing to listen to *tseena* as to where his next spirit calling might be. With the encampment having swelled to more than 150 Comanche warriors, squaws, and children, he was already giving thought to organizing a serious hunt, as there were many mouths to be fed. That would mean assembling a large hunting party, including the best hunters as well as women, to tend the temporary camp. A successful hunt would mean tending to meat preservation, tanning hides, repairing equipment, feeding hungry hunters, tending horses, guarding the camp, and more.

Three months had passed since Three Toes' hunting party had set out eastward. Their encampment due south of San Antonio offered easy access to water, avoided trails commonly used by the White man, and provided plenty of game. They were interested mostly in venison, but an occasional javelina, lynx, or mountain lion was welcome. Three Toes had even managed to kill a bear, though it had cost him a nasty slash across his chest. The bearskin and the rakish claws, however, were worthy trophies. Bear fat also provided arguably the best lubricant of any of the frontier game animals.

"It is time to return to our people." Three Toes looked out almost wistfully across the wide river as he shared his thoughts with Long Feathers. "Great Spirit give plenty." He wondered how many more hunts there'd be before the White man overran his people.

Long Feathers looked off toward the setting sun. "Great Spirit keep White man away."

Three Toes nodded. Indeed, there'd been some near brushes with occasional travelers but no incidents. The younger warriors were always a worry, as they yearned to prove their manhood. He'd overheard three of his best young warriors talking of attacking the homesteads of the hated White man. Three Toes felt claustrophobic, as though a new world order was slowly crushing the Comanche in from all sides. The mere thought tightened his chest and made breathing momentarily difficult. The day before, he had seen a column of heavily armed men on horseback pass perilously close to the Penateka encampment. He'd heard of these men, called Texas Rangers, and they were to be feared by all accounts.

"What troubles you, my chief?"

Three Toes shook off his trepidations upon realizing they'd become physically obvious. "We break camp at rising of sun." He began to walk off. He paused and turned as if to say more, but chose not to and headed toward his teepee. Perhaps a dalliance with his new second wife, Moon Woman, would ease his thoughts?

Long Feathers watched the war chief limp away. The effects of having lost a couple of toes had had a lasting impact. The warrior turned his attention to his own sons. He, too, had heard talk of raiding homesteads. It didn't seem like so bad an idea, though it was clear that Three Toes wasn't inclined to go to war against the Anglos. He shrugged and went to look for his sons, Coyote Who Runs and Hawk Nose.

Three Toes emerged from his teepee with a self-satisfied smile, cinched his breechcloth tighter, and let his eyes scan the encampment. Preparations for leaving the next morning were already underway. He looked over at the remuda and sensed that ponies were missing. He couldn't be fully certain, but he prided himself on keeping track of these sorts of things. Thus, even three ponies of the nearly one hundred in the remuda were noticed as missing by his practiced eye. He saw Long Feathers and Mandog talking animatedly and strode over.

Mandog's son, Bear Slayer, had left camp along with Long Feathers' two sons. They'd been seen by Mandog's wife, who noted that they had carried full quivers of arrows and their lances and clubs. Most significantly, they'd painted their faces as if for battle.

Three Toes asked the obvious. "What worries you, my brothers?"

Mandog's facial expression showed anger at the impetuosity of his son. He was unable to speak.

Long Feathers, furious as well, also found words difficult. "Our sons are hunting." He choked. "They headed into the rising sun."

Three Toes strove to suppress his own anger. "You dance with words, my brothers."

Mandog finally blurted it out, "They go to kill Whites."

"When did they leave?"

"Before sunrise."

Three Toes realized there would be no time to catch the three young bucks and stop their attack. He shook his head. "We wait," he said resignedly.

Mandog and Long Feathers wore apologetic expressions, but the damage was already underway.

Three Toes turned to them. "We must break camp quickly." He knew that it wouldn't be long before the bluecoats would be avenging whatever havoc the young Comanche braves wrought.

★★

Two nearly spent ponies galloping hard into the encampment weren't missed by Three Toes' practiced eye. The riderless third pony was of greater concern.

The two young Comanche warriors pulled up not far from Three Toes' teepee. They acted as though they didn't want to face him.

"Coyote Who Runs, come here." The chief was not about to let them avoid answering to him. Coyote Who Runs and Hawk Nose walked over, their eyes glued to the earth. "Where your brother? Where Bear Slayer?"

Coyote Who Runs' eyes remained glued to the ground. "He count coup, kill, scalp White man." They were touting Bear Slayer's bravery, as if to distract from having to answer Three Toes' question. The warrior paused, breathed deeply, and barely whispered, "Bear Slayer killed."

"How die? Where scalps you take avenging him?"

Hawk Nose sighed and resigned himself to the inevitable. "White woman kill him." They dared not admit that the woman was a young girl.

"And you left him to die?" Three Toes worked hard to contain his anger. What was happening with the young Comanche warriors these days? Where was their sense of honor? "We talk with Council...tonight." He waved them away. The Council would not likely result in a desirable outcome for the two; there would be some punishment. Bear Slayer had two wives, children, and several horses. He would likely have become a chief one day.

Coyote Who Runs and Hawk Nose, fearing punishment, snuck away from the encampment ahead of the Council meeting in hopes of avenging Bear Slayer's death.

Three Toes, having seen them slip away and telling Moon Woman to say he'd gone hunting if anyone asked, followed the two warriors at a distance. Thus, the chief patiently watched from afar as the warriors met their fate at the hands of a tall, red-haired man and a young woman. This was hardly the outcome he had expected. Three Toes had at least been confident in the warriors' prospects of killing the woman and bringing back Bear Slayer's body. Despite his sadness at losing Coyote Who Runs and Hawk Nose, he was none-theless impressed with the fighting skill of the big White man and the bravery of the young White woman. He had faced Texas Rangers with Buffalo Hump in the past and recognized the shiny badge on the man's chest that caught the rays of the afternoon sun.

The chief had seen where the big man had buried Bear Slayer, and he was thus deeply impressed by the Texas Ranger's respect for the dead Comanche. He was doubly respectful when the White man similarly buried the bodies of Coyote Who Runs and Hawk Nose. This White man seemed different. He was sure the young woman had called him Dunn; he figured this must be his name. He was appreciative of Dunn's attempt to lay the bodies out respectfully. It wasn't the Comanche way, but the White man's care was duly noted. Because of this, he might only kill him and spare him any torture.

Three Toes thought about tribal custom. Traditionally, he would wrap the dead warriors' bodies in blankets, place them on horses behind riders, and then ride in search of a burial place like a secure cave. After burial, the bodies would be covered with stones. The riders would return to the encampment, where the tribe burned all the deceased warrior's possessions. He sighed. There simply was no time, and there were too many people nearby. Three Toes continued to observe the homestead until Dunn rode off. Even with the Ranger gone, there were too many Whites around for even a brave Comanche chief to attack. He'd bide his time; there would be other days to avenge his warriors. He waited until the Whites had left the homestead before satisfying the spirits by uttering songs and incantations appropriate to the spirits of the dead over the bodies where the Ranger had buried them. Three Toes would pay his respects later to Long Feathers and others of the tribe. He reflected on his vision quest and the images of *tseena* and *kwihnai*. The calls for war and loyalty roiled in his head.

Then, there was still the matter of his curiosity about the Texas Ranger. He waited until morning before searching for and taking up the Texas Ranger's trail. Finding Dunn's trail hadn't been difficult for a Comanche of Three Toes' experience. While he remained determined to avenge the deaths of his warriors, he was just as determined to find what it was that seemed different about this White man. The eagle vision, the image of *kwihnai,* was strong, and he felt obligated by loyalty to his tribe to better understand the enemy.

As he tracked this man named Dunn in the days that followed, the chief found himself impressed by the White man's skills at doubling back and hiding his trail. The Ranger was tracking someone, but he clearly suspected he was also being tracked himself. Three Toes found himself respecting the lawman, albeit grudgingly. He felt at times as though he was tracking a spirit, a ghost of sorts.

On the afternoon of the third day of tracking his prey, Three Toes suddenly found it necessary to hunker low in the tall grass. He made his pony lie down. Man and beast would lay low and stay quiet for however long it took for his prey to move off to a safe tracking distance. Three Toes had been careless, inadvertently following within sight of the Texas Ranger. He could only hope that he hadn't been seen.

That was not to be. Too soon, Three Toes found himself staring down the barrel of Texas Ranger Dunn's Colt revolver. The hammer was cocked, and the lawman's finger was curled around the trigger. The chief's head spun with a combination of surprise, anger at his carelessness, and fear at his possible fate. Should he fight, or try to escape? The primary Comanche warrior instinct was to fight, but such a choice meant certain death. Why hadn't the Ranger pulled the trigger? His eyes swept the White man from hat to boots. He was a big man with fiery red hair. The gray horse he led was also big by any measure. They presented a formidable enemy...or might this White man be a friend?

Three Toes cautiously raised his hand as a sign of peace.

Dunn smiled and motioned with the barrel of his gun for the chief to stand. Then, much to Three Toes' surprise, the Texas Ranger released the hammer on the Colt and slipped it back into his holster. The Ranger smiled. He surely recognized that Three Toes was at his mercy but had chosen to not kill the Comanche. "My name is Luke Dunn." He spoke slowly and distinctly, pointing to his chest as he introduced himself.

Three Toes closed his eyes. Images of *tseena* and *kwihnai* swept through his mind. As he opened his eyes, he relaxed and attempted to smile. "Me Three Toes...chief of Penateka Comanche."

It was as though some invisible barrier had been struck down. Luke stepped forward, his hand extended.

Was this the man who had, just days before, killed and buried Three Toes' warriors? Could he trust the White man? Then again, this White man had respected the dead Comanche; this White man could have killed him quite easily. His instinct was to trust this human who had surprisingly made himself vulnerable before a savage Comanche chief.

Had he been able to climb inside the Texas Ranger's head to know that he really didn't want to have to kill another Indian, and had he known of the advice this White man held dear that peace was a preferable outcome, he might have more readily understood Luke's motives. He took Luke's hand in his and clasped it firmly. It was though some sort of bond was forming, a bond built upon mutual trust and respect. Three Toes eyed the Ranger guardedly and spoke respectfully, "*Atsabi tuhuya karu*."

Luke cocked his head inquisitively.

Three Toes pointed to Dunn's horse and made a stepping motion with his fingers, then pointed to the sky and made a wave with his hands as if to erase the image he was depicting. *"Atsabi tuhuya karu."*

Luke cogitated on the chief's hand motions, and his eyes grew wide. The chief was telling him he was like a ghost who rode a horse. To Three Toes, he was Ghost Who Rides. He repeated the chief's words, *"Atsabi tuhuya karu."*

Three Toes smiled.

Luke motioned toward the shade of a nearby live oak motte. "Want grub?" Luke pointed to his mouth and made a chewing motion with his jaw. With that, he mounted up and urged Three Toes to follow.

Soon, they would become acquainted and begin a friendship over beef jerky and coffee.

NOBLE SAVAGES

Ponies prance nervously, bathed in breaking shards of
     morning sun,
A breeze wafts ever so gently across the buffalo run;
Red, yellow, magic images dance across the horses' hides,
Snorts, bobbing heads, swishing tails into havoc, they'll soon
     ride.

The Cheyenne village sleeps, lies silent; a dog sniffs the air.
A meandering wispy haze tempers sun's early glare;
Spires of dying campfire smoke hint of life the day before,
Mother and child emerge from a teepee; she stretches, yawns.

Comanche eyes scan the scene, glow black with savage fury,
The chief sits astride his pony, headdress in full array.
Scalps adorn his lance; bow and arrows will soon terrify.
Up he thrusts his black-striped face to the Great Spirit on
     high.

The sound begins deep inside, guttural, then a blood-
     curdling cry.
Lance held high, he leads the charge to be the first to count
     coup;

In a heartbeat they're among teepees, ash and dust kicked
   high,
Fleeing squaws, screaming children, old men standing ready
   to die.

Cheyenne warriors rally for naught as arrows fill the skies,
Run down, cut down, scalped as they breathe their final
   goodbyes.
Children killed before their mother's eyes, women raped,
   impaled;
No prisoners, no mercy, the Comanche have prevailed.

The Comanche chief, bronze skin glisten with sweat, with
   blood, this day,
Hand held high with bloody scalps, soon on his lance will
   display.
His long trilling war whoop signals the end of the gory fray,
Off they gallop, a hundred prized horses leading the way.

Mourning wails fill the air, rising mists reveal the horrid
   void;
Warriors bloodied, women defiled, children destroyed.
A panicked stray pony, lost dog, dying fires, dying race,
A burned-out teepee falls; of Cheyenne peace, there is no
   trace.

The Comanche chief pauses at the live oaks, turns, gazes
   back,
A final whoop, lance raised high, Armageddon on horseback.
Comanche, enemy, new stories to tell of this day,
Then he looks beyond. Dust? Wagons? Comes end of
   Comanche way.

COMANCHE RAID

The author's family emigrated from Ireland and settled in South Texas beginning in 1845. The frontier could be unforgiving. Comanche roamed the prairies seeking to acquire horses to trade and breed toward building their herds. They trusted no one. Their tortures were legendarily horrible. This poem is based on accounts of encounters with Comanche raiding parties during those early years of building ranches, farms, and families on the prairie frontier of South Texas. From 1855 to 1912, the poet's great-great-grandfather, Nicholas Dunn, raised longhorns and horses on his twenty-thousand-acre spread west of Corpus Christi. The Dunns and other families endured despite the challenges wrought by weather, disease, bandits, and not-so-noble savages. The following poem is about a Comanche raid that Dunn may have faced.

Bert is the name we gave our breeder bull,
A prize longhorn with six-foot horn span.
His bellow shook the afternoon lull;
An arrow struck clean through his feed pan.

I shouted for my family to hide,
While ducking behind the water trough.
I grabbed my rifle, quarters were close;

TUMBLEWEED TUMBLINGS

No time to aim, just got shots off.

Arrows and war whoops pierced the air;
A warrior's lance whizzed past my head.
Dust and horse hooves seemed everywhere;
Now, my pistol spewed forth its deadly lead.

Faces adorned with black war paint bands,
Eyes wildly aflame with passion's rage.
Warriors and ponies joined as one,
Better their lethal fury engaged.

For a breath, time froze, battle stopped;
The chief's steely eyes fixed on mine.
Proudly astride his prize pinto steed,
Chin raised, war lance held high as a sign.

Raw hate spewed 'neath his horned headdress,
His gaze fell to the warrior I'd undone.
Then a change, a saddened mournful look.
A shrill whoop, clouds of dust, all was gone.

Six horses stolen, but Bert was unhurt;
My loved ones safe in the cold cellar's dust.
Blood from an arrow's tip stained my shirt.
Had I won? Had the proud Comanche lost?

A BAWDY LADY

SCARLETT'S ESCAPE?

Scarlett Rose is a character from the Tumbleweed Sagas who, when we first meet her, sells her body and soul as a prostitute in Laredo, Texas. Her tale is all too common in the annals of the Old West, as she epitomized the second-chancers that built Texas.

THE MIRROR HELD THE TRUTH. Scarlett Rose's svelte figure was fifteen going on twenty-one. Waves of red hair framed deep green eyes, passing the most luscious lips before cascading down her shoulders, and for the moment, hiding her ample but firm breasts. She turned first to one side, then to the other, and could not contain a most demure, sensually provocative smile.

The door to her room crashed open. Her grandmother stood in the doorway, mouth agape. "Harlot! That will be quite enough, young lady." Mrs. Rose held the strap tightly in her hand, her lips tightened and brows furrowed. Her gray hair, tied in a tight bun, seemed to want to turn as red as the angry crimson of her face. She stalked toward Scarlett, arm raised to strike.

Scarlett turned away as much for protection as to cover her nakedness.

Her grandmother delivered the strap across her young back, leaving a deep-red welt in contrast to her perfect ivory whiteness. Again and again, the old woman lashed with the dreaded strap across her granddaughter's innocent shoulders, then lowered her target. Three...four...she finally caught her breath. It seemed her rage might know no bounds. "You'll not bring shame on this house! There'll be no common whores under this roof!" She raised her arm to strike again but found her wrist imprisoned in an iron grip.

Carl Rose found himself conflicted between viewing the naked beauty of his granddaughter while restraining his wife from doing further damage.

Scarlett made no attempt to hide her nakedness, thrusting her chin defiantly outward until the redness in her grandparents' faces nearly matched her hair.

Carl Rose was aghast and sputtered, "Cover yourself, young lady. There'll be none of this in my house."

Mary Rose had been taken momentarily speechless. Her husband had wrenched the strap from her grip, and she now broke down and began to wipe away tears with her handkerchief. "Oh my, Scarlett, what would your mother and father have thought?"

Scarlett had finally grabbed a shawl hanging on a hook beside the mirror and wrapped it around herself. Despite the softness of the wool, its very touch to her skin quickly reminded her of the swelling red welts across her back and buttocks. It at least covered her most womanly assets. She strove to be contrite. "I'm sorry, Grandma. My head wasn't right. Guess it's my bleedin' time."

That was just a little too much information for Mary Rose. She twisted free of her husband and sulked as she left the room.

Carl Rose gave Scarlett an appraising stare, a cross between compassion and outright lustfulness. He shook the latter image from his mind; it wouldn't do to be thinking in so lecherous a way about his own granddaughter. "Get dressed, Scarlett, then come downstairs. We must talk."

Scarlett's parents had been killed in a carriage accident when she was only twelve. Driving rain and gusty winds had swept the rig from the road, down a steep embankment, and into the swelling waters of the James River. Her folks and younger brother drowned, but by some miracle, she'd been ejected from the carriage and was able to cling to shrubs just above the flood. She'd been found by passersby, and her maternal grandparents had been good enough to take her in. Scarlett had lived the past three years under their strict rule. There was a yearning in her to be free of the yoke of what she saw as persecution.

There, in her grandmother resided the strong oppressiveness that had mentally abused her mother, defeated her spirit, such that Scarlett's last memory before the fateful accident was of her mother cowering before some remonstration by her father. She was determined to not be her mother, and certainly not her grandmother. Scarlett was awestruck that her grandfather endured the woman. Now, she sat at the table in the spacious kitchen with her grandparents sitting opposite her.

"We figure it's time to get you the education we are unable to give you, Scarlett. There's a fine finishing school in nearby Richmond. It's time you learned social graces in addition to book learning."

Scarlett nodded. She absentmindedly watched a roach scramble across the edge of the table. At least it was free…until her grandmother crushed it with her hand. The next thought to sweep through her mind was to be free of this imprisonment without being crushed like the roach. It never really occurred to her that she might trade one form of imprisonment for another. She shook off her dreamy distraction. "When will I go, Grandma dear?"

"Week from tomorrow. We've made the arrangements."

Carl Rose nudged his wife.

"And I'm sorry to have whipped you so, Scarlett." It was barely a halfhearted expression of contrition, but it was spoken nonetheless.

"I forgive you, Grandma." Not an ounce of sincerity could be found in her words, but they'd been said. Any fence erected between them was at least partially mended so far as was necessary.

Carl Rose buttoned his trousers. "Don't you be saying a word to your grandmother, Scarlett, or I'll lay a whippin' on you like you will never forget. Never!"

Scarlett shuddered, as much at what she'd just been forced to do as what she'd seen…or been forced to see. It was an ugly thing, and it stunk to high heaven. She'd never forget that smell, or the taste. She wretched involuntarily.

Her grandfather smiled. Carl Rose had finally delivered on those lecherous thoughts he'd held for so long.

No, Scarlett wouldn't be telling her grandmother. All of a sudden, she couldn't get to that finishing school in Richmond fast enough. Questions lingered. Were all men like her grandfather? That thing between his legs, the thing he called a carrot—did it always smell so terrible? It sure was no carrot.

Her eyes followed him out the door of her room. She wiped away a tear, determined that it would be her last. When she was sure he was gone, she closed the door, staggered over to the wash-basin, filled her mouth with water, swished it, and spit it out into the basin. The foul taste yet lingered on her tongue. She rinsed again. No, she'd not soon forget.

Saturdays were special days at Mrs. Brown's Finishing School for Girls. The young ladies were permitted to freely roam the grounds for three hours in the afternoon so long as they didn't stray to the nearby river or the fence surrounding the remainder of the school boundary. So it was on this particular Saturday as Scarlett lay on her back staring up into the wispy clouds against the deep azure sky. She wore a blue dress that her grandparents had sent for her sixteenth birthday. She recognized it as her mother's but paid that no mind. She closed her eyes. The dress still held just a hint of her mother's scent, but that was soon overtaken by the aroma of wild-flowers as their strong fragrance wafted across the meadow and caressed her soul. She was perhaps fifty yards from the riverbank, yet hidden from the view of the distant manor house that served as dormitory, dining room, and classroom for the boarders. Scarlett closed her eyes. She heard a strange sound, a jingling of a sort unfa-miliar to her.

"Pardon, miss?"

Scarlett opened her eyes and lifted herself such that her elbows supported her. She blinked. It was a man. What in the world was a man doing on the grounds of Mrs. Brown's school? She shielded her eyes from the brightness. Before her was the most handsome man she'd ever laid eyes on. He stood erect before her with his braided blue coat, gold epaulets, plumed hat, white trousers, black boots, and a gilded sword that had most certainly been the source of the jingling she'd heard. "Get down, sir. You'll be seen." She motioned toward the manor house and the girls frolicking beside it.

He bent to one knee. "Lieutenant McCall, at your service, ma'am."

Scarlett contained a blush. Was this a dream? Where had this vision come from? She strove to act more mature than her years. "Who? What?"

"As I said, I'm Lieutenant McCall. I've seen you before from the other side of the river and felt compelled to make your acquaintance."

"How did you get in?"

He smiled. "'Twas easy, ma'am." The look he gave her could have turned cane sugar to liquid. "Pray tell, may I learn your name?"

"Scarlett…Scarlett Rose."

McCall took the liberty of sitting himself beside her. "It's a beautiful day."

Scarlett gathered her feelings as best she could.

"There is nothing so lovely as a beautiful day with a beautiful woman."

"Oh my, sir, but you are rather bold."

"Yes, but I'm an honest man. I can only speak in truths."

Scarlett blushed and found her fingers twisting her long red locks. It was only at this moment that she realized that her mother's old blue dress was a bit revealing, as the swell of her breasts was all too obvious to the discerning eyes beside her. "You…you must go. I must go back." She stood.

McCall arose, bowed, kissed the back of her hand, and smiled broadly. "May I have the pleasure of your company again, Miss Rose?"

Scarlett disconcertedly caught the utter sincerity of his expression. She looked about in search of any prying eyes…or ears. "Be careful."

McCall strutted off with an all-too-obvious spring in his step.

They managed to maintain the secrecy of their liaisons. They'd even stolen a kiss now and again. The Saturdays seemed to run together until one in August. On this particular day, however, the young lieutenant arrived with a decidedly serious expression.

She sensed his distress. "What is it, John?"

"I'm to ship out next week. They're sending us to New Orleans."

"Oh my! What are we to do?"

"Let's steal away and be married! Wives can accompany officers."

Scarlett blinked. Marriage? This had not come up before. She snuck a peek at the manor house and had a fleeting thought of her grandparents. This was her chance at the freedom she so dearly sought. This McCall fellow seemed honest and caring enough. "When? Where?"

"Can you sneak out Tuesday after sunset and meet me at the gate?"

There was no turning back now. "Yes. Yes, I can, John. I'll be there."

"Pack light, my sweet, as we'll travel by horseback to a nearby church. The pastor will be waiting."

McCall was a passionate lover. With his gentleness and especially his cleanliness, the predation she'd endured with her grandfather and his carrot was relegated to distant memory.

They'd been married barely two months and set up housekeeping in a cabin for married officers outside the gates of Fort Pike when she realized she'd missed her monthly bleeding. Their lovemaking had been passionate beyond her wildest dreams and produced a not wholly unexpected outcome. The cold reality of her situation set in a couple of days after she'd informed him of the upcoming blessed event.

She lay languidly in their bed. He'd been especially passionate in his lovemaking the night before, almost as though it'd be their last. His ardor had seemed to know no bounds. It suddenly occurred to her that he'd failed to kiss her this morning before leaving for his daily duties. She sat up and looked about their cozy little living quarters. Where were his spare uniforms? Where were his—

"John?" She stood and wrapped a blanket around her shoulders. She whispered, "John?"

Scarlett scanned the cabin. All of his personal effects were gone. She opened the door and gazed out toward the fort. An enlisted man was passing a few yards from her front door. "Excuse me, soldier. Have you seen Lieutenant McCall?"

He paused long enough to pass on what he knew, though it wasn't much. "He didn't appear for morning roll, ma'am. Can't say where he might be."

At that moment, Captain Bridger appeared. "Mrs. McCall, I'm sorry to inform you that your husband has left his post without permission. We've sent out a search party." The officer cleared his throat. "If he's not returned within the week, I'm afraid you cannot be staying here, ma'am. I'm sorry."

"Thank you, Captain. Good day." Scarlett pulled herself back inside the cabin. She didn't want to believe it at first. Her lieutenant had run away. What was churning through his mind that he'd take so drastic an action? She'd, by all appearances, been abandoned. Scarlett sat by a small table to take stock. If he was returning, why would he take all his possessions? If he didn't return, where was she to go? She couldn't return to Richmond.

What, indeed, becomes of an unaccompanied pregnant woman? She had a week to decide, and no close friends to turn to. Her neighbor, Mrs. Smith, had seemed friendly enough.

Scarlett put on a clean dress and strolled over to the neighbor's cabin. They made small talk before she revealed the purpose of her visit. "My dear husband has apparently deserted."

Mrs. Smith shook her head, dismayed. "Oh my, dear. He seemed as though he'd be a fine officer...and such a gentleman." She strove to contain a blush of embarrassment as she recalled her own impromptu dalliances with Lieutenant McCall.

Scarlett persisted, "I don't know where to go. New Orleans is far too wild for my liking."

Mrs. Smith's mind raced to refocus on the problems the wife of her paramour was facing. Her romantic aspirations were also being brought to a wholly unexpected halt. She fought back the urge to tell Scarlett but demurred. "There are schooners plying the gulf between here and Corpus Christi, my dear. Or perhaps you might consider one of the steamboats heading north to St. Louis."

The steamboats plying the Mississippi became fertile ground for Scarlett, so far as keeping herself in food and clothing. She partnered with a riverboat gambler named Henderson that exchanged his protection for her womanly charms. It was toward the end of the third month of her pregnancy that she awakened bathed in sweat, lying in a spreading pool of blood and the tiny form of her baby. Thankfully, the bleeding stopped, but her child was not to be. A mix of sadness and relief swept over her. Henderson offered no sympathy but decided that it was time for her womanly charms to be shared with others. After all, Scarlett Rose was strikingly beautiful in an incongruous joining of sultriness and innocence.

The first paying customer treated her well and paid well, too. Even after she gave a portion of the money to Henderson, she retained a goodly amount. Perhaps this wouldn't be so bad...for the present, at least.

As for Henderson, he sought to add more women to his stable of prostitutes. He didn't always win at the poker table, so his growing side business offset any losses. So it was that one especially hot evening, one of his gambling victims had become drunk and unruly. The man knew of Henderson's side business, had feasted his eyes on Scarlett, and demanded her services. He figured to take out his gambling losses on a quickie with a good whore.

Scarlett appraised the man whom Henderson had just introduced to her. He stunk to high heaven, had a scraggly beard with bits of day-old food stuck in it, was missing a couple of teeth, and had a belly that seemed to droop to his knees. But then he waved five gold coins before her.

He snarled with alcohol-laced breath, "Let's go, woman!"

She nearly fainted at the foul-mouthed odor, but Henderson motioned for her to take care of him. She led him to her room.

The oaf grabbed a bottle of whiskey from a nearby table as he followed her. They stopped three times for him to take generous swigs of the booze. He'd begun to unfasten his belt and trousers just before they'd reached her cabin. He almost tripped as they staggered through the door, and then he began to tear at her beautiful brocade dress.

She stammered, "Please, there's no hurry." She playfully pushed him onto the bed.

The drunken sot pulled her on top of him, forced his lips against hers, then rolled on top of her. His weight was crushing as he tried to force his way into her. He was unsuccessful and quickly grew angry in his inability to perform. He struck her face with the back of his hand. "You ain't much of a whore, bitch. I want my damned money back." He balled his fist as though to hit her again.

The explosion rocked the tiny room. It surely must have been heard about the boat. Scarlett's free hand had found the Deringer hidden beneath her pillow. The bullet had planted a hole just about dead center in the man's forehead. She squeezed herself out from under his dead weight. Then, the horror of the moment swept over her. The dead monster's vacant eyes stared off into space. Scarlett shuddered involuntarily. Panic set in, but she quickly took stock with the maturity borne of being a sixteen-year-old whore on a Mississippi River steamboat.

What was she to tell Henderson? She could be hanged for this. Was escape possible? What to do with the body of whomever this man was? The steamboat was nearing New Orleans.

It had been three weeks since Scarlett escaped the cruel punishment Henderson had exacted upon her. They'd dragged the dead body to the deck rail under cover of darkness and thrown it overboard into the roiling wake of the boat. Henderson now held her in his grip, intending to turn her in to the authorities as a murderess, effectively extorting her into servile compliance. He took an ever-greater percentage of her earnings and was more demanding in his own

availing of her services, even to the point of bizarre sexual perfor-
mances. It was blackmail of the ugliest sort as he figured to lock her
into his growing business.

Scarlett may have been young, but she was ever less naïve. She
knew that staying with Henderson was untenable if she hoped to
have any life beyond selling her body to men. It didn't take her long
to wrestle from under Henderson's bondage, and having found
passage on one of the schooners heading to Corpus Christi, she
escaped in the dead of night after getting him to pass out from the
whiskey laced with peyote.

"Unimpressive," came to her lips as she scanned the landing at
Corpus Christi. Despite shallow waters, the town did have a fair
cattle shipping trade, and cotton too. However, there wasn't much
to the town for the sort of profession Scarlett had sunk to. It seemed
to have none of the hustle and bustle, the relative excitement of New
Orleans or St. Louis.

The schooner captain had been good enough to give her the
address of a rooming house. Now she stood before the ramshackle
dwelling, sighed, and knocked lightly on the door, lest it fall apart.

A burly looking matron with a toothless grin opened the door.
"Kin ah help you?"

Scarlett showed her the note the captain had scribbled.

"Oh, my God, another of them." She shook her head resignedly.
"Come on in. I've got one room left. Cost two bits in advance."

Scarlett gave her the money and nearly wretched in disgust as
the woman dropped the coins between her overly ample breasts.

"I lock up at midnight. Be sure any, er, *guests* are out afore then."
She gave Scarlett a patronizing look.

Who was she to talk? thought Scarlett. She quickly settled into the
room, though she was already determined to be gone from the town
as soon as possible.

Scarlett's long, lustrous red hair spread over bare shoulders
had the effect of quickly attracting men, so she donned an emerald-green satin brocade dress to set off her hair. She soon found
her way to the Longhorn Saloon, a drinking hole that was a
favorite of cowboys visiting Corpus Christi, and sidled over to
the bar.

The barkeep was an old-timer and right quickly figured what

she was up to. "There are three rooms upstairs. Cost two bits an hour in advance."

She sighed and forked over the money. He gave her a key, and she silently slunk off into a corner where she could easily observe the comings and goings. She had become pretty fair at judging who had money enough to afford her wiles, so she waited as evening set in and the saloon began to fill. Two other women had designs similar to hers, but they both looked pretty much worn out. They'd be waiting to prey on customers too drunk to care about appearances.

A tall, red-haired cowboy strode in. He spoke briefly to the barkeep, scanned the room, and eased back out of the saloon. She caught a glimpse of a lawman's badge on his chest. Damn, but he was incredibly handsome. She saw that several of the customers watched the tall man come and go, so she gathered he must be well known. Scarlett nudged a man at a nearby poker table, smiled demurely, and asked, "Who was that?" She was tempted to add the descriptors running unfettered through her mind. "Handsome" wouldn't have done the apparition of manhood justice.

"Texas Ranger, ma'am. Fella named Luke Dunn."

"He seems to get attention."

"Outlaws and Injuns avoid him like a plague."

"Married?"

"Not yet. Spends his time chasing down human varmints. Don't know as he's got a woman."

Scarlett smiled and turned back to the room. She'd place the vision of the Texas Ranger in the not-so-deep parts of her memory. She sighed and noticed a well-dressed man with a dark mustache seated on the other side of the room. His appraising eyes had already found her. She took a deep breath such that it forced her breasts to swell a bit more above her bodice. He noticed.

In but a heartbeat, he'd sauntered over to Scarlett's table. "Howdy, darlin'. Care for a drink?" He was broad-shouldered and smelled at having just come from a bath and shave. A sizable mustache that twisted up at both ends graced his upper lip, and a scar traced its way down one side of his face. It told of having endured tougher days. Some might have said it added character.

There weren't many men in such fairly pristine condition who sought her attentions; most were grimy, sweaty, and stinking of booze and livestock. "Why certainly, sir. Whiskey would do just fine." She knew the barkeep would water it down, so she'd be keeping her wits about her.

He nodded to the barkeep and led her to another table off to one side. He sat and pulled a second chair in close. "Come sit, darlin'." It was more a command than request.

"You been to Corpus before…" She searched for a name.

"You can call me Bart."

As Scarlett slid into the chair beside him, her hip bumped into a .44 caliber Colt revolver stuffed into his holster. "Where you from?"

"Sorry about the gun." He paused and took a swig of whiskey. "Come down from Kansas…been ranching. Figured for a fresh start in Texas." He smiled.

The nature of Bart's ever-so-slightly twisted smile sent an involuntary chill up Scarlett's spine, but not so much as to deter her. "You looking for a little fun?"

"I was about to ask."

"Why don't we slip upstairs and see what's up?" Her meaning was hard to miss.

They reemerged about an hour later. Bart had been a generous client, so Scarlett sported a satisfied smile. For his part, he didn't hang around, exiting the Longhorn right quickly after paying his tab.

The barkeep motioned Scarlett over to the bar. Curious, she eased on over. The barkeep put his hand aside his mouth and spoke in hushed tones. "Do you know who that was, Scarlett?"

"Why? Should I?"

"That, my dear, was Bad Bart Strong, one of the meanest, toughest killers in the territory. They say he's killed maybe ten men, all bushwhacked."

Scarlett didn't quite know what to make of the barkeep's story. She smiled demurely. "I can only say that bushwhacking isn't the only thing he's good at."

The barkeep persisted. "Word has it, he's lookin' to avenge the death of his cousin. Strong is aiming to put that Ranger you saw earlier in his rifle sights."

Her eyes grew wide as her mouth dropped a little. "Does the

Ranger know?" She thought on what a waste it would be for the Texas Ranger to be lost.

"I expect he knows. Not much he can do until Bad Bart tries something. The fella ain't broken any laws down this neck of the prairie."

Scarlett shook her head in wonderment. "That doesn't seem right."

The barkeep chuckled resignedly. "Nope. But be sure Luke Dunn is keeping a keen eye out for Strong. They say Strong is a patient killer. He'll wait for the perfect opportunity. Something could happen tomorrow, or a month from now."

Over the next few days, Scarlett picked up a trick or two each night at the Longhorn and began to learn what opportunities South Texas might yet afford. Some men told of San Antonio, but it sounded busy and overly competitive like New Orleans, and others spoke of Laredo. The possible adventure of nearby Mexico that Laredo afforded had some appeal, so she began to come around to thinking that the little town at the westernmost reaches of the Nueces Strip might suit her. Geographic distance might even enable her to put her lascivious trade behind her, though she pondered just what other skill might suit her. Far as she knew, no one was tracking her for killing Henderson.

Texas Jack's Saloon in Laredo wasn't the cleanest watering hole along the Rio Grande Valley, but it was the best the region had to offer. Sawdust on the floors absorbed spilled booze, urine, and occasional spatters of blood while the air was permeated with the associated odors coupled with gun smoke now and again. Scarlett had done reasonably well in Corpus Christi but had gotten word that a US Marshall was coming from New Orleans to inquire around about a murder on a steamboat. She decided it was best to seek new horizons sooner rather than later.

As she lounged at a table near the bar, she yielded to her occasional curiosity as to what became of that Bad Bart Strong character and the Texas Ranger. Her reminiscences were soon broken by the doorway filling up with a huge man. He exuded money by his dress and manner. He was tall, but exceedingly overweight.

Scarlett sidled over to the bar. "Do you know him, Ramey?"

The barkeeper smiled. "That's none other than Horatio Thorpe. Owns a huge plantation east of Austin. Lots of other business interests. They say he takes his baths in gold dust."

"He's awful big, Ramey." She held back on saying "fat;" big would do for now. She couldn't help but wonder what else of this man's physique was big. But then there was that prodigious belly…

"And rich. He can buy just about anything he wants. I hear tell he runs a string of brothels across Texas just for the fun of it." The barkeep raised his eyebrows at her. "I expect he's looking for new talent, Scarlett."

Thorpe strode into the saloon and looked about. All the tables were occupied. He looked over at Ramey, briefly caught Scarlett's eye, and motioned to the barkeep for a table to be cleared.

Ramey shrugged.

Two heavily armed men came up on either side of Thorpe. He pointed to a table off to his left, and the two men strolled purposefully over to the table occupied by three card players and said something to them. The men looked at each other, then at Thorpe, nodded, and left the saloon.

Scarlett whispered to the barkeep, "Dang, Ramey, there was no arguing. Not a hint." She shook her head in true wonderment, then looked over at Thorpe.

The big man motioned for her to join him.

Ramey handed her a bottle and gave an extra cleaning wipe to two glasses. "Better get on over there, Scarlett. Don't keep the customer waiting."

Scarlett stood before the table opposite Thorpe and placed the bottle and two glasses on the well-worn wood surface. She seductively, almost absentmindedly, moved her hand across the surface nooks and crannies that embodied the table's character. She took a deep breath that lifted the curvature of her breasts gently above the green satin of her bodice. "I haven't had the pleasure of your acquaintance, sir."

Thorpe smiled. "That's a big word for…" He held himself back from saying "common whore." He shifted his weight in the chair, and it squeaked as though it might collapse under his weight. His jaw dropped. Damn, but she was drop-dead beautiful—gorgeous, even. "Er...pleasure to meet you. My name's Thorpe. Horatio Thorpe."

Most of the men she serviced didn't offer their actual names. The name this oversized potential customer used had already been confirmed by the barkeep. Seemed he was sufficiently confident to be straight-up about whom he was. She smiled as demurely as she could. "My name is Scarlett. May I join you?"

"Had that on my mind, darlin', when I waved you over." Thorpe tried to be as invitingly friendly as was in his constitution. He motioned to the seat beside him.

As Scarlett slid in beside the behemoth of a man, he poured two drinks. They clinked glasses, and as he quaffed his, she poured most of hers into the sawdust. He didn't seem to notice as he poured himself a second.

Scarlett felt his hand on her thigh. Midway up her thigh. Thorpe was wasting no time. His hand stopped a mere hairsbreadth from her nether region.

Thorpe was clearly excited by the softness of her inner thigh, but he shook off his momentary drift into passion's grip. "I have business later at Fort McIntosh, Miss Scarlett." There was a hint of lecherousness in his smile as he delivered his invitation. "I'd be happy to have you accompany me."

It was hardly what she'd expected, as evidenced by her inquisitive glance toward him.

"Well, I figure we might do that after we get better acquainted upstairs."

The proposition came almost as a relief to Scarlett. "Are we in a hurry, Mr. Thorpe?"

"Please do call me Horatio, Miss Scarlett."

She could feel his bulging hips pressing against her as his hand continued to explore her innermost thigh. She stole a glance toward his crotch but could see nothing, thanks to his belly. She reached beneath her dress and gently took his hand. "Shall we go upstairs... Horatio?"

He smiled. At least, she noted, he had decent teeth.

Horatio Thorpe had stayed around for an extra couple of days, availing himself of Scarlett's charms. He'd taken great pleasure in her accompanying him to Fort McIntosh, as she was such an incredibly attractive adornment that surely raised the libidos of the troops.

Scarlett deftly managed to pleasure Thorpe without finding herself suffocating underneath his considerable bulk. While she'd never mention such a thing to a customer, she was underwhelmed by the size of his manhood. It was actually a bit of a challenge to service Thorpe.

At last, the time came for Thorpe's departure. He'd been quite generous to Scarlett, lavishing her with two new dresses and an impressive amount of gold coin.

"Must you leave, dear Horatio?"

"Ah, my dear Scarlett, I'm afraid I must return to Magnolia." He'd described Magnolia Plantation to her a couple of times while recovering his libido beside her in the bed, along with telling her of the shipping business he operated out of Galveston. He was married to a shrewish wife, by his account, and had a couple of children. Ramey had confided to Scarlett that it was said that several of the slave children at Magnolia had Thorpe's eyes.

"Well, Horatio, do come back to Laredo any time." She raised to her tiptoes and kissed him full on the lips while delivering a memorable rub to the small bulge in the man's trousers.

"My offer to join me in Austin stands, Miss Scarlett." His eyes rolled dreamily at her touch. "I can arrange for all you would ever need."

She shook her head gently. "I'll give that serious thought, Horatio, dearest." She broke away with a final caress of his cheek as he boarded the wagon that would carry him eastward. A final wave, and Horatio Thorpe and Scarlett Rose had parted ways…at least for now.

Scarlett slowly walked into the saloon. She hadn't noticed the big gray stallion tied to the hitching post out front, but it was hard to miss the tall, red-haired Texas Ranger leaning into the bar and questioning Ramey.

Dunn's peripheral vision caught her entry. He looked at her as though he might have seen her before but turned back to his dialogue with the barkeep.

Scarlett batted her eyes slightly but to no effect.

Luke Dunn tipped his hat toward Scarlett as he exited Texas Jack's. He was on a mission, and nothing distracted him from a mission. Plus, for all he knew, he was as much prey to Bad Bart Strong as he was hunter. Attractive women, especially those of Scarlett's profession, were distractions to be steadfastly avoided.

Scarlett nodded to Ramey and left out the back door to the saloon. She'd have to decide which of her new dresses to wear that evening. Thorpe's invitation to Austin lurked in the deeper recesses of her mind, but she consciously pushed it back ever more deeply. The idea of effectively becoming a concubine simply didn't sit well with her, though it was tempting. That Texas Ranger, on the other hand…well, she'd trade her soul for a night with him.

Texas Jack's was unusually busy. Seemed like every cowboy and itinerant traveler had rendezvoused in Laredo and the saloon was a logical gathering place. Scarlett struck a seductive pose at the far end of the bar, trying to shake loose images of Luke Dunn and get Thorpe's offer out of her mind. The squeak of the swinging entry doors caught her attention, but she found herself doing a double-take. A slim apparition dressed in black and sporting a pair of Colt revolvers on his hips strode purposefully into Texas Jack's. He paused and scanned the room, catching Scarlett's open-mouthed expression as he made for the bar. His glacial-blue eyes only left hers to avoid tripping as he eased his way along the bar toward her.

"Name's Dirk…Dirk Cavendish."

Scarlett's eyes were drawn to his like a magnet.

"'Tain't seen you here before."

She struggled to break away from his gaze. "Er, yes…my name is Scarlett." Her mind was already swimming with thoughts of how this would be a night to remember. "Are you staying long?"

"Just tonight, Miss Scarlett."

"Where you headed?"

"East. Corpus Christi, I expect."

She looked seductively into his eyes, took his hand, and led him toward the stairs.

Upon awakening disappointedly to an empty bed, Scarlett heard shouting and all manner of hollering up the street. Those Mexican hiders were coming to town to celebrate. Every now and then, the hiders would have their fill of rustling and skinning cattle to sell hides. It was a tough living, and the rustling part was illegal. The hiders were a smelly, rough lot. They stunk to high heaven: wore clothes encrusted with all manner of caked-in prairie dirt, blood, and manure: drank as though every drink was their last: and sported mostly toothless grins under greasy mustaches. To the hiders, Laredo whores were disposable, and passing the women around as suited their particular lascivious demands was as nothing to them. Scarlett dreaded the contrast to Horatio Thorpe...and her dream of that Texas Ranger. Where was it that Dirk Cavendish had said he was headed? How soon could she get free of Laredo? She felt a dampness in her loins. Damn, but Cavendish had been incredible.

As she entered Texas Jack's, her visions of Cavendish faded and she was quickly reminded where she was.

A voice from among several hiders shouted out, "*Hola, señorita. Mi nombre es Carlos Pérez. Estás listo para follar?*" It was the hider leader, Carlos Pérez.

"*Para follar,*" she whispered. The words of the crass proposition haunted her. Most customers at least *pretended* some level of civility. She apprised Pérez from afar. Little distinguished him from the other hiders—large sombrero, grimy clothes over a wholly unwashed presence. He was armed to the teeth, given that few of his teeth remained. The only difference was that he was their leader, which meant that he was tougher, meaner, and rougher than any of the others.

"*Ven aquí, moza!*" He had begun to show off for his compadres. Pérez had already consumed most of a bottle of cheap whiskey.

Wench? thought Scarlett. She'd begun to pick up a bit of Spanish on her occasional trips across the Rio Grande to shop in Nuevo

Laredo. It served her well in this increasingly undesirable border town.

"Ven aquí, ahora!"

Scarlett slowly strode across the floor toward meeting her immediate fate.

Pérez stood, staggered a couple of steps to meet her, and nearly knocked her down as he grabbed her arm. He pulled her roughly toward the stairs. He knew Texas Jack's layout and wasn't wasting time in his desire to avail himself of the red-haired whore's charms.

Scarlett grabbed a bottle from Ramey and barely kept up with the drunken hider.

They reached the first room, and Pérez tottered through the door ahead of her. He grabbed the bottle from her, took a long drink, and proceeded to pass out.

Scarlett looked aghast at the hider leader, now crumpled on the floor. This was enough.

She tried to recall where that Cavendish fellow was headed. He'd be far and away the lesser of evils, and she craved more of his lovemaking. The Texas Ranger, meanwhile, seemed out of reach.

Scarlett had dared not go downstairs to face other hiders. She gathered what she could of her personal effects, grabbed a couple of biscuits, and stuffed them into a large travel satchel. She sighed as she glanced around the room and took a last fleeting look at Carlos Pérez's passed-out form lying prone on the bedroom floor. She exited out the upstairs side door of Texas Jack's, carefully descended the stairs, and headed to the livery stable up the street. In the dark of the moonless night, she easily found her way.

With her limited funds, buying a horse in the dead of night became an unexpected challenge. She gently shook the half-drunk stable boy awake. "Please...I need a horse."

Ferd shook off enough cobwebs to see the tops of a woman's breasts lingering over him. "Whah?"

"A horse. I need a horse."

He shook his head again. It hurt. "Ya got money?"

"Yes."

Ferd had begun to realize that he was talking with the whore from Texas Jack's Saloon. "Two hundred dollars plus tack will put ya in the saddle."

"That's outrageous!" Scarlett was appalled and leaned back in horror at the price.

A devious, devilish smile creased Ferd's jaw. "There might be another way." His tongue seemed to dart out like a serpent.

He was about as physically ugly an apparition as Scarlett had ever seen. It didn't take a mental giant to see what was coming. There was no way this abomination was going to sully her already sin-laden body. She sighed resignedly. "Give you fifty dollars and a look. You must include the tack."

Ferd's eyes lit up. The horse was an old nag, and the money would be a bonus for the worthless hunk of horseflesh. He vigorously shook his head despite the oncoming hangover headache.

Scarlett lifted her skirt.

"Higher, dammit. Gimme fifty dollars' worth."

She lifted her skirt higher, blocking Ferd momentarily from sight. She heard his hard breathing and a thumping sound. She dropped her skirt to see him pleasuring himself. "Pervert!" She was aghast, though not at all surprised. "Get my horse."

Ferd took a step toward her only to find himself facing the muzzle of the revolver she'd had the presence of mind to bring with her. With that, he slunk away to fetch the horse and tack.

Scarlett was soon enough mounted and on her way. She'd gone but a mile or so when an involuntary shudder swept over her. The parting view of Ferd had been enough to set her stomach churning. She strove to conjure thoughts of Dirk Cavendish, the Texas Ranger, and even Horatio Thorpe's money. It all swirled round and round in her head. What, indeed, might the future hold for Scarlett Rose? Could she yet put the label of "Laredo whore" behind her?

HEART AND SOUL ARE ONE IN TEXAS

Bluebonnets stretch 'cross verdant meadows far as eyes
　　can see,
Soft velvet petal clusters dance in a breeze so free.
As though the land is painted to blend as a prairie sea,
Heaven's almighty artist shares His manifest glory.
God bless, but my heart and soul are one in Texas.

God's bounty offered up in nature's soliloquy,
Motts of live oak and mesquite shout the Creator's plea.
Cool shades shelter creatures of this vast unbound country,
Majestic creation in but a simple bluebonnet prairie.
God bless, but my heart and soul are one in Texas.

TEXAS ON MY MIND, TEXAS IN MY BLOOD

Visions of rolling hills dance a Texas two-step in my mind,
Live oak and mesquite beckon under a great azure sky.
Blankets of bluebonnet and primrose undulate with the
    breeze;
Yeah, oh yeah, Texas runs ever deep in my soul, in my blood.

I see cowboys on horseback herding Brahmans and
    longhorns,
Trail-worn boots mix with jingling spurs and clouds of dust.
Lariats reach out with waving hats and choruses of yeehaws,
It's all deep in my heart, oh yes, deep in my heart of Texas.

Pumps spread 'cross the land lapping up precious black gold;
Cotton, hay, pecan, and soy hold the vastness hostage to the
    soil.
Javelina, coyote, and gray fox run free while eagles soar,
This is Texas, so very much the place I was born to be.

From Big Bend to the gulf, the panhandle to Nueces Bay,
I see wide-open spaces of Texas swathed in peach-toned
    twilight.
My forebears' blood runs in its soil, where they fought and
    ranched,

And Texas, oh Texas, sets ever deeper in my soul.

DISCRIMINATING TREACHERY
A SECRET PLOT TO ASSASSINATE ABRAHAM LINCOLN

Colonel Rex Rucker is a Tumbleweed Sagas character that comes to represent the tragedy and triumph of the War Between the States. He and his brother Stephen are cadets at West Point when war breaks out. To the chagrin of their army colonel father, they take opposite sides and eventually meet in combat. They suffer the depths of fate from which only Rex arises. This story, first published in the second annual anthology of the Gettysburg Writers Brigade, For the Love of Gettysburg, *tells of his fate.*

EXASPERATED! Frustrated! Colonel Rex Rucker sat alone in the dimly lit confines of his office. Washington, DC, was not exactly living up to expectations. Bureaucrats hadn't a clue as to the sufferings of soldiers battling for causes that grew ever more blurred. Deceit was rampant. Decisions were slow.

What was to be expected of a used-up relic of the Texas front? His right arm hung pretty much useless. The Union officer had been seriously wounded near Port Lavaca during the campaign to take the port of Galveston, TX. He was rescued from certain death in a prisoner camp by his brother and fellow West Point student Stephen, who was later killed by Cole Younger's gang as part of Quantrill's Raiders' campaign in Texas. Rucker's wound had healed, but he'd never be firing a rifle with any accuracy again. He'd had his tunic designed such that he could place his left hand in a pocket,

93

thus easing the weight of his arm pulling from what remained of his shoulder.

His office was actually reasonably comfortable, given the October morning chill. The little wood stove took the edge from the coldness. His relic of a desk replete with dings, splits, and scrapes on its top surface contrasted with the beautiful deep-red grains of the dark mahogany wall paneling and matching bookcases left behind by the previous occupant. He'd even managed to find a book or two to ease the barrenness of otherwise empty shelves.

Rucker leaned back in his chair and pivoted to afford himself a view from the single window to the parade ground beneath his second-floor office. His thoughts were laden with the recent past. It was certainly a far cry from leading his troops at Corpus Christi and Port Lavaca in the Texas Campaign. He'd been on his way to support Commander Renshaw in Galveston when he'd run into units under Colonel Thomas Green rushing to support Confederate Major General Magruder. Not realizing that Rebel scouts had discovered his movements up the Gulf Coast, Rucker had fallen into a trap. A mini ball in the shoulder had taken him out of action, and he'd have been sitting in a prison camp had his younger brother Stephen, a Confederate cavalry captain, not happened by with his unit of the 2nd Texas Cavalry. Rucker had been near death from loss of blood, but his brother had managed to get him to his parents' home near Corpus Christi. There, he'd fended off a doctor's recommendation to amputate the arm and managed to heal sufficiently to garner the desk job in Washington, DC.

This day was made all the more somber by the news of the previous evening. He had learned that Stephen had fallen into an ambush by Cole Younger's gang while escorting Yankee prisoners to San Antonio. Younger, a member of William Quantrill's rogue Confederate cavalry, apparently chose not to distinguish blue from butternut gray. Captain Stephen Rucker's unit had been massacred. So much for the high hopes of the two sons of a distinguished army officer. They'd planned to graduate from West Point and serve their nation together. Rex Rucker fought off a dark cloud of bitterness.

A crisp knock disrupted his meditations. "Enter." Rucker pivoted back to his desk.

The immaculately uniformed courier entered and offered up a smart salute. "Colonel Rucker, sir."

"At ease, Private." He greeted the courier with a reciprocal salute and an ironic sort of smile. The trim and cleanliness of the man's uniform seemed almost incongruous to the colonel's dark thinking. "State your business."

The courier thrust forward an envelope.

Rucker took the proffered missive. "Anything else?"

"No, sir."

"Dismissed."

Again, the exchange of salutes, and the courier turned on his heel and was gone.

Rucker took a deep breath and hefted the envelope. It was from the War Department. He sighed as he broke the seal. A seal? These were orders of some sort. He extracted and unfolded an important-looking single-page document. A small card fell out nearly unnoticed and fluttered its way to the floor. He placed the document on his desk as he reached to the floor for the card. Upon righting himself, a perfunctory scan of the document led him to the signature of Secretary of War Stanton himself. He placed the card aside for the moment.

Slowly, ever so slowly, the colonel read what were apparently his new orders. It seemed that President Lincoln was planning to personally attend the dedication of a national cemetery at Gettysburg, and he, Colonel Rex Rucker, had just received orders to head the security detail to be certain of the president's safety.

Rucker absentmindedly picked up the card that had fallen from the envelope. It turned out to be an invitation to a reception. The card was initialed by Stanton, so it was not to be ignored.

"Mrs. Faltress, ma'am, it's a pleasure to make your acquaintance." Rucker had just shaken hands with Roland Faltress and was acknowledging the industrial scion's beautiful young wife. His eyes couldn't help but shift from Faltress's cane to the exposed bounty of his wife's bodice and thence to her decidedly flirtatious green eyes.

The husband nodded to Rucker before ambling unsteadily off to greet some fellow on the other side of the room. It was as though he'd suddenly fully forgotten about his wife.

"It seems you've been abandoned, Mrs. Faltress. Would you care to enjoy a taste of Washington's finest champagne?"

"Why, Colonel Rucker," she rejoined in a silken Southern accent. "I'd be pleased for your company."

Rucker offered his right arm and escorted her to a nearby service table. The striking presence of him in his stately dress uniform with saber, epaulets, gold buttons, and other accouterments, and this young woman in an eye-catching emerald-green dress that set off her long raven curls and those green eyes, could hardly be missed by guests. At just over six feet tall and sporting a dark mustache and goatee, Rucker cut a rather handsome vision despite or even because of his battle wound.

"So, tell me, Colonel, what is your role in this national drama?"

Rucker was well aware that his assignment was of a sensitive nature, hardly something to share with someone he'd just met. "I push papers now and then, ma'am."

She cocked her head inquisitively. "Really? I cannot imagine an officer of your standing being relegated to simply pushing papers around a desk, Colonel."

In his peripheral vision, Rucker caught the gaze of Secretary of War Stanton from the other side of the room. He sensed a signal of concern. The colonel resolved to ascertain later just what that meant. Meanwhile, he had arguably the most fetching young woman in the room capturing his attention. "I'm afraid I met with an inconvenient fate in Texas, ma'am." He pointed to his left shoulder.

"Wounded in battle? And survived? How brave." She batted those green eyes again. "I'd love to hear more of your battle exploits, Colonel Rucker." She stole a quick glance toward her aged husband, who was fully engaged in some sort of negotiation. "You may call me Morticia, Colonel."

It was a bit quick to achieve such familiarity, but the colonel was what might be described as vulnerable. He hadn't received the attentions of a woman in quite some time. Married or not, the attention was welcome—welcome, if not a shade careless. "Texas at war is a wild place, ma'am...er, Morticia." The name actually came off his tongue more comfortably than he'd expected.

"Texas, Colonel?"

"Why yes, Morticia." He thought back to the running battle he'd fought around Matagorda Bay and the Gulf Coast. "The Rebs were mostly Texans fighting on their home ground. I had grown up some in Texas, but it was only because my father had been assigned there with the army. Those Texans knew every nook and cranny of the battleground."

"But the battle? How did you get hurt, Colonel?"

Rucker wasn't quite ready to have her calling him Rex, but it was sure appealing to talk with someone who actually cared about his exploits. "Led us into an ambush at Aransas. We'd just about broken through their lines when this happened." He cocked his head toward the wounded shoulder.

"But you survived."

Rucker was about done with discussing the battle. Morticia was seemingly enraptured with his story, but her probing was beginning to touch a raw spot in his psyche. He sought to shift the conversation. "It appears that you are married to a quite well-respected gentleman, Morticia. Where did y'all meet?"

"I grew up in Charleston, Colonel. Charleston, South Carolina, not far from Fort Sumter." She looked distracted for a moment at the thought. "That is where we met, Colonel. Does that answer your question?" She rolled her eyes ever so slightly as she took a sip of champagne. She surprised Rucker with a sort of whimsical smile. "I'm tired. I'd really like to go home." She yawned half-heartedly. "My escort must...oh, dear me, Colonel. My husband is my escort, and he seems to be very engaged."

The colonel found himself drawn to a hard gaze leveled upon him by Stanton. He caught the Secretary of War mouthing something at him. He seemed quite concerned. From what Rucker could gather, it was to be careful. He turned his attention back to Morticia. "I'd be pleased to ensure your safe return to your home, Mrs. Faltress." He'd rather judiciously decided to return to a more formal mode of address. He quaffed the last of his champagne, smiled at Morticia, and went off to fetch the lady's cape.

Cord Whelan—Sergeant Cord Whelan, that is—had watched as Rucker helped Mrs. Faltress into her waiting carriage. The colonel tied his own mount to the rear of the rig and proceeded to join the woman in a seat opposite her.

Whelan had served the colonel for a couple of years now, pretty much ever since Rucker had left West Point to join the army and his unit's assignment to Texas. The sergeant was rough around the edges, a born and bred frontiersman who had honed his skills in north Texas and even up so far as Wyoming. He'd taken the measure of many a Crow, Blackfoot Sioux, and Comanche while coming once or twice within a hairsbreadth of losing his own long blond hair. If there was an inventor of intuition, it could well have been Cord Whelan. Something just didn't seem right with this woman luring his colonel along like a puppy on a leash.

Whelan had endeared himself to Rucker by helping him endure the seemingly capricious orders of a hotshot US Navy Lieutenant Kittredge ensconced in the schooner *USS Arthur* off the coast of Corpus Christi. Kittredge was part of the Yankee blockade harassing the Texas coast and harbored visions of capturing the city. Rucker detested the naval officer's condescension toward the army, and thus, Whelan was there whenever needed to listen to Rucker's protestations.

Colonel Rucker alighted from the carriage as it came to a halt at the front of the mansion that served as home away from home for Morticia. He proffered his right hand to assist her in stepping down from the carriage, then excused himself for a moment to hitch his horse to a nearby post and waved the carriage away. "Mrs. Faltress?" He offered his arm to escort her up the broad stairs, past the stately Georgian columns, and to the front door.

She released her grip on his arm, smiled, and gave a bit of a curtsy. Not just any curtsy, mind you, but one that revealed just a bit too much of what was within her bodice. "Thank you so very much for your gallant assistance, Colonel." She acted hesitantly. "I do have one more small favor to ask."

Rucker looked curiously. "Favor, Mrs. Faltress?"

"Oh, do stop with the formality, Colonel." She smiled. "It's quite dimly lit inside and the servants are gone. Would you be so kind as to look inside to be certain it's safe for me?"

The colonel's suspicions were a tad aroused, but he shrugged and nodded assent. Actually, the shrug sent a slight twinge of pain through his left shoulder, but the moment transcended any hurt. He opened the door and stepped inside with Morticia following closely behind. Too close. "Er, Morticia...ma'am. I need a bit of spa—" His words were muffled as she turned him and kissed him full on his lips. He pulled away. "Ma'am!"

"I–I'm so grateful, Colonel," she cooed. "Thank you so very much."

"You're welcome, Mrs. Faltress," he offered disconcertedly. "I expect I'd best be going now, ma'am." He turned toward the door.

She smiled disarmingly. "Just one more little thing, Colonel."

Rucker paused in midstride.

"I usually enjoy champagne before turning in. Would you be so kind as to open a bottle for me?"

Sergeant Whelan waited patiently for what seemed like hours. He'd quickly surmised that the colonel could be in considerable difficulty were J. Roland Faltress to return home too early. Finally, he could contain himself no longer. He strode purposefully up to the door and rapped with the butt of his revolver so there'd be no mistaking the knock from within. Moments later, the colonel, after a peek through a side window, opened the door. He was still in the process of pulling himself together. Being disheveled was the least of his present worries. "Sir...pardon, but the master of the house should be along any moment." He attempted to say it as respectfully as possible, though his thick Texas accent drew out each syllable to a seemingly interminable length of time. Whelan was embarrassed for the colonel and attempted to refrain from direct eye contact.

"How'd you find me, Sergeant?"

Whelan took that as a rhetorical question. "My job, sir."

"Rex? Rex...who's there?" The female voice wafted down from

the top of the grand staircase, leaving little doubt that she'd had a bit too much champagne—and likely an overdose of Rex Rucker.

"I must go, Morticia," he shouted over his shoulder. Rucker offered no impassioned goodbyes as he bolted out the front door with Whelan.

So it had begun. Morticia and her newfound love found an out-of-the-way tavern where they could consummate their occasional dalliances without raising the suspicions of either the elder Faltress or the War Department brass. If Secretary Stanton knew anything, he gave no indication, as he met regularly with Rucker to map out security plans for the Gettysburg dedication event. A date of November 19 had been selected for President Lincoln's train ride to the site of the horrific battle of just four months earlier. There had already been more than one assassination plot foiled, and logic held that there'd be more. Rucker's assignment was to ensure that nothing happened to the president.

Sergeant Whelan was ever present, protecting Rucker's backside from any intrusions on his little affair.

"Rex, dear Rex. I so want to leave Washington. Tell me more about Texas."

Rucker lay back on the pillow. In a mere two weeks, he'd be accompanying President Lincoln to Gettysburg. From there, and assuming all went well, he'd been assured of a promotion, perhaps even a return to command. His father, a retired colonel, still had some influence, and maybe, just maybe, Morticia Faltress's husband could sway the higher command…so long as he never learned of his wife's sordid little affair. At least the colonel's situation had yet to become fodder for the gossip around the nation's capital. He felt a bit sorry for his compatriot, George Armstrong Custer. While the brevet major was gallivanting about the countryside leading cavalry, his strikingly beautiful wife was grist for the local rumor mill. His wandering mind was brought back to the here and now by a soft hand stroking his bare chest.

"Rex? Are you returning to Texas?"

"I'm hopeful. My folks still live there, and they're not getting any younger."

"Will you be given a command?" She gently touched his wounded shoulder for not-so-subtle emphasis. Her fingers traced his scars.

He nearly flinched at her touch but caught himself. "I may know in a couple of weeks. I must complete my assignment here first."

"Oh, yes…your big secret." Her hand moved from his chest to explore elsewhere. "Can't you tell me your secret?" She pulled back her hand and licked her fingers one by one.

My God, but she's so desirable, went through his mind. He turned to her, but she coyly pulled away.

"Gettysburg. I'm going up to Gettysburg in a couple of weeks."

"Oh my. Can I go, too?"

"Perhaps I can get an invitation for your husband." The colonel had opened the door to his secret and now sought cover.

"He'd be no fun to have along." She turned back to him and resumed the soft but increasingly passionate strokes of his chest. "Couldn't it be just the two of us, Rex?"

Rucker knew they needed a cover. It wouldn't do to blatantly go off with another man's wife. Not yet, at least. "I've already said too much, Morticia. If you do want to attend the president's address, you will have to be accompanied by Mr. Faltress." He stroked her long dark hair. "There's no other way."

"Can we get close to President Lincoln?"

"I'm sure the president is aware of your husband's contributions and influence, Morticia. I expect I could arrange a seat close to Mr. Lincoln."

"I'm sure you can, Rex." She slipped on top of her colonel. "I'm certain of it."

★★

"Colonel…a word, sir." Sergeant Whelan normally wasn't so forthcoming when approaching Rucker. But then, circumstances were fast calling for greater boldness on his part. If all went well, he might live out the war with his body intact and mind at peace.

"Cord? What is it, Sergeant?" He returned the man's casual salute. Rucker respected Whelan's inattention to crisp spit-and-polish bearing such as he's seen in his own father and learned at West Point.

Whelan shifted uncomfortably. "There's something you need to know, Colonel."

The sergeant's uncharacteristic uneasiness got Rucker's undivided attention. Whatever made the normally unflappable soldier uneasy must have been important. "Well?"

"It's about Mrs. Faltress, sir."

Now, he had the colonel's full attention. "Mrs. Faltress? What about Mrs. Faltress?" Rucker felt a warm rush sweep up across his face. "Is she all right?"

Again, Whelan shifted uncomfortably.

"Sergeant, out with it. What's happened?"

"It's what's *been* happening, sir."

Rucker immediately thought the affair had been discovered. "Am I compromised, Sergeant?"

The sergeant attempted to speak, but the words caught in his throat.

"Sergeant, you're testing my patience. Is it truly that bad?"

"Worse, sir."

"Does Secretary Stanton know?"

"Not yet, sir."

"Damn it, Cord, what the hell are you trying to say? Out with it. I'm a man—I can take it."

"I have reason to believe that Mrs. Faltress may be a spy, sir."

"May?" Anger welled up in Rucker's expression. "You come to me with so heinous a suspicion! How dare you, Sergeant!"

"I saw her talking in whispers with known Confederate sympathizers, sir. She secrets away from her home to meet with them each week." He ignored Rucker's angry countenance. "I'm sorry, sir, but I took it upon myself to follow her. I managed to get close enough to overhear some of her conversation. I believe they are planning to harm President Lincoln."

Rex Rucker's anger subsided like the air popping from an exploding balloon. "Oh my God! What have I done?"

"I have a plan, sir." Whelan went in with newfound confidence.

"I hope so, Sergeant. I hope so, or I'm undone." That he'd been played by a beautiful woman was now secondary to saving his career, and thus, Colonel Rex Rucker was all ears.

"Yes, Roland. I won't be long. I just have a quick errand to run."

"Hurry back, sweetheart." The old man rapped his cane against the massive mahogany desk as he spun the chair toward his departing wife. He smiled lecherously as he watched her leave. If he was lucky, he figured he might even take her to bed upon her return. It seemed an ever-rarer occurrence of late.

For this errand, Mrs. Faltress had donned a rather unassuming gray riding outfit with tastefully understated black piping. Her raven locks were tied back and mostly hidden beneath a stylish but simple hat sporting a black plume. The big chestnut stallion was waiting in the courtyard. "I won't be long, Joseph," she assured the stable boy. She might have been most any lady of means heading out for a recreational ride.

Within the hour, she found herself waiting beside a huge oak tree a few yards from the highway. She soon enough heard the telltale sound of horses approaching, and within a few moments, they pulled up a few feet from her. "You're late, gentlemen. My time is precious. We dare not be discovered."

The older of the two men dismounted and took a folded and sealed note she passed to him. He was a grizzled old veteran, while his companion was considerably younger. They wore no uniforms but were well-armed. "We'll see that General Lee receives this, ma'am."

She gasped angrily. "Never mention names, you idiots! The woods have ears." She glanced about furtively, smiled, and whispered excitedly. "I'll be so close, I can't miss."

The men instinctively looked around. They held back chuckles, as it was clear that no one was nearby. The younger man smiled sheepishly. "Begging your pardon, ma'am, but we seem to be alone." In any case, they were just couriers, clueless as to what her comment about not missing was about.

The courier couldn't know that not fifty yards away lay one Colonel Rex Rucker. He'd watched intently through his spyglass and saw that she'd passed a note. He wasn't able to hear any conversation but knew that Whelan was nearby and pretty fair at reading lips. He would know what had been said soon enough.

The older courier helped Morticia to mount her horse. His mind momentarily drifted to pleasant thoughts as he took in the sweet aroma of her perfume, and he looked up at her a bit too fondly.

She raised her riding crop but did not strike the courier. "Know your place, mister." With that, she galloped off.

The couriers watched her disappear. "Damn, Clyde. Did you catch a whiff of her?" The words had barely left his mouth when he crumpled in a heap. The younger man followed. Cord Whelan had done his job. He wiped his knife on the shirt of the younger man and slipped it back in its sheath. With that, he stooped down and rifled through the older courier's pockets.

The colonel rode up with Whelan's horse in tow. "Did you find it, Sergeant?"

Whelan smiled broadly. "Here 'tis, sir." He handed it up to Rucker.

Rex opened it carefully. His eyes grew wide as he read the message. "My, but she travels in heady company, Sergeant."

"Sir?"

Rucker shook his head somewhat ruefully. "Damn...such a beautiful woman. What a waste." He shrugged, then winced, as he'd momentarily forgotten the pain in his shoulder. He figured there was nothing to hide, at least not from his ever-loyal sergeant. He displayed the note to the sergeant. "It's addressed to none other than General Robert E. Lee."

"She said that she'd be so close to President Lincoln that she couldn't miss."

"Note confirms that. She plans to murder the president of the United States."

"What now, Colonel?"

Rucker found himself enveloped with a certain bitterness at having been used. He murmured, "I expect that I should be honored that she chose me. She was discriminating in her treachery."

"Excuse me, sir?"

The colonel collected himself and turned to Sergeant Whelan. "We have evidence, Sergeant...but we need to catch her in the act, and do it without endangering President Lincoln." The colonel scratched his chin thoughtfully. "I think I know how." He smiled deviously. "Indeed, I'm sure of it."

Morticia double-checked the round in the Deringer. They'd be leaving in about an hour, and she dared not miss the train. Mr. Faltress was taking his sweet old time. She'd had to accede to his wishes for sexual favors that morning to assure his being on the train with President Lincoln. She knew the train would be full of military and politicians as well as leading citizens like she and her ever-so-frail husband. Deep in her evil mind, she wished he'd simply die and leave his fortune to her so she could return to Charleston as a grieved widow and live in luxury. Morticia was the only heir to the Faltress empire. The scion's first two wives had passed away of disease, but not before each had borne him a son. Both sons had died coincidentally in horsing accidents.

"Roland...hurry, love. We must be on our way." Lurking in her mind was the irresistible thought of placing a .41 caliber slug into the president's head. A chill of excitement coursed through her body. It was not unlike the surge she had admittedly felt in more impassioned moments with that crippled colonel she'd had to seduce. Perhaps the Deringer was not enough to eliminate the perceived barriers in her life: the colonel...her husband. Alas, the single-shot pistol would have to suffice. Just in case, she slipped a couple of more cartridges into her delicately-beaded purse. As for the Deringer, that was neatly tucked away in a special pocket sewn into her beautiful silken dress. It was November 18. President Lincoln would be dedicating the cemetery the next day.

They arrived just as the locomotive was building steam in preparation for pulling out. President Lincoln was already onboard.

Morticia tried mightily to hustle her husband along the platform to catch the train before it could depart and thus foil her plans. A soldier suddenly stepped out to block their path. "Halt!"

"Halt? Can't you see we're late?" She saw the station master signaling the engineer. Desperation was overwhelming her. "See?

We have tickets." She brandished her passes before the eyes of the guard.

"Sorry, ma'am…sir. Orders are to allow no one to pass."

"Corporal!" a commanding voice shouted from the rear deck of the train. "Let them pass!"

In the brief moment, the guard turned toward Colonel Rucker to better hear the order, Morticia and her husband moved past. It was all she could do to hurry the old man along.

She and Roland climbed on board just as Rucker nodded to the stationmaster. In but moments, the train belched huge clouds of steam, and in a surge of brute force, began to pull away. Whistle, steam, smoke, a cheering crowd beyond the station…the cacophony all merged together as a single demonic force in Morticia's ever more disordered mind.

Rucker escorted his charges to seats in the passenger car forward of that carrying the president. Roland lagged a bit, and his steps were uncertain as the train gathered steam, lurching and rocking its way from the station. "I hope you find this satisfactory, Mr. Faltress… Mrs. Faltress." The train lurched as if to punctuate the colonel's words. He grasped an overhead bar with his right hand to steady himself. The move brought him close enough to brush against the overhanging folds of Morticia's dress. It was pure chance, but he was certain that he felt some sort of object hidden away. Given the circumstances, he logically concluded it to be a weapon of some sort.

He straightened himself and nodded to the couple. "If you'll be kind enough to excuse me." He offered a casual salute and marched himself toward the rear entrance to the car. Slowly he opened the door, taking a quick, guarded glance back at the woman who'd used him. She was beautiful…on the outside. Rucker shook his head ruefully and took a deep breath.

As he passed between the moving cars, he scanned late autumn's foliage-denuded countryside passing by and took a moment to further collect himself. The loss of greenery, loss of life, seemed symbolic to him. He saluted the two guards standing at the door, straightened his tunic, and entered the president's car.

He nodded toward Secretary of State Seward and Interior Secretary Usher as he took his seat. Postmaster General Blair was out of sight, apparently huddled with President Lincoln, who was feeling under the weather. He noted that Secretary of War Stanton had remained in Washington. Rucker scanned the coach and felt comfortable with the well-armed soldiers he had strategically stationed. If nothing else, it gave the passengers some sense of security. Maryland, after all, was home to a few folks that were hostile to the Union. He smiled at the irony of having a known provocateur already onboard.

Rucker reviewed the program for the next day's dedication. Lincoln would speak after the windbag orator Edward Everett spoke. There was to be some music before the president would rise and deliver his dedicatory remarks. The colonel assumed the attending crowd would offer some applause, and this would present Morticia with her opportunity. The president, clueless to her intentions, had requested that Roland be seated in the front row of the podium in appreciation for the man's service to the Union. Morticia could not have hoped for better.

Rucker decided to avoid Morticia, at least for the trip to Gettysburg. He wanted no suspicions either way to squirrel his plan to foil her devious plot. She dared not suspect that he knew of her treachery.

The train rolled into the Gettysburg Railroad Station, where President Lincoln disembarked and was efficiently ushered with his entourage to the Wills House on the town square. The president was clearly not feeling well, as Rucker noted that the man appeared a bit gaunt, even haggard. The colonel was told that Lincoln would be refining his speech and was not planning on leaving his quarters that evening. An armed guard at the Wills residence would be sufficient. This freed Rucker to work out his plan.

With all his money, Roland Faltress did have friends. He had managed to arrange lodging at the Farnsworth house on Baltimore Street. Importantly, and in consideration of his aged legs, it was a convenient distance from the cemetery.

Morticia was not satisfied with spending the evening captive to her husband. He tended to nod off to sleep before sunset these days, so she figured to enjoy an evening in Gettysburg preparatory to the big day ahead.

Once Faltress was asleep, Morticia donned a wool wrap and headed to a nearby tavern. She made sure the Deringer was secure in her dress.

Crowds of folks had already begun to gather in Gettysburg with the aim of witnessing the cemetery dedication. The honoring of those who'd died defending their country held strong in every breast. In any case, the tavern was crowded, the air thick with smoke and the aroma of beer and whiskey. It was hardly a refined atmosphere. Morticia surveyed the scene critically. This was certainly not her beloved Charleston.

She sighed with disgust and had just turned to exit the tavern when who should appear before her but one Colonel Rex Rucker.

"Morticia, my dear. What brings you to this foulest of speakeasies?" He mouthed the words in as distasteful a manner as he could muster.

"Why, Colonel Rucker. It's a pleasure."

"The pleasure is mine, ma'am. Permit me to escort you from this den of iniquity to a place more suited to your discriminating tastes."

She smiled fetchingly, parting her ruby-red lips ever so coyly. *Perhaps one more night of sexual debauchery.* She placed her hand on his cheek. "I'm yours, Rex."

He offered his arm and led her in silence up the avenue to a nearby residence. They stood a moment before the entrance as he produced a key. Before inserting it, he turned her to him and kissed her full hard on those luscious ruby-red lips. Her hand slipped down beneath the bottom of his tunic. He pressed her tightly to him. He must convince her that he held no suspicions. "Patience, my sweet," he anxiously whispered.

A few strides down the hallway, they entered a bedroom with an exceptionally plush four-poster bed. Rucker lit a candle and produced a bottle of wine.

Morticia needed no urging, no seduction. She unbuttoned his tunic, being careful of his shoulder as she slipped the suspenders from his shoulders, and he was as quick to release her breasts from the confines of her bodice. A kiss, and then she dropped to her knees as she drew his trousers to the floor and revealed his readiness. With his passions strained to their utmost, Rucker lifted the raven-haired seductress and guided her to the bed.

Once they'd satisfied their carnal desires, the wine seemed merely an afterthought, a dessert of sorts. "Are you enjoying your visit to Gettysburg, ma'am?"

"I am now," she cooed. She stroked his bare chest and fluttered her eyelids. "Oh my, Colonel. You seem to be ready again." Her smile could have melted ice as she straddled him.

Rucker bided his time. Soon enough, the wine had taken effect. Whatever Whelan had given him to put in her wine had worked. The sergeant had claimed it was some sort of Comanche remedy. In any case, she was sleeping quite comfortably.

The colonel's work was done; now, he could rest easy. As he lay back on the bed and watched her sleep, he couldn't help but lament what a waste of womanhood she represented. He thought back to his mother, the dutiful military wife. She held principles so high it would be a formidable challenge to ever hope to match them. Rucker's mother? She was the antithesis of Morticia Faltress.

Rucker's ruminations were suddenly interrupted.

"Damn it, Rex Rucker! How could you have let me sleep?" Her sudden rage brought the colonel to full attention, albeit prone. "I must get back to Roland before he awakens."

"I can assure you, dearest, that he still sleeps." Rex couldn't know how fully true his words were. Roland Faltress would not wake ever again. "Get yourself together, and I'll escort you back to Farnsworth."

"Oh, Colonel...I'm sorry." She tried to seem genuinely remorseful at having scolded him. "I'd be grateful for you to accompany me." She moved to him and kissed him full on the lips. She'd already felt for her Deringer in the hidden pocket of her dress and was secure that it was still ready. As she smiled at Rucker, she thought that it was a shame that she'd had to dupe him so. He'd been a vast improvement over her husband so far as performance in bed, and he was quite handsome. The colonel was quite the dashing figure despite his crippled shoulder.

Upon entering the suite, she casually hung her bonnet. "Roland? Roland? Are you awake?" she called from the anteroom. Silence. "Roland?" Morticia cautiously peeked into the bedroom. Her husband appeared to be enjoying a peaceful slumber. In fact, she could not ever recall his countenance appearing so relaxed. But wait...he wasn't breathing. "Roland!" She ran to the bedside and shook him gently. There was no response. She put her head to his chest. No sound, no heartbeat. J. Roland Faltress had met his maker.

Morticia ran from the room and out the door to their suite. "Help! Help! My husband has died!" she called out to anyone that might hear. It was now the best of times and worst of times for Morticia Faltress. She was a wealthy widow and soon-to-be assassin.

The president's speech was to be delivered that afternoon. Between now and then, she was faced with dealing with the police, coroner, and all manner of distractions. She had failed to bring a black dress, so she had to see to that as well. She was not encouraged at having to find a reasonably fashionable black mourning dress in this little backwoods farm town. Lastly, she figured she'd have to come up with a few tears as well.

The show had to go on. The cemetery dedication would not be delayed on her account. She arranged for her deceased husband's body to be transported by hearse to Roland's estate in eastern Maryland. She calculated that after her sordid work was done, she'd make her escape, collect what was hers from the manor house on the eastern shore, and find her way back to Charleston. If her note had been received by General Lee, she should have an escort on hand ready to spirit her away in the chaos following President Lincoln's demise. They were to be disguised in Union Army uniforms to avoid any suspicion of impending doom. Her only discomfort was that she had received no response from Lee. She checked the Deringer to be certain it was loaded.

She managed to get a message to her dear Colonel Rucker. Hopefully, he'd be sensitive to her vulnerable situation and ensure her comfort at the speech. She had no appreciation of his having to soon perform one of the most important duties of his brief military career.

The brisk afternoon Gettysburg air filled her head as she enjoyed the brief walk with a gathering crowd to the new National Cemetery. Pressing forward, she couldn't miss sensing the peaceful freshness of the surrounding graves even though the carnage of battle had been wrought but four months earlier. The platform from which the program would be delivered soon loomed ahead. There was a swirl of activity as the carriage transporting President Lincoln parted the mass of people and eased past her. The rig was escorted by four cavalrymen. She felt as though Lincoln had looked directly at her as he rolled by and even nodded in acknowledgment of her black dress. She smiled inwardly. There wouldn't be enough security to stop her. Morticia looked about, paused, tapped the hidden Deringer as though further reassuring herself, and resumed her walk.

She showed her pass and was escorted to a seat behind where the president would be delivering his address. She tried to relax but nevertheless fidgeted a bit beneath the black veil that covered her face. It wouldn't do to look suspicious. Folks were conversing all around her as they waited for Lincoln to ascend the platform. She heard boots approach and looked toward the sound to see her Colonel Rucker approaching. "I hope you're comfortable, Mrs. Faltress. I'm sorry for your loss."

"Why thank you, Colonel. It is a time of grieving, my own and for our nation."

Rucker nearly blanched. "Yes, indeed, Mrs. Faltress. Yes indeed." He bowed slightly and kissed her hand.

Morticia looked deeply into his eyes. She wanted him right then and there. A peck on her black-gloved hand was a sorry substitute. She sighed. Her grief was certainly not for her husband. "Thank you for your kind words, Colonel. Perhaps, later…"

Rucker stood erect, nodded, and strode to his position at the far end of the platform. He caught the eyes of two members of the president's security detail who awaited his signal.

After a rendition of *Homage d'uns Heros*, a prayer by Reverend Stockton, and a piece by the Marine Band, the Honorable Edward Everett was introduced. Morticia's feet danced nervously as the orator droned on for the next two hours. She lifted her veil so as to breathe better. Would he ever conclude? She glanced at her colonel every now and then, smiling and rolling her eyes at the speech.

Rucker merely smiled distractedly back at her. He was keeping his eyes on President Lincoln, who was still not feeling so well. Now and then, Rucker scanned the assembled multitude to confirm that there were no unexpected threats lurking about. The crowd seemed at ease and anxious to hear the president's words honoring the fallen heroes of Gettysburg.

Finally, Everett was finished. There was a not-so-respectful sigh with mixed polite applause that emanated from the onlookers. A Baltimore Glee Club hymn was met with somber respect as the crowd awaited Lincoln's remarks.

Abraham Lincoln brought his lanky frame easily to the front of the platform. He was greeted with much applause, and then he cleared his throat. "Four score and seven years ago, our fathers..." It only lasted a few minutes; it was but ten heartfelt sentences. The crowd applauded occasionally during the delivery but was mostly stunned to near silence by his heartfelt words. At last, "...shall not perish from the earth." Applause erupted. Everyone on the platform stood.

Morticia slipped the Deringer from under her cloak. She pulled back the hammer, stepped forward to directly behind the president, aimed, and squeezed the trigger. Her jaw dropped. Nothing happened. She tried a second time. She fumbled in her purse. *Where were those damned bullets?* raced through her mind.

Colonel Rucker and the two security guards were already moving toward her as the president, others on the platform, and even the audience remained fully unaware of what she'd just attempted.

"Arrest her." Rucker's cold command echoed in Morticia's ears. He strode easily behind as her arms were firmly grasped, and she was escorted from the platform.

"You...you son of a—"

"Silence!" Rucker would truck no speech from this treasonous viper. He took the Deringer from her hand and extracted the bullet. Once free of the platform, the colonel turned to face her. "Danged if this isn't a dud. Can you believe that?" He reached into his pocket and pulled out a half dozen live rounds. "This what you were expecting, ma'am?"

Angry tears streamed down Morticia's face. She twisted in the grasp of the guards. "It could have been so good for you." Her venomous petulance masked any truth in her plea. She spit at him.

Rucker offered a rueful shake of his head. "Take her away, men."

As he watched her being led off, Cord Whelan slipped alongside Rucker. He smiled broadly. "Going back to Texas, Colonel?"

"Could be, Sergeant. Could be." He offered Whelan a congratulatory tap on the shoulder. "You saved my rear end, Sergeant. Likely saved the country. I'll not forget that. Now, let's get our president back to Washington."

IT'S IN OUR BONES

Here he come, limpin' along, him an' that goldarned crutch.
He shoulda damn well taken better care of hisself.
Hurts watchin' him jammin' that stick in the stable dirt;
Jam an' step, ache an' pain, simply not his old self.
Truth be told, it's sorta my fault; fence was too high.
Stopped sudden-like an' o'er my head he went, poor old elf.

He gazes up at the halter on the hook 'side my stall;
He pauses, winces as he reaches an' grasps the browband.
Couple more jam an' steps, an' he slips it o'er my head;
He gently strokes my neck with one gnarled old hand.
Graspin' the saddle pommel, he grunts, slings it on my back,
He cinches it tight an' gasps a bit as straight he stands.

Our eyes lock. I know what's next. Been doin' this a while.
We jam an' step to a li'l hill; he swings up to make us one.
The twinkle in his eyes hints of the fire still lit in his belly
He be a cowboy's cowboy in our day, ridin' till settin' sun.
He makes a clickin' 'tween teeth an' gum an' pats my neck.
Off we go like old times, but at a walk rather than run.

We used to ride far 'cross the prairies checkin' our beeves;

114

We'd stop at live oak mottes to drink an' take the shade.
More than once he saved us both from rattlers an' wild boar,
Even chased off some bad dudes an' shot a renegade.
They say that cowboy is in our bones, an' it's true, it's fact;
Far too soon our trails will end, but our souls will ne'er fade.

GOLD ON THE GUADALUPE

Eddies bend around bald cypress and box elder roots,
Laying bare twisted creations and soul-bending marvels,
As the Guadalupe carves its way through the Texas hills,
Meandering its way to San Antonio Bay.

Golden leaves flutter in the crisp autumnal breezes,
Heralding the frigid winter frosts yet to arrive.
A solitary cypress leaf braves the churning rapids,
Carried twisting and turning on its eastward journey.

Towering escarpments guard the river's chosen path,
Lending majesty to the moving munificence;
A white-tail deer drinks at its edge, ears on high alert,
While yellow eyes silently watch its every move.

A golden ceiling reflects in the swirling currents,
As soothing sounds bely the danger lurking near.
A squirrel chatters a warning, drops a cypress cone,
The startled buck leaps into the river's gold—too late?

Tongue sweeps 'cross lips, a turn, a rueful padding away,
The white-tail quivers, shivers in the swirling waters.

God's bounteous glory in wonder ever displayed,
Autumn gold's been struck on the Guadalupe this day.

WHITE SLAVER
OBSESSION-DRIVEN EVIL

Horatio Thorpe represents an evil force throughout the early Tumbleweed Sagas, as his wealth, coupled with his huge ego, self-centeredness, promiscuity, and obsessive-compulsive nature, combine to wreak mayhem upon the good citizens of Texas. His Magnolia Plantation east of Austin eventually houses a dysfunctional family and features nearly two thousand slaves cultivating cotton and tobacco.

HORATIO THORPE WAS A TALL MAN. Well, actually, he was tall and quite wide...borderline obese. He'd been that way since the completion of his Magnolia Plantation not far from today's Conroe, Texas. He was as much a culinary overindulger as he was sexually promiscuous, much to the distress of his psychologically abused wife. One of the wealthiest men in Texas, Thorpe was descended from a Carolina plantation family that had afforded him the resources to build his own vast plantation on the Texas Gulf plains. Money served as the elixir, feeding his obsessions and especially his insatiable desire for more of his most sought-after tastes—more money, more food, and more sex. His wealth wrought power, which in turn was artfully applied to strongly sway Texas politics. But his habits bred a certain contempt for the law, enabling him to not only stoop to but also get away with fraudulent and deceitful practices.

Had he not been so corpulent, he might have been judged a

handsome man, as he dressed well. Notably, he abhorred guns, a consequence of a near-death experience during the Mexican-American War. A disgruntled junior officer had tried to assassinate Thorpe but missed. Ever since, he kept his distance from firearms. It might have been just as well, as he was unlikely to find a gun belt that would fit easily around his prodigious waist.

Growing up, Horatio Thorpe enjoyed the fruits of his parents' labors —or more correctly, their slaves' labors. By the time he was fifteen, he'd bedded nearly every female slave on the plantation and developed a special talent for promiscuity that would follow him throughout his life.

Young Thorpe had just celebrated his eighteenth birthday when his father took him aside. "Horatio," he sputtered through lips wet with whiskey, "I'm likely not going to live past a couple more months. The infection's got me." The old man—he was a mere forty years old—coughed up blood into a handkerchief. "This"—*cough*— "all of this"—*cough*—"will be yours."

Horatio thought on the words. His mother had died birthing him. His father? Well, he had satisfied any sexual needs just as Horatio would learn to. Learning to objectify women, especially slave women, came easy to these Thorpes. Horatio had fully expected to inherit the Carolina plantation. He was an only child; who else was there?

Nevertheless, he listened patiently and respectfully to his father. In the back of his mind, roiled thoughts of opportunities promoted by some fellow named Stephen Austin in a place called Texas. The lure caused a seemingly insatiable case of wanderlust in Horatio's very core. There'd surely be greater opportunities there than in Carolina with its staid plantation elite.

Thorpe buried his father beside his mother on a grassy knoll at the far northeast corner of the plantation. Stuck in the young man's pocket at the funeral service were the signed papers transferring title of his legacy to some folks newly arrived from Europe. Horatio wasted no time. As his father had drawn his final breaths, he'd already begun loading a veritable parade of ox-drawn wagons with any necessary possessions for the long trip to Texas. He'd purchased a hundred thousand acres of rich farmland sight unseen a hundred miles northeast of Austin. Horatio even had a name picked out: Magnolia. He'd packed a couple of dozen Magnolia seedlings in one of his wagons with which he planned to flank the envisioned pathway leading to the big Georgian-style plantation house he would build.

One hundred days. Oxen were not exactly a speedy mode of transportation; they did well to make a dozen miles a day. Thorpe was not a patient man. He, at least, had his own perceived pleasures met by the concubine embedded in the over one hundred of his slaves making the journey to Texas. Food and sex became his ready substitutes for enduring the slow, plodding travel.

Ultimately, the caravan reached what was to become Magnolia Plantation. The big house construction was already underway per instructions sent ahead. Another month existing in wagons and tents was a small price to pay for the anticipated grandeur of the Georgian edifice that was to be. While the big house was under construction, Horatio put his slave chattel to work clearing fields for planting and building cabins in the evenings. Wise in the selection of prime slave stock, he brought only the best of the four hundred slaves from North Carolina. The rest? Well, they had been sold to the new owners of the plantation.

Thorpe dug into his coffers, bought up more land, and grew plenty of cotton over the next dozen years. By the time he was thirty years old, he'd doubled his acreage, amassed nearly a thousand slaves, and expanded his plantings to include tobacco. He early on recognized the importance of controlling his cotton from seed to cloth. It didn't take long to discover Galveston and its potential. He built a mill in the port city to turn his cotton into thread, weave it into cloth, dye it, and produce far more bolts of fashionable fabrics than any other plantation owner in Texas.

What did he do next? He bought a shipping company and established trade relations with France. He'd seemingly overnight become one of the wealthiest and most influential men in Texas. And yet there was an underlying ruthlessness, a coldness about him. His wife, Martha, barely knew him, though she surely was aware of his many dalliances with pretty young slave girls. His sons were essentially estranged, though the younger son, Gascon, less so than his older sibling Edward. Their daughter, Mattie, had died by rattlesnake bite at age seven but barely knew her father. Horatio was barely at home during the children's formative years.

Thorpe's roving libido didn't stop with slave girls. No, he'd frequented pretty much every bordello in Texas, Louisiana, and down into Mexico. The French ladies of the night surely tasted his affections. Money and power, coupled with an insatiable lust for food and women, led Thorpe to buy up brothels such that he'd have his needs met whenever and wherever he traveled.

It didn't take long for Thorpe to discover that providing food and sex to influential folks was a great strategy for compiling even greater wealth and power.

Imperfections aside, Thorpe recognized that his plantation chattel were far from stupid. Disadvantaged by circumstance, for sure, but not stupid. Those whom he judged the brightest—or in the case of slave girls, most comely—got to be household servants. Thus, a slave named Samuel came to be entrusted with his master's office operations, including tracking and even helping manage Thorpe's vast holdings. When Horatio Thorpe left town, Samuel ran operations. Throughout Austin, the slave became grudgingly accepted as Thorpe's surrogate.

While prostitution was viewed by many as an amoral pursuit, it was nevertheless tolerated. Thorpe was known to operate what might be described as high-class brothels. While prostitution brought Thorpe a few notches down morally, it was his underlying deteriorating sensibilities of being so powerful as to be above the law that brought him to new business interests that piqued his leanings toward greed.

This day, he sat contemplating his next venture. He'd begun to weigh the ugliness of political storms brewing in Washington, DC, over slavery and in Austin by extension. He figured it was about time to get his due from the state and national governments. He'd not especially benefited from the Mexican-American War, and prospects ten years later hadn't appreciably improved. He ran his hands over the glassy smooth surface of the huge mahogany desk that served as centerpiece for his office in Austin. The office was well appointed and easily accommodated his ample girth, though the chair he presently occupied behind the desk was undergoing a trial of its physical limits.

Thorpe's gaze looked off to the hill where the new Texas capital would be built. But it was no ordinary stare into space. He'd broken just a bit of a sweat, and his breathing had become just a tad heavy. His pulse quickened. Samuel's knock at the door broke the spell.

"Massah Thorpe. Your guest is here, Massah."

Thorpe's eyes went to the ceiling. He pushed back from the desk and began to button his pants. He spoke in an intense whisper. "Side door, Delilah. Go. See you later."

The comely slave forced a smile as she wiped her lips and then bolted for the side exit to Thorpe's office.

Thorpe cleared his throat, pulled himself up from his chair, and prepared to greet his guest. "Send in the general, Samuel." He flinched reflexively as General Booker Truax strode in with the measured steps of a West Point graduate. The flinch? Thorpe's aversion to guns ever since that damnable Mexican-American War. He'd bought himself a commission, a high enough rank to enable his service as a brevet colonel. Given his wealth-bought political influence, he served more as a sutler and adjutant, acquiring hard-to-find supplies from a tent far behind the battle lines. His role hadn't been to wave a saber and rally troops.

Turned out, however, that a major in General Taylor's command felt that Thorpe was the cause of his having been passed over for a promotion. The major attempted to kill Thorpe but failed and was summarily tried and executed. Ever since that narrow miss, Horatio didn't permit guns in his office. Thorpe noted that the general had not surrendered his sword or sidearm, but he realized he'd simply have to tolerate it. He eased around the desk and shook Truax's hand while motioning to a table and chairs at the far side of his cavernous office. "Care for a drink, Booker?" There was a sort of diabolical satisfaction in using the general's first name. He didn't want Truax drawing on rank to play any high-and-mighty games.

Truax wasn't one to waste time. He waved off Thorpe's affront and sat purposefully. "What's with Thaddeus Brown demanding a bigger share, Horatio?"

Brown wasn't ever supposed to contact the general. His point of contact was a Colonel Horace Rucker, under Truax's command. Thorpe sighed, then grunted as his ampleness found the chair. He poured himself a glass of whiskey and quaffed it down. "He's out of order, General. You can be assured it will never happen again."

Truax cleared his throat. "When are you moving our merchandise overseas?" The general was anxious to be rid of anything that might link him to Thorpe's profitable scheme. But for the damnable plantation owner having given him a free pass to his string of brothels, Truax wouldn't have permitted himself to be lured into the sordid business of stealing government property.

"In due time, General. We don't want to arouse suspicion." He was careful to not reveal where the stolen merchandise was stored. The less folks like Truax and Rucker knew, the better.

Thorpe calculated that Thaddeus Brown had at least one more circuit of the Indian agencies and posts to make. Brown had the responsibility of delivering supplies to those facilities but was skimming a hefty portion of the inventory and routing them to a barn near Laredo for storage. Soon enough, they'd cart the lot of it off to Brownsville and thence to an overseas buyer that served as the tentacles for Thorpe's vast commerce empire. They'd bide their time for a few months before beginning the cycle again. "I will have Colonel Rucker see to it." For Thorpe, it was less about the money than the sheer audacity of stealing government property right under its inept nose.

"When?" The general was just a tad more anxious than his fingers tapping on the table revealed. "My honor is at stake here."

"You will know, Booker. Trust me. You will know." Thorpe smiled.

Honor? Truax wasn't in this for honor, not his nor anyone else's. This was purely and simply about voracious avarice; it was greed that could never be sated. Yet for Truax, it assured retirement in far greater comfort than he might otherwise ever have imagined.

Truax had received the surreptitiously delivered envelope filled with cash once before. The general nodded resignedly.

"I apologize, Booker, but I'm about to head off to follow up on our venture. I do hope you will excuse me." The chair seemed to groan with relief as Thorpe stood. He politely escorted Truax to the door.

When the general was out of sight, Thorpe turned to Samuel. "My carriage, Samuel. I must visit Laredo." As he was about to return to his office, he paused and scribbled a few words on a piece of paper. He folded it and handed it to Samuel. "See that Colonel Rucker receives this."

Texas Jack's Saloon was the sort of establishment that Horatio Thorpe hated but knew better than to turn up his nose at. While he owned no brothels in Laredo, the likes of dives like Texas Jack's often spawned lovely soiled doves for his establishments in Austin and San Antonio and Galveston. It was a matter of discovering them before they were too despoiled.

Scarlett Rose, seated across from the swinging front doors of Texas Jack's, caught his eye immediately. She was one of those women that could cast an indelible impression on the likes of Thorpe. Raven-red hair framing ruby-red lips, falling in graceful waves across ample white breasts pushed up from her green satin bodice, coupled with long slender legs crossed so as to reveal just enough thigh captured the wealthy Texan's soul. Thorpe knew then and there that he must have her.

Scarlett spent three days enduring Thorpe's crushing weight and undersized manhood. However, Horatio Thorpe paid extremely well. Yes, extremely well. He told her he had business at nearby Fort McIntosh, though didn't share any details. He even brought her to a dinner at the commanding officer's residence. For her part, it became increasingly obvious to Scarlett that this man wanted more of her than a simple sexual dalliance.

Upon leaving Laredo, Thorpe made her an offer he was sure she couldn't refuse. He saw her as an important addition to his Red Rose Brothel in Austin. Importantly, it would place her a mere five-minute walk from his office through hidden alleys. He cleared his throat and stroked her naked back as he lay beside her. "Scarlett, my dear."

"Yes, Horatio. Are you ready again?" She half turned toward him.

"No, no, not that." He smiled. "I want you to come to Austin. You will live in luxury, Scarlett. Any desire you have will be met."

Scarlett had grown ever wiser to the ways of men. "And you, Horatio?" She knew this stood to benefit him somehow as well.

"You'd only be there for me, Scarlett. You would not be bedding other men."

Scarlett's eyes connected with his. Did she want to be held captive to this man's sexual fantasies, and realistically, to his crushing bulk? Did she want to be available at this man's whim? She averted her gaze.

"Well?" Thorpe stroked her thigh.

"I'll think on it, Horatio dear. I'll think on it."

Thorpe's expression turned serious. "Don't wait too long, Scarlett Rose. I may have to come steal you away." He broke into a laugh that cut the tension.

A chill coursed through her as she sensed that he would indeed kidnap her. As young and still naïve to worldly ways as she was, it wasn't hard to recognize obsession.

Thorpe pulled her to him. He'd have her once more before departing for Austin.

Thorpe had wisely stayed clear of the barn just north of Laredo. He had to trust that Thaddeus Brown was good to his word. Little did he know that but a couple of days after his departure, Scarlett escaped to avoid giving pleasure to a gang of Mexican bandits and to pursue a handsome customer that had caught her fancy. She was headed toward Corpus Christi on what would turn into an odyssey, eventually bringing her back into Thorpe's life.

"Good morning, Samuel." The master strode past the slave's

desk and into his office. The desk was stacked with papers for Thorpe to sign. Samuel was nothing if not efficient. To Thorpe, Samuel was the antithesis of what so many folks assumed about the intelligence of black folks. He sat at his desk and signed each document, scanning each before putting his signature to them. Signings done, he stretched his prodigious bulk and considered what to do next.

"Samuel!"

The slave appeared in the doorway, respectfully bowing his head. "Yes, Massah Thorpe?"

"Get Roy Biggs here for me." He paused. Thoughts of Scarlett Rose swept through his imagination. A smile crept across his lips as the delights he had enjoyed with the red-headed Laredo whore swirled from his brain to his crotch. He cleared his throat. "Oh…and fetch Delilah."

"Yes, Massah Thorpe." Samuel closed the door behind him, sighed, and rolled his eyes. Fetching Roy Biggs would be easy, but Delilah was Brody's woman. Brody, a tall, well-muscled slave who had been saved from field hand work precisely because of Delilah, worked as security at Thorpe's Red Rose Brothel. So far as Samuel or pretty much anyone else knew, Brody was oblivious to Horatio Thorpe's carnal use of the comely slave woman he thought was his and his alone. Were he to ever find out, well…Samuel hoped and prayed that would never happen.

Roy Biggs stood, hat in hand and with an empty holster, before Thorpe's desk. He shifted his weight ever so slightly from foot to foot. For as tough an hombre as Biggs was, he tended to cower just a tad before Horatio Thorpe. Go figure. The oversized plantation owner had, in effect, become the outlaw's meal ticket to his well-cultivated, sleazier side. While Biggs had amassed a sizable fortune stealing claims in the gold fields of California and owned a huge fortress-style hacienda secreted away in a remote part of western Texas, he found himself drawn to Thorpe. Perhaps it was a sense of kinship.

Despite being married to a beautiful Mexican woman by which

he'd had a couple of children, Roy Biggs was far from domesticated. Wasn't in his nature. He had, for some perverted reason, taken to the occupation of killing for hire. He'd already been jailed twice for murder in Texas but went free both times thanks to Thorpe's graciously deep pockets. Biggs admired the man simultaneously for the business acumen that enabled him to amass a large fortune, for the deviously evil cunning that stole from the government, and especially the obsession over women that led to a string of well-outfitted brothels. As he stood before the big man's desk, Biggs couldn't help but think on the contradiction of how Thorpe's wealth made his lawbreaking all the more unnecessary. He nevertheless wondered what sort of task the rich Texan had in mind.

Thorpe cleared his throat. He didn't hide the fact that Delilah was taking care of business under his desk. The big man's face contorted, then relaxed. In but another moment, Delilah darted for the side entrance to the office. Thorpe smiled. "How unhospitable of me, Roy. Would you like me to call her back?" He followed with a satisfied grin.

Biggs shook his head. "That's okay, Mr. Thorpe. I can find my way to the Red Rose later." He smiled uncomfortably.

Thorpe buttoned his trousers as he arose from the desk. He locked onto Biggs's eyes, taking a contumacious, almost capricious satisfaction in the dark wickedness he found there. It was as though they connected with some even blacker part of the man's soul. He nodded toward the nearby side boy and half staggered toward it. "Can I get you a drink, Roy?"

Biggs figured to fully keep his senses about him. "Thanks, Mr. Thorpe. I'll pass today." He moseyed over to a chair and sat, all the while keeping his eyes locked on Thorpe's. He sensed that Thorpe took some sort of perverted pleasure in staring him down.

Thorpe blinked first. "You been to Laredo lately?"

The desperado's eyes got just a bit darker and tad wider as he recalled the border town as the site of his most recent killing. It had been a bushwhacking a couple of months back that Thorpe had paid handsomely for. "Not since..." His voice trailed off.

"I need you to get down there and fetch somebody for me."

Biggs smiled. He was all too well acquainted with Thorpe's tastes and methods. It was surely an exceptionally beautiful woman that Thorpe had bedded and now obsessed over. He flashed back his own sort of evil smile. "And?"

"One thousand, plus your usual expenses."

The outlaw's mind began to calculate how many men this whore would have to bed to compensate for satisfying Thorpe's desires. "Her name is Scarlett Rose."

"Texas Jack's?"

"Of course she's at Texas Jack's. Speed is essential, Roy." Thorpe drew an envelope from his coat pocket, placed it on the table, and pushed it toward Biggs. Then, as if a shroud had been dropped over them, he grew deadly serious. His dark eyes bored into Biggs. "Touch her, and you're a dead man."

"Not to fret, Mr. Thorpe." Biggs paused. This must be hugely important to the man, he gathered, as the scion of Texas had never threatened him before. "And if she's not there?"

Thorpe hadn't considered that his bird might have flown the cage. She sure hadn't seemed happy with Laredo and her chosen profession. In fact, he was still just a bit hurt that she hadn't leaped at the chance to come directly to Austin with him. "If that's the case, find out where she went and track her down. I'll double your pay." Thorpe stood and fished a piece of red paper from his vest pocket. He strode to his desk, initialed it, and handed it to Biggs. "Here, Roy. Enjoy one of the ladies. My compliments."

Moments later, Biggs stood outside Thorpe's office reloading his gun. He finished, nodded friendly-like to Samuel, who had returned his revolver and ammunition, and headed to the Red Rose. He figured he had enough time before heading to Laredo. It would be a long ride, and with any luck, the Scarlett woman would have left town. Biggs didn't cotton to spending time in Laredo.

Thaddeus Brown alighted from the wagon and marched to Colonel Rucker's office. He'd easily passed the guards at the gates who knew him for who and what he was.

The guard standing outside the colonel's office moved in front of Brown before he could barge in on Rucker. "Dammit, man. At least let me announce you." He was well acquainted with Brown and even helped occasionally with the man's skullduggery.

Brown stopped, an impatient look on his face.

The guard knocked on the door. "Colonel, Mr. Brown is here."

There was a long silence, then, "Send him in."

The guard let Thaddeus Brown pass. The two smiled at each other. It was as though everybody knew the chicanery that was afoot. Somehow, Brown was a master at ensuring that participants benefited just enough to hold their tongues. Everybody also knew that a wagging tongue could result in a less-than-desirable end.

Colonel Horace Rucker remained seated. He didn't look up. "What the hell are you doing here, Brown?!"

"Got an especially big inventory this trip, Colonel Rucker."

"Well, dammit, you know where it goes! Just tend to business and get your sorry ass out of here."

"Gonna cost more. Had to add two wagons."

Rucker shook his head. A caravan was an attention-getter. General Truax would be none too pleased. The colonel only had a very vague idea from where the general was taking his orders. Keeping the bosses happy was a top priority in any case. He shook his head and looked up at Brown. "It'll be taken care of. Now, get out of here…quietly."

Brown tipped his hat and was gone.

Rucker rubbed his nose. There was a decidedly offensive odor left in Brown's wake.

Horatio Thorpe was none too pleased at the message from Roy Biggs. It was properly cryptic. All it said was, "The bird has flown the cage." Thorpe mumbled something unintelligible under his breath, then cursed a little louder. It had been nearly a month, and he truly craved a tumble with the ravishing Laredo whore. The memory of her fragrant scent swirled through his very soul. Her essence lifted his senses, and he'd have sworn she was right there lying with him. The spell was broken by Samuel knocking at the office door. He shook off his dreamy meanderings. "Yes? What is it, Samuel?"

"You said to awake you at noon, Massah Thorpe."

"Thank you, Samuel. That will be all." Thorpe stood, wobbled, caught his balance, and straightened out his vest while looking in the mirror. He told himself that he really needed to lose the bulges protruding over his belt; he was asking a lot of his suspenders. The wealthy scion snorted, held his chin high, and headed for the door. If he couldn't have Scarlett, he'd bury his obsession with one of his ladies at the Red Rose. He glided past Samuel. "I'll return in a couple of ours, Samuel."

"Excuse me, Massah Thorpe. A word, please?"

Thorpe froze. It was most unusual for Samuel to interrupt him when he was on one of his brothel missions. "Yes, Samuel." He couldn't hold back just a bit of impatience in his tone.

"It's Brody, Massah. He know 'bout you an' Delilah."

Thorpe sighed. Brody was good breeding stock; it wouldn't do to remove any threat by having him killed. Hell, good strong black men were bringing top dollar in the markets. Was there the remotest soft spot in Thorpe's heart? "Send him to Magnolia, Samuel. He's to be whipped. Be sure he understands that if he shows up in Austin, he'll surely die."

Samuel had been through this once before, and it hadn't turned out well for the slave. "Yes, sir, Massah Thorpe." He swallowed hard and nearly shed a tear at the prospect of a fellow black man suffering such a beating.

Thorpe took a few steps before pausing. In just an instant, he'd rethought the matter with Brody. He knew Delilah loved the big slave. "I've changed my mind, Samuel."

Samuel winced imperceptibly. These sorts of second thoughts didn't usually go well.

"Have Brody and Delilah sent to the market in New Orleans. They should be worth a pretty penny." He gave a hard look at Samuel.

"Yes, sir, Massah Thorpe. I'll see to it, Massah." Samuel shuffled over to his desk with his back to Thorpe, trying to conceal the tears already streaming down his cheeks.

Thorpe exited, giving the door a good-riddance slam. He figured Brody was just savvy enough to seek revenge over any punishment his master might mete out. At New Orleans, it was just possible that

Brody and Delilah could be sold as a pair and fetch a higher price. He smiled at having solved his problem. After all, Samuel would quickly find the comeliest of the young Magnolia slave girls to substitute for Delilah's duties.

As Horatio Thorpe strode confidently up the alley toward the Red Rose, he sensed that he was being followed. While he had an aversion to visitors to his office being armed, it didn't stop him from carrying a loaded Deringer in his vest pocket. He slowed, then sped up his pace. Whomever was behind him was quite clearly following his pace and quite likely up to no good. Thorpe stopped and pivoted as he drew the gun from his vest.

Upon Thorpe stopping, the masked man behind him had begun to draw his gun. He was a swarthy-looking character and quite clearly was planning to rob Thorpe, or worse.

Thorpe reacted, planting a round from the Deringer between the assailant's eyes. At a mere five feet away, it was next to impossible to miss. Thorpe scanned the alley. There were no witnesses. Despite his bulk, he bent down and pulled away the man's mask. "Damn," he muttered under his breath. The man had worked as a supervisor at Thorpe's Galveston shipping operations. He'd been caught stealing from the company and summarily fired. As Thorpe began to turn away, he heard a murmur.

"Son of a bitch…you…you cost…me…" The man took his final breath.

Scanning the alley again, Thorpe shrugged and headed for the Red Rose. He desperately needed a woman and a drink; he'd leave it for someone to find the body. No one could know that he'd shot the man. Besides, it was self-defense.

"What the hell are you doing here?" Two weeks had passed since he'd heard from Roy Biggs, and now the man sat in his darkened parlor. "How'd you get in?"

Biggs lit a match and put it to the end of one of Thorpe's finer cigars. In the dim light cast by the match, his dark eyes looked even darker. Hollow, devoid of the least bit of emotion. "Getting in wasn't a problem, Mr. Thorpe. You need to lock your back door." He smirked and took a pull on the cigar.

Horatio recalled that he'd left the door unlocked for one of his liaisons. She was due in about an hour. "And?"

"We have a problem, Mr. Thorpe." Biggs sent a smoke ring skyward. "Your little Laredo whore has a guardian angel." He leaned back and crossed his legs. "Still, she's a feisty little thing."

"What are you talking about?"

"I was hanging at the Longhorn Saloon in Corpus Christi. Seems your Scarlett Red has been up to all sorts of no good with some outlaw named Dirk Cavendish. But it gets complicated, Mr. Thorpe."

The big man strode across the parlor and lit a lamp before pouring himself a drink. He saw that Biggs's eyes had gone to Thorpe's crotch and embarrassingly realized he'd not buttoned his pants after his most recent love poking. He got himself together and stood with his back to the fireplace facing Biggs. He gave the desperado a look that demanded the story be continued.

"Seems there's this Texas Ranger named Luke Dunn. He's out to get the Cavendish fellow but seems to have a soft spot for the whore. Don't understand that, being as he's married."

A bit of red began to creep into Thorpe's face. "So, you couldn't dispose of this outlaw, this Cavendish fellow, and the Texas Ranger as well? Where the hell is Scarlett?" Roiling through his thinking was questioning what he was paying Biggs for.

"Damn, Mr. Thorpe. This Cavendish fellow is right careless. I expect the Texas Ranger will see to him."

"And the Ranger? And Scarlett?" Thorpe was growing ever more irritated.

"You never heard of Luke Dunn, Mr. Thorpe?"

"Can't say as I have. Is he a problem?"

Biggs offered a sardonic smile. "You might say."

Thorpe took a long pull of whiskey straight from the bottle.

"He's built a reputation as a very effective, no-nonsense lawman who always gets his man. Dunn is so good at bringing outlaws to justice that he's become a favorite of the powers that be in Austin. None other than Rip Ford is partial to him."

Thorpe was well aware of Ford's reputation against Comanche and Mexican bandits, so he quickly surmised that this Luke Dunn fellow must be something extra special to have earned the famous Texas lawman's admiration. "How much?"

"Well, here's the interesting part, Mr. Thorpe." Biggs's smile broadened. Had he been a snake, his tongue surely would have been darting from his lips. "I expect she'll be heading this way. I heard that she wanted to escape her whoring fate and was looking to head north. Her travels would naturally take her through Austin."

Thorpe's eyes widened and he nodded slowly as he grasped the scenario laid out by Biggs. He eased over to a high boy, opened a small drawer, and pulled out a sack of coins. "I appreciate your efforts, Roy." He smiled and handed the sack to the outlaw. "Your job is done for now. I may call on you later about that Texas Ranger."

Biggs took a final pull on the cigar, stuffed the sack of coins in his pocket, and headed for the door. "Been a pleasure, Mr. Thorpe."

General Truax felt dirty, but was already far too deep in this business with Thorpe. The plantation master needed a legitimate-sounding ruse to capture Scarlett without her suspecting he was behind it. Thorpe had concocted the perfect plan for waylaying her travels northward.

"It's an order, Colonel Rucker."

"If I may speak freely, sir?"

General Truax nodded.

"I have a perfectly good housekeeper. She's been loyal...almost like family."

Truax sighed. "This woman, this Scarlett Rose, will be in Austin briefly. You might say she is destined to escape one fate only to find another."

"What of Rex and Stephen?"

The general smiled ironically. "Be assured those young boys of yours will appreciate Scarlett Rose. I understand that she's ravishingly beautiful and excels at her profession."

"Sir?" Filthiness swept over Rucker. He felt like some sort of White slaver. *Duty? Honor?*

"Damn it, Horace! She's a prostitute looking to find a new life. Our job is to guide her to recapture her virgin virtues, fashion a new beginning for the young woman." Truax dared not reveal from whence his orders came or what that supposed new life entailed. "Just get it done, Colonel."

Rucker saluted smartly and departed. He paused outside and wiped his hands on his tunic. His mouth felt dry.

Truax smiled. Horatio Thorpe would surely be pleased.

Thorpe's eyes took himself in. The big mirror didn't lie. He sucked in his portentous belly as best he could, promising himself to shed a few pounds. After all, he owed it to the red-headed Laredo whore to make himself as attractive as possible. Better for her to enjoy his charms, at the least. If the general and his acolyte colonel did their duty, he'd be bedding his White slave sooner than later.

He looked toward his office door. "Samuel, get Calista in here! Make it quick." His libido had arisen at mere thoughts of Scarlett. He plunked himself behind his desk. "And bring me those papers about the cotton shipments to France." Horatio Thorpe could be nothing if not efficient, even when it came to combining pleasure with business. Importantly, Calista had no secret paramour like Delilah had enjoyed. He wondered for a moment how Delilah and Brody made out at the auction blocks in New Orleans. *Were they sold as a couple?* Samuel would tell him soon enough what price they had fetched. Ah, but here came Calista. He pushed back from the desk just enough and picked up the shipping documents.

Soon enough, he expected to hear word of Miss Scarlett Rose having taken the position with Colonel Rucker. He'd bide his time.

TEXAS DEEP WITHIN MY SOUL

My soul is fully laden with deep dreams of Texas life,
Yearning to embrace my birth blood, grasp it, and fill my
   soul.
Oh, there's more; I hunger to
Travel bayous to Big Bend, Panhandle to Rio Grande,
Sate my hunger for Texas beef brisket and barbeque,
Absorb Austin music and lights of San Antone's Riverwalk.
Indeed, Texas lies so very deep within my soul.

I long to simply go, to fulfill these dreams I harbor,
Touching my loved ones near and far while yet within my
   reach.
And still more; I hanker to
Caress God-carved shapes on Palo Duro Canyon's palisades,
Savor perfumes of yellow roses laced with bluebonnet
   bouquet,
Consume the dazzling sun rays on Padre Island's gulf-kissed
   shores.
Oh yes, Texas lies so very deep within my soul.

No one can know, none can feel the deep ache of days that
   pass,
Sharing tales of family and dreams of all yet to come.

My soul cries out; I ache to
Climb the pink-hued granite escarpments of Enchanted Rock,
Take in vast prairies dotted with live oak and mesquite
    mottes,
Breathe in living stories from my Irish ancestors' graves.
You see, it's in my blood, it's deep within my soul.

TRUE TEXANS

Anglo-Celts were as a human wave crashing upon Texas
   forest and plain;
Real frontiersmen blazed Daniel Boone's rugged trail beyond
   Kentucky's bounds.
Fighters all, long rifles in hand, seeking land, fortune, on they
   pressed.
The land and its peoples were harsh, unforgiving despite
   unbounded beauty;
These men too well knew brutality 'tween Anglo and Indian
   cut both ways.
They spread beyond Sabine and Red Rivers, first true Texans
   carving their way.

Colonists came next, braving an untamed world, carving
   farms to eke a life;
A protestant ethos of God, work, and money clashed with
   their Mexican hosts.
They faced a world reeking of treachery, of promises unkept,
   danger lurking;
Dread Comanche beset from the west, Mexican thieves
   harassed from the south.
The clash of cultures could be plaintively heard 'cross the
   vast prairies and hills.

Independent, free, ever stronger men and women, true
  Texans fighting free.

Land was plentiful, drawing planters from bayous of the
  deepest south;
Cotton might be king, but land and slaves were its deviant
  barter, its legal tender.
Wealthy planters, few in number, held most Texans hostage
  to their whims;
A consciousness of race, a bitterness wrought of farming,
  ranching, and gentility.
Tribalism emerged against the constant of blood memory in
  winning their place.
Colony to republic to state, flags change, true Texans forged
  in land and mind.

Rinches, Tejanos Diabolos, Tejanos Sangrientes, the Mexicans
  called them.
They were Texas Rangers, a warrior class of men, a fully
  masculine culture;
Drawn to open spaces, enforcing the peace, ranks filled with
  camaraderie.
Quiet, decent honest men, their horses valued more than
  their women;
Notoriously brave, never boastful, but "catch and hang" their
  brutal motto.
Armed to the teeth and wed to the saddle, true Texans in
  every way.

Cattle, cotton, and railroads offered but a brief twilight
  'gainst the Texas of old,
For wildcatters stepped into Texas lore, bred of civic
  barbarism of days long past.
Farm and prairie soon enough earned the bounty of black
  gold's largesse;
A tectonic shift was ushered in, a change of economics but
  not the Tejano soul.

Myths influenced by the Alamo and Comanche spears, one
    hundred years of wild frontier.
Texan lives and values forged in a land of plenty, these are
    the true Texans.

REDEEMED

AVOIDING THE HANGMAN'S NOOSE

Walker Carson represented Luke Dunn's first opportunity to decide between justice and redemption, as Dunn encountered the teenager on the run from a failed bank robbery attempt. It was a hanging offense. As Luke faces the unarmed, dehydrated young man walking his lame horse, he accepts the young man's story and decides to give him a second chance. Luke's faith in Carson is ultimately proven, but not without stumbles along the way.

THUNDER BOOMED, and lightning streaked the night sky across the northern reaches of the Texas Nueces Strip. Walker Carson was born under firebolts and ear-jarring crashes on July 14, 1839. He was the seventh Carson brought into the world, and this childbirth nearly killed his mother. Perhaps that alone foretold a future of living on life's edge.

Hap "Hoss" Carson, Walker's pa, had tried his hand at pretty much everything a man that couldn't read or write might do to make a living. He could lasso a yearling, mend a fence, drive cattle to the Kansas railheads, split logs, outfight most any polecat he met in a saloon or camp, and drink most any man under the table. He was a mixed bag of failure and success, depending on any judge's perspective. Aside from his undying love of horses, the single most reliable distinction to be said of Hoss was that he always came back to his wife and kids at their ranch about thirty or so miles south of San Antonio.

Horses were Hap Carson's lifeblood. Hoss was known to whip his sons but lay nary a feather lash to a cayuse no matter if it misbehaved. He likely gave more affection to any one of the two dozen or so steeds in his pastures than he did to his wife, Mary Maude, save for the times he managed to lie with her long enough to get her pregnant. Nevertheless, it was said that Hoss was a better breeder of horses than sons.

The Carson sons tended to lean toward all kinds of trouble once they reached their teens. The oldest two got into drinking early on, wound up shooting a lawman in Uvalde, and were lynched side-by-side on the local hanging tree. The next couple in line didn't profit much from their brothers' transgressions but managed to escape to Arizona Territory and were never heard from again.

Hoss expected his boys to carry most of the chores once they were old enough to walk and talk. This was important so as to enable his far-flung adventures. As the boys tired of being horse-whipped and berated, they'd be encouraged to leave if they hadn't already made up their minds to escape. Once escaped, they knew better than to come back, as Hoss would never stop reminding them of their cowardice in not finding a means to survive. Any returning Carson quickly escaped again as soon as possible rather than endure their pa's wrath.

Feeding a large family cost a bit, and Mary Maude did all she could to keep food on the table while Hoss was off on his exploits. Of course, she could never truly count on his return. That lent a touch of uncertainty to her life, enough to hedge her own bets, so to speak. She took in a bit of sewing, but her real moneymaker was evidenced by the smiles on men's faces as they left her cabin before sunup. For the gossip-minded, it left one to wonder just how many Carson boys were of Hap Carson's doing. For his part, Hoss was either too dumb or too disinterested to keep track of the birthings.

This was the life little Walker Carson was born into. Maybe that thunderstorm at his birth would be a reliable predictor after all.

One of Walker's habits that annoyed the very bejabbers out of Hoss was the boy's habit of daydreaming. 'Course, he didn't call it that or even know what it was. He'd find the boy leaning against a fence-post he'd just planted, staring off into space all dreamy-like.

"Walker! Dammit, boy. Whatcha stoppin' for?"

Walker would blink a couple of times, shake his head a tad, and shrug. He'd say nary a word.

"Stick to yer knittin', son. We got plenty of work needs doin'." And he'd give Walker a not-so-gentle cuff across the back of his head. Of course, he never bothered to ask what Walker was thinking about. Even if he did, the youngster would have been too fearful to honestly tell his father. Thus, Hoss Carson was oblivious to the river of dreams running through Walker's very soul. He had no idea how much the boy dreamed of escape from his father's rule, escape to the perceived freedoms of the Texas prairies. Even Walker Carson's rides out across the ranch to check fences and strays felt limiting to the young man's constitution. He'd continue to dream private-like. His pa needn't know; nobody did.

By the time he was fifteen years old, Walker's family had added two more sons, and unexpectedly, given past history, two daughters. Walker recalled being quite curious about the absence of certain private parts on these female humans referred to as "sisters." In fact, the absence of said parts left the boys to teasing the girls until Mary Maude complained to Hoss, and such untoward revelries were forever ended.

Sisters aside for now, Walker was about to make his first big mistake. It was a hot July afternoon a few days after he'd celebrated his birthday by himself that he found himself out riding beside the creek that meandered across their ranch. There were plenty of swimming holes, and it was an especially hot day that seemed to demand a break from searching for maverick beeves and stray horses. He dismounted near his very favorite spot, tied his horse to a nearby tree limb, and began disrobing. He was just about naked and had begun easing into the cool waters when a voice gave him pause.

"Why, Walker Carson, how you has growed."

Walker cringed. There he was butt naked in front of Daisy Warner, one of Uvalde's more active prostitutes. "Who? What the hell are you doing here?"

"Have to ask yer pa 'bout that, Walker, sweetie." She smiled fetchingly. "I was heading back to town when I spied you ridin' long 'side the creek."

"Well, keep on riding." Walker slunk down into the waters to cover his privates. "What do you want, anyway?"

"Bet you ain't had no woman afore, have you, sweetie?" She'd dismounted and was unbuttoning her blouse as she headed toward Walker. "We gonna change that, sweetie."

A large hole suddenly appeared between Daisy's breasts just after an explosion shattered the air. Walker dove toward the creek bank and the revolver lying atop his clothes. Still naked as a jaybird, he grabbed the gun and looked about him. Whomever fired the shot was too far away and likely long gone. There was nary a sound save the running waters and Daisy's final rasping gasps. What was he to do? Leave her body lying by the creek to rot in the sun or be devoured by coyotes? Someone knew she was there. Would anyone think he shot Daisy?

Walker dried himself off as best possible. He was still pondering what to do as he gazed down at her inert body. A couple of flies were already gathering on her remains. The thought of her being eaten by varmints caused him to shudder. He sighed resignedly and grabbed the shovel he always carried behind his saddle. He wasn't going to take her to town and arouse suspicions, but at least he could offer a decent burial. He still had no clue as to who shot her, but upon reflection, as he dug, he had his suspicion. After all, dead whores tell no tales.

Long about sunset, Walker rode up to the barn and began tending to his horse. He was hanging his tack when his pa appeared from the shadows.

Hoss took a casual posture, as though he hadn't a concern in the world. "How'd yer day go, son?"

Walker returned a squinty-eyed look, trying to take the measure of this man who claimed to be his father. "Not much, Pa. Couple beeves got mud stuck. Fixed a fence."

Hap Carson shrugged, offered a knowing smile, and headed off to the cabin.

Walker watched his pa stride away, feeling pretty much convinced that Hoss had shot Daisy. Problem was, he'd never be able to prove it. As to Daisy, she'd be another whore chewed up and spit into an early grave by the rigors of an often harsh and unyielding frontier life. Walker's mind momentarily drifted to what it might be like to have his way with a woman. He'd never really considered it until Daisy had come upon him. He shook his imaginings off as disrespectful of the woman whose body lay in a shallow grave just beneath the surface of the Nueces Strip. He figured coyotes were likely already digging her up. He ruefully shook his head, let his horse loose in the corral, and headed to the cabin.

Dinner would be a silent affair with curious expressions on the faces of mother and children at the usually talkative Hoss's unusual quiet demeanor. For his part, Walker kept his gaze mostly down toward his dinner. Mary Maude knew something had happened between father and son but dared not inquire. Besides, Walker was actually the product of one of her dalliances with the local banker, Will Singletary. She'd kept track of the months and was pretty certain of that. Singletary even paid her a handsome bonus to not tell his wife. Mary Maude understood blackmail, and Hap Carson never needed to know.

July 30, 1855, would not be soon forgotten by young Walker Carson. A buffalo hunter named Grog Jones had come by the ranch the previous day on his journey northwest toward the buffalo herds. Hoss had taken a liking to the man and invited him for a meal and a cool, dry place to spend the night.

Jones was like no one Walker had ever laid eyes on, a strapping hulk of a man with long white hair, a scraggly beard, penetrating icy-blue eyes, and a red scar across his forehead ostensibly from a Comanche's failed attempt to scalp him. The man was decked out in fringed stained buckskins despite the July heat. Only later would Walker learn that the stains were from buffalo fat and gore mixed with the dust and dung that hung about the vast herds of the beasts.

Above all else, Grog Jones had a wide, infectious smile and could tell more tales than most anyone around the region ever imagined. Most significantly, Jones sensed a wanderlust lurking in young Walker and played upon it. Thus, it was that they found themselves sitting around a campfire down alongside the creek.

Jones had just wrapped up another of his tales about staving off Indians and stalking buffalo when Walker broke the hunter's repertoire. "How many buffalo do you kill and skin out in a day?"

Hoss laid a piercing look on his young son, his eyes slicing into the teen's soul like hot knives through butter. The message was crystal clear: *Don't you even think about running off.*

Walker ignored him.

Jones had missed the eye signal Hoss was sending to his son as he simply smiled and answered the question. He figured his stories had already gotten the lad hooked on hunting buffalo. "Depends on how many skinners we have son. Typical day, we might do twenty or more buffs. It's not just skinnin', boy. The tongue is what they call a delicacy. We butcher and smoke the hams and humps and make the backstraps into brisket."

The conversation lingered on for a couple of more hours until Hoss signaled that it was time to pack it in for the night. Jones headed for the barn, thanking Mary Maude and letting the family know that he'd be headed out before first light. Hoss grabbed Walker's arm before the question-filled youngster could follow Jones out from the cabin.

The morning broke with an uneasy quiet. Hoss Carson strode out to the barn to find Jones gone along with his horse and pack mule. Nothing seemed amiss...except that Walker's bedroll was also gone. Hoss's eyebrows knitted in anger as he stalked around the barn and headed for the corral. *Damn!* he thought. The buckskin was missing from the corral, and Walker was nowhere to be seen.

Grog Jones rode at an easy pace as he continued to answer his new companion's seemingly never-ending questions.

Young Walker absorbed the answers like a sponge. It impressed Jones that the teen never asked the same question more than once.

What sort of rifle was best? What's the difference between a ripping knife and a skinning knife? How did the horse help with the skinning? How were hides processed for either toughness or suppleness?

Finally, Jones brought his horse to a halt. "Young Mr. Carson, I'm pleased to have you along, and I appreciate your curiosity. I do prefer to ride quiet-like and enjoy the natural sounds of the prairie." He offered up a smile. "In a couple of days, we'll reach camp and most of your questions will be answered." With that, he nodded, smiled again, and kicked his horse into a trot while the pack mule jostled along behind on a tether.

Walker paused to take in Jones's words before nudging his buckskin to follow a few feet behind. He figured Pa and Ma had discovered he was gone by now and wondered whether Pa would come after him. He was actually pretty certain that wouldn't be happening.

On the fifth morning, they crested a rise on the prairie. Before them, as far as the eye could see, were thousands of buffalo. Smoke from a campfire off to Walker's left signaled the location of the buffalo hunter camp. After pausing to take in the scope of the scene, he followed Grog Jones down below.

Reality sank in as Walker drew closer to the camp. All manner of odors permeated the hot July air. Putrefying flesh, buffalo dung, piss, whiskey, and sweat offered a nauseating concoction not fit to breathe. He saw only three rifles that Jones had described as buffalo guns. A half dozen men were busy skinning buffalo, butchering the carcasses, tanning hides, repairing camp equipment, sharpening knives, and more. A couple of the men looked up, shared toothless grins, and bent back into their tasks. There was nothing the least bit glorious, much less romantic, about the scene.

Jones broke the conversation lull, such as it was. "Gotta start from the bottom, son." He pointed to what was apparently some sort of makeshift privy. Jones meant his words literally. "Looks like it could use some cleanin'." Jones dismounted. "Dinner's aroun' sunset."

Second thoughts began to creep into Walker's head. He'd escaped from his father's abusive rule only to fall into a situation he already wasn't so sure he was up to. It was fast dawning on him that his chances of shooting a buffalo were about as good as getting the privy clean. But there he was, no money and no plan for any other future.

Walker was awakened by the sound of rifle fire. Jones was already picking off choice buffalo. The hunter sat with the barrel of his Sharps nestled in the nexus of a pair of sticks tied together and set as a gun barrel rest. Old Grog would kill a buffalo, then take a swig from the whiskey bottle alongside him. He fired five times and felled five buffalo. Jones took a final swig before motioning to the skinners to get to work.

The dead buffalo were roped and brought into the camp, where processing quickly got underway. The ripping knife began the skinning process, followed by the skinning knife, whereby they skinned the beast just enough to attach it to a rope. The rope was handed up to a mounted skinner and tied to the saddle horn. With the help of the skinners on the ground, the tough buffalo hide was slowly pulled away from the animal's body. Care was taken so as not to tear or otherwise damage the valuable pelts.

Jones saw Walker and motioned for him to join the men dragging skinned hides over to stretchers to begin drying.

As Carson eased on over to help, he watched as other men butchered the skinned carcass. Most every part of the buffalo was being salvaged.

By day's end, young Walker was bone tired. He was so hungry that the hot bowl of beans tasted every bit like prime steak.

Jones sidled up to Walker. "You did right well today fer a beginner, boy." That was all, then the big man strode off and hunkered down into his bedroll. Soon enough, his snores filled the air with nearly enough volume to stampede the herd.

By midday, Walker Carson found himself about a dozen miles clear of Grog Jones and the buffalo hunters. He was heading southeast in what he judged to be the general direction of San Diego. What he figured to do when he got there was anybody's guess. He'd have chosen San Patricio but feared he might be likely to run into someone he knew or, worse yet, his father.

He'd had the presence of mind to grab some leftover beans and a canteen filled with barely drinkable water. The whiskey was tempting but stored too close to Grog Jones's bedroll.

Walker harbored vague hopes that he could hire on with a local ranch as a cowboy. He pretty much thought he was capable enough. Maybe he could catch on with a trail drive. He needed some money, and his paltry stash of beans wouldn't be lasting very long.

As the sun dipped toward the horizon, he rode atop a ridge and feasted his eyes on distant lights. He turned the buckskin and headed toward what turned out to be a small ranch. The light? Well, it was from the dying embers of what had been a cabin. Then the cold truth hit him as he saw arrows protruding from two bodies lying near a water trough. In the failing light, his peripheral vision caught the horrific sight of a woman tied naked to a fencepost, obviously having been tortured before being mercifully put to death.

He vomited involuntarily. Walker closed his eyes a moment and took a deep breath. Should he bury them? The image of coyotes or buzzards ravaging the bodies made him shudder. He knew deep in his soul that he'd feel forever guilty if he left them to rot. Steeling himself, he grabbed his shovel as he dismounted.

After burying the victims, he looked around for anything of value to no avail. The Indians, likely Comanche, had already pilfered what hadn't been burned. The only thing the savages missed was a gold coin hidden under one of the dead men. He scraped down the last of the cold beans and decided to bed down for the night so as to strike out again for San Patricio in the morning. He shoved the coin into his boot for safekeeping.

Walker finally rode into San Diego. Over the next couple of days, he first tried his hand at being a farrier. Unfortunately, one overly spirited horse near broke a couple of the teen's ribs with a well-aimed kick. That abruptly ended his horseshoeing career. He spent as night helping the barkeep in the local saloon, but he was challenged to keep up with the service demands of inebriated customers. He was fired right quickly.

The gold coin had gotten him a couple of breakfasts and even dinner in San Diego, but his money was running thin. Now, Walker found himself sitting in a card game. His pa had taught him a little about poker, but he'd never played for money or with folks serious about playing for money. He was a neophyte, and it showed. It didn't take but a half hour to blow through what little remained of the gold coin.

One of the card players, the dealer, turned to Walker. "You done, boy?" He offered up a grin nearly devoid of anything resembling teeth.

Walker sighed. He was hungry again. Desperation was creeping into his thoughts.

"What's it gonna be, boy? How 'bout that fine buckskin pony ya got?" The dealer stared hard at young Walker. "That'll keep ya in the game. How 'bout it?"

Walker sighed and nodded. He was holding two pairs: aces and tens. *Fair hand*, he figured.

But a minute later, the hand was called. The dealer revealed his hand last, slowly displaying a full house. He laughed. "Gonna love yer hoss, boy."

The teen was beside himself. How could he be anything without his horse? What had he been thinking? He felt incredibly stupid as he slowly pushed back his chair, stood, and slinked from the saloon. As he stood on the wooden sidewalk, he looked across the street at the bank. How could life get much worse? Far as he could see, he kept being dealt losing hands. Abusive father, promiscuous mother, ill-fated buffalo hunting venture, losing his horse in a card game, hunger, abject poverty, and life in general, seemed to weigh a ton on his now sixteen-year-old soul.

He checked the load in his revolver and unhitched the buckskin. No two-bit card shark was going to have Walker's horse. As he strode across the dusty street with buckskin in tow, the dealer hollered from the saloon doorway. "Hey, boy! Where ya goin' with my hoss?"

Walker turned, drew his Colt revolver, and fired just over the head of the dealer, who promptly ducked inside. The commitment had now been made. In but two bounds, Walker crashed into the double doors of the bank. They were locked! Confused, he turned back to the street. Men, some with guns already drawn, had begun to appear. What to do? He slammed into the doors again and broke through. He dashed to the teller window, grabbed a money bag, and threw what little money he could find into it. Shots began to ring out. He headed for the buckskin, dropping the money bag as a bullet grazed his shoulder. He hadn't figured on a bank teller working overtime in the back office. Carson could be thankful that the teller only had a peashooter of a pistol that wasn't especially accurate nor packed much of a wallop.

A couple of bullets sailed over his head. There was no time to waste as he leaped onto the buckskin's back and galloped up the street in a hail of misaimed gunfire…excepting the one that blew a hole in his canteen.

He pulled up at what he figured was a couple of miles out of San Diego. The buckskin was game but spent from the hard ride. Worse, a horseshoe had come loose, and Walker realized that he'd turned his ankle a bit when he assaulted the bank doors. *Lame—lame horse, lame man, lame excuse for a human being.* He limped west on the road toward Laredo, hoping the town folk wouldn't assemble a posse. Other than running off with the card dealer's ill-gotten cayuse winnings, no real crime had been committed. Was attempted bank robbery a crime? He had no idea. Here he was stumbling along on a tender ankle with a gimpy horse, both growing ever thirstier. Hot… dry…dusty…the Nueces Strip was unforgiving. He found himself praying that neither card dealer nor posse would pursue him.

Walker had no idea how far he'd walked. His limp was turning into a desperate, labored stagger as lack of water began to take its toll. He lapsed into something akin to delirium as his old river of dreams flowed through his head. The freedom of the prairie was now his, but at what cost? In a moment of lucidity, he looked westward into the distance. The shade of a live oak motte beckoned. It was maybe a quarter mile off.

As he drew close to the shady motte, he saw what appeared to be burial mounds. Was that smoke, too? He was striving to clear his head when a voice from behind nearly startled him. Fear and panic coursed through his desperately tired bones.

"You looking for something, friend?" A big man on a big horse had a rifle pointed at Walker. "Turn real slow-like and keep your hands where I can see them."

Walker obeyed.

The big man smiled at him easy-like but kept the rifle pointed at Carson. "I'm Texas Ranger Captain Luke Dunn. Appears you've had some trouble, pilgrim." The Texas Ranger apparently was a master of understatement. "What's your name?"

Walker found himself face-to-face with a man a half foot taller and with what seemed like the biggest rifle muzzle in the world aimed at his midsection. To make matters worse, the sun reflecting from a Texas Ranger badge lent emphasis to the big man's words. He'd been caught by the long arm of the law. Something about this lawman jogged the depths of his brain. In his travels, Carson vaguely recalled having heard of some especially tough Ranger bringing law and justice to the Nueces Strip. It'd be just his luck to fall into that particular Texas Ranger's clutches.

"Um...name's Walker Carson," he offered up through parched lips. "I'm traveling to Laredo, Captain. Had a bit of a scrap in San Diego, sir." He'd quickly recognized this as a time for humility and respect, not swagger. No point in hiding the truth, either.

Dunn began to dismount, all the while keeping the rifle aimed at Walker. "What happened to your horse?" It was more a rhetorical question.

"Pulled up lame."

Dunn deduced that the buckskin had been ridden too hard for too long. It appeared otherwise to be a healthy horse. "Where's your water?"

Lots of questions. Carson couldn't admit that he'd escaped without any. His mind was racing to concoct a plausible story. "Somebody shot at me and put a hole through my canteen. Wouldn't hold water no-how."

The Texas Ranger's instincts were now working in overdrive. This character was on the run and had obviously been up to no good. There was no way the man would make it to Laredo with no water and a lame horse.

The two men stared at each other momentarily.

Dunn offered a somewhat sardonic smile, as though knowing the answer to the question he was about to ask. "You want help getting back to San Diego?" The silence was deafening. This was the last thing Walker Carson wanted to hear. There was no way he was going back to face his crime. "I'm scared to go back. Just as soon keep heading toward Laredo, if it's all the same to you."

The Ranger guffawed and shook his head dismayingly. "So, tell me what really happened."

Seemed Walker couldn't fabricate a story if his life depended on it. He was exhausted and hurting. He sucked it up and sighed. "I've been down on my luck. I tried to rob the bank in San Diego." He let that sink in. "Lucky to escape with my life. Teller shot me, I turned my ankle, my horse went lame, leaky canteen, and I didn't get any money."

Dunn figured he was finally hearing the truth. He could arrest the boy for attempted robbery or bet that he'd learned his lesson. It was hot, and he really yearned to get back to Nuecestown. Was redemption possible? The Texas Ranger thought back to the advice Ranger Captain Jim Callahan had given him. Walker might still be young enough to change his ways; lawbreaking likely as not wasn't bred into his character. Would he go straight if freed of the dark clouds of his past? Did this mere boy deserve a second chance? Perhaps it would change the boy's life.

Dunn lowered his rifle. "Tell you what, Mr. Carson, I'm inclined to give you a second chance. If you'll mosey over to that motte over there, you'll find a pot of coffee sitting on hot coals. You're welcome to a drink. Set a spell in the shade while I see to your horse."

Walker couldn't believe what he was hearing. He'd been totally unaware that the motte was occupied. The Texas Ranger had easily skirted around behind the teen and gotten the drop on him. Yet, he wasn't going to arrest him. It'd been so long since life had given him such a break.

"Thanks…er, thanks very much." There wasn't much else to say. He made his way to the motte while Dunn saw to the buckskin. It felt good to sit in the shade of the live oak. The coffee was perfect.

Carson looked about him, and his eyes focused on the three fresh burial mounds. From their decorations, the occupants were obviously Indians. He wondered whether the Ranger had killed them.

Dunn checked out Carson's horse, noting the loose shoe. Ever handy, he secured the shoe properly. He was truly getting into the role of being a sort of Good Samaritan. Now, he had to decide how to supply this traveler with water. He walked over to where Apache paraphernalia lay near the freshly-dug graves. There appeared to be at least one serviceable water skin, and it even still had water in it. He opened it, took a whiff, and quickly closed it. "Mr. Carson, the water in this thing isn't the greatest, but you'll find at least two cisterns between here and Laredo where you can refill it."

The failed bank robber humbly hung his head and used his bandana to wipe beads of sweat from his brow. "Captain Dunn, I'm ever beholden to you. How can I..." His words trailed off.

"Mr. Carson, you can thank me by never ever doing anything that'll put you in my gunsight again." Luke scratched something on a piece of paper from his saddlebag, folded it, and handed it to Carson. "Give this to Sheriff Stills. He owes me for clearing some lawbreakers out of Laredo. By this note, I've asked him to give you a job."

Walker was overwhelmed and grateful nearly to tears. He'd been given a gift that he dared not mess up. They chatted a bit while Carson sipped coffee. "I don't understand, Captain."

"Long story, son. The Good Book advises not to hold folks' faults against them." Dunn measured his words. "That doesn't mean lawbreaking should go unpunished, but out here on the prairie, judgments often must be made. My judgment is that in your misery, you've paid for your crime." Dunn smiled sardonically. "Failing at a bank robbery figures in, too. I believe you failed big enough to never try it again. Now, I'm counting on you to live a law-abiding life, Mr. Carson."

Walker nodded. "I'll surely try to do that, Captain Dunn." He took a final sip of coffee. "Captain Dunn, what about these graves?"

Dunn smiled easy-like. "Apache. They were on the losing end of a fight with Comanche. I just happened on them and figured to give them a decent burial."

Carson's expression revealed total amazement. Most passersby

MARK GREATHOUSE

would have let the bodies of the savages rot in the heat or be eaten by scavengers. This Texas Ranger was unlike anyone he'd ever met. "Right good of you, sir."

Dunn nodded. "Always respect the dead, Mr. Carson. No matter what brought them to their final breaths."

Soon enough, it was time for the big Texas Ranger to resume his travels. "Mr. Carson, rest your bones for a bit. Be sure those coals are out before you leave." Luke walked over and mounted Big Horse. He tipped his hat at the young man. "Safe travels, Mr. Carson."

Walker thought on what had just transpired. He had come to realize that like most young men, he thought only in the short-term. He hadn't even listened to his own dreams of the future. He had shown neither the experience nor imagination to come up with legitimate solutions to meeting his living needs. Walker Carson had been in danger of turning to the evil side of life's ledger, of becoming a predator rather than a protector. He'd been given a second chance before he'd turned into lawman's prey. It was up to him not to blow it.

154

THE COWBOY'S POSSIBLES
BAG

The cowboy rides tall in the saddle, drivin' beeves up the old
   Shawnee Trail.
He's hummin' a song a bit off-key, followin' the longhorns'
   twitchin' tails.
Watchin' for strays, lookin' fer savages, an' keepin' them
   doggies movin',
The cowboy's possibles bag chronicles his meanderings an'
   rovin'.
Yep, that bag 'twas filled with possibles, things he might
   need, no room fer swag;
'Twern't no man purse, nor satchel, and fer sure no Injun'
   wampum bag.
Not dust, nor rain, swollen streams, nor arroyos, that stuff
   didn't matter none,
Bedroll, slicker, rifle, 'twere 'portant, but his pos'bles bag was
   number one.
Extra ammo, jerky for snacks, a small knife, New Testament
   tore up a tad,
Old bandana, fire starter, tobacco, they was pretty much all
   he had.
Yep, that old leather possibles bag held the creature comforts
   of his life.

Why, the dang-blamed thing came just short of that cowboy
     needin' a wife.

The years go by; todays and tomorrows come and go.

The pickup roars to life headin' up the dusty road to the back
     hundred,
Cowboy hummin' that off-key tune to the drum of the beast
     beneath the hood.
Gonna catch up with some stray beeves, saddle's in the truck
     bed ready to ride,
Hopin' the buckskin is huggin' the fence waitin' fer his
     cowboy's backside.
The possibles bag has seen better days; old Shawnee Trail
     dust fills its seams.
Those gnarled old hands have rubbed over the leather so
     many times it gleams.
Right handy it sets on the seat beside, screwdriver, Bible still
     tore up,
Fire starter, small sharp knife, first aid kit, bug spray,
     sunscreen, an' shiny tin cup.
Caliche roads replaced prairie trails, but the old cayuse is
     always there,
The old pickup truck? Well, the buckskin could take him just
     about anywhere.
Yep, that possibles bag pretty much still held the creature
     comforts of life.
Why, that dang-blamed bag had just been mended by the old
     cowboy's lovin' wife.

WANNA BE A TEXAN?

So, you wanna be a Texan?
Well, how sharp are the tips of a longhorn's horns?
How much grit does it take for eight seconds on a bull?
Do you know chaps from saddle bags?
How many pumps can an oil pump, pump?
Can you tell Mex from Tex-Mex delicacies?
Does the sight of acres of bluebonnets fuel your fantasies?

You really wanna be a Texan?
Do you know 'bout the Alamo an' Goliad an' San Jacinto?
Can you stare down a rattler or javelina and win?
Can you rope a calf while astride a galloping bronc?
Are Tony Lamas and Stetsons your second skin?
Is your wanderlust fed by a mountain echo or a hill country
    breeze?
Do you love mottes of live oak and mesquite trees?

You truly do want to be a Texan?
Have you driven the Chisholm Trail to Abilene?
Can you climb o'er a barbed wire fence without a snag?
Do you know a quarter horse from a mustang?
How many tumbleweeds have tumbled 'cross your trail?

Have you kayaked Spanish moss-bedecked lakes and
    bayous?
Do you know armadillos from horny toads?

You just might get to be a Texan.
Can you shoot a nasty varmint 'tween the eyes?
Know the difference 'tween gallery and porch? Ain't none!
You ever climbed to the top of Enchanted Rock?
Have you watched the sunset make Palo Duro Canyon glow?
Does brisket an' chili an' barbeque make your dining list?
Do you own a fancy belt buckle big as your fist?

Hey, pard, welcome to Texas.

HIDDEN REVENGE

This short story was first published in the third annual anthology of the Gettysburg Writers Brigade, "On Hallowed Ground: Stories of America's Favorite Small Town." It is what is called alternative history, an actual event embellished with a fictional outcome.

PROLOGUE

WHILE THE WAR *Between the States raged, President Abraham Lincoln was necessarily distracted by the often-violent stirrings of savage tribes intent on fending off the seemingly endless migration of settlers and prospectors onto ancestral lands promised to them by the Great Father in Washington, DC, no matter that the lands weren't the Great Father's to give. The Bureau of Indian Affairs hoped to broker peace by bringing a delegation of tribal chiefs to Washington to meet with the president. Meetings tended to be brief, owing mostly to language barriers, so much of the chiefs' time was occupied with tours arranged by the government. As a matter of historical fact, the delegation headed back to their homes on April 30, 1863, but here is where our fiction begins. In this story, the delegation is rescheduled to head home on July 5, giving the chiefs the opportunity to visit a little town named Gettysburg behind the US Army lines on July 3, 1863. The chiefs were tired from being on display and understandably frustrated at what they perceived as the duplicity and disinterest of the Great Father. Revenge by humanity's badly behaving children was in the air.*

159

Chief Lean Bear of the Southern Cheyenne stared stoically at the onlookers who'd paid for the privilege of viewing genuine American savages at P. T. Barnum's American Museum in New York City. It was hard to judge what might be running through his mind. His thoughts most likely were to endure being Barnum's sideshow until he could return to the vast prairies, forests, and hills that were his heritage. He must have wondered what his wife and children might think were they to see him displayed like a circus sideshow. Nevertheless, he was decked out in his full ceremonial regalia, from ornately beaded moccasins to a majestic feathered headdress.

Several scalps hanging from Lean Bear's shield and lance added a sense of the savage macabre that Barnum fully exploited in attracting the crowds. Lean Bear's fellow chiefs represented bands of Comanche, Kiowa, Arapahoe, Caddo, and Cheyenne. The chiefs didn't need to speak, as their painted faces, buckskin scalp shirts, buffalo robes, long braids, ornate feathered headdresses, fringed leggings, and beaded moccasins spoke plenty loud enough for gawking crowds. They were at once diplomatic friends and sworn enemies of each other. The irony was palpable in the deferential ways they interacted. The paying customers were clueless as to the dynamic at work within the delegation. Barnum sensed it but strove to keep the chiefs preoccupied while trumpeting the curious to come and see the chiefs before they returned forever to their wild frontier homes.

The four-tiered theater of Barnum's gallery on Broadway Street was regularly packed with a public both captivated and simply curious. Barnum, ever the showman, paraded his fierce-looking guests through the streets of Manhattan periodically along with a marching band to promote his guests. They even stopped at local schools where children would perform for the delegation, much to the delight of everyone. After having endured Barnum's patronizing but lucrative show, the chiefs expected to board a train for Denver on April 30. They surely craved the freedom of the wide-open spaces of their wilderness homes.

Chief Lean Bear was a leader of what was referred to among his people as the Council of Forty-Four. His Cheyenne name was *Awon-*

inahku. Although their decisions were nonbinding, the Council of Forty-Four was a governing body viewed by the tribe as peacemakers. The label "peacemaker" might be subject to interpretation, as the Cheyenne trucked no aggressive incursions by neighboring tribes. The Cheyenne did have an aggressive part of the tribe called Dog Soldiers, and they accounted for much of the violence attributed even to the peaceful Cheyenne.

Chief Lean Bear and a handful of Council chiefs had received an unexpected visit nearly a year earlier from a contingent of soldiers. The term "unexpected visit" is used loosely, as few humans could approach an Indian encampment without being spotted beforehand. Lean Bear was thus well prepared to meet these visitors. He stood impressively in full regalia, though he wore no war paint. He waited until the interlopers were within roughly fifty feet before raising his hand to call them to a halt. "You no bluecoat." Lean Bear spoke broken English and simply expressed the Cheyenne's initial observation. These soldiers wore gray tunics. There were only a half dozen soldiers plus the driver of the accompanying wagon with its mule team. They appeared to be a bedraggled lot, likely as a consequence of travel over rough terrain.

"Y'all are right, Chief. We fight your bluecoat enemies."

Lean Bear was well aware that there was a war underway far to the east and south. There were some Cheyenne chiefs who had seen this as an opportunity to halt the migration of White settlers into their ancestral lands, but the peacekeepers had advised against going on the warpath, and if not for the Dog Soldiers, had mostly prevailed. Lean Bear saw no distinction between the graycoats and bluecoats other than their uniform colors. They were soldiers; they were enemies to be wary of. The Cheyenne were vaguely aware of slavery being an issue, but it concerned them not, as they practiced it themselves with prisoners from other tribes. He also surmised that once the war was over, the winning army would turn its attention back to persecuting his people.

"What do graycoats seek from Cheyenne?"

The Rebel lieutenant was surprised at Lean Bear getting right down to business. He'd expected some level of ceremony. The Indian agent had assured them that the Cheyenne were mostly peaceful.

"We give you guns to kill bluecoats." The lieutenant conjured up an almost devious smile. "Have firewater, too."

The chief fought to keep from rolling his eyes at the soldier's sheer audacity. A quick glance at his fellow chiefs confirmed the response he'd already settled upon. "Graycoats go. Leave wagon here."

The lieutenant was quite aware of the contents of the wagon. Rifles, ammunition, whiskey, and other trade goods were to be traded in exchange for the Cheyenne becoming allies against the Yankees. "We cannot do that, Chief."

More than three dozen armed warriors appeared as if from thin air. War paint only served to enhance the threat imposed by nocked arrows and lances decorated with enemy scalps. Lean Bear gave as savage a glare as he could muster so as to make sure his threat was clearly understood. "Go! Now!" He deferentially swept his arm toward the trail from whence the graycoats had come.

The lieutenant reflexively ran his hand under his kepi as though assuring himself that he still had his hair. He glanced meekly at his fellow Rebels, shrugged ever so slightly, and led them away amid an uneasy quiet.

Barely a year later, on March 26, 1863, Indian agent Sam Colley and an interpreter accompanied Chief Lean Bear and the other tribal chiefs into the East Room of the White House. They had to negotiate a smoke-filled corridor filled with gawking diplomats, cabinet secretaries, journalists, and other invited guests. The delegation members seated themselves in a semicircle on the carpet. The chiefs wore their best tribal trappings awash in intricate beadwork, soft yellow buckskin, luxurious fur, and colorful feathers. Only their lances, war clubs, and bows and arrows were missing and kept them from appearing overtly savage.

President Abraham Lincoln arrived fifteen minutes late, as he'd been reviewing reports of troop movements, an exercise that invariably left him frustrated. Having to face a collection of hostile Indians from the westernmost reaches of the nation was not exactly a desirable task at this moment. He'd been cursorily briefed enough to know that Lean Bear was the delegation leader.

Lincoln stood tall before the seated Indians. Colley was standing behind the chiefs and pointed at Lean Bear for the president's convenience. Lincoln reached out to offer his hand to the chief. "Pleasure to meet you." They shook hands tentatively, then purposefully. Lincoln wasted no time. "What do you have to say, Chief Lean Bear?"

The chief was momentarily taken aback but gathered himself quickly and stood up. "Need chair."

Two chairs were brought in, and the chief and the president were duly seated opposite each other. There was an uncomfortable silence.

Lean Bear cradled a long-stemmed pipe, which he finally lifted and swept the room as if holding some sort of pointer. He spoke in his halting but intelligible English. "We travel long way to hear counsel of Great Father. Cheyenne no fight bluecoat, no fight gray-coat. Live in peace. We live as one people." His eyes fixed on Lincoln's, addressing him as an equal. He swept the room with his pipe once more. "Great Father chief of his people, live in big lodge. Lean Bear also great chief of his people."

Lincoln nodded his understanding, though he was anxious for the chief to get to his point so he could get on with other presidential duties.

Lean Bear sensed Lincoln's impatience, but he was an orator among his people; he wasn't about to shorten his remarks for this man. He finally began to reach a conclusion to his speech. "Great Father must tell his White children to stop their attacks against my people, so both peoples can travel safely across our lands." The chief wasn't convinced that Lincoln was fully grasping his message. "Cheyenne, Kiowa, Comanche, Arapahoe, Caddo join in wishing for end to White men's great war." The reference to the ongoing insurrection seemed to resonate with Lincoln's sensibilities. "We must return to our homes, and we ask for the Great Father to offer peace and speed our travels."

The president smiled an awkward smile that bordered on condescension. "You have all spoken of the strange sights you see here, among your pale-faced brethren: the very great number of people that you see, the big wigwams, the difference between our people and your own. But you have seen but a very small part of the pale-faced people. You may wonder when I tell you that there are people here in this wigwam, now looking at you, who have come from other countries a great deal farther off than you have come. We pale-faced people think that this world is a great, round ball, and we have people here of the pale-faced family who have come almost from the other side of it to represent their nations here and conduct their friendly intercourse with us, as you now come from your part of the round ball." He'd had a globe brought into the room along with a professor who pointed out in basic terms the essence of land masses and seas.

Lincoln pointed to Europe and swept his hand across the globe to America. "Pale-faced people have journeyed far." His hand paused over the Great Plains. "You ask for my advice." Lincoln folded his hands and leaned toward Lean Bear. "We have people now present from all parts of the globe—here, and here, and here." Lincoln's fingers danced across the globe. "There is a great difference between this pale-faced people and their red brethren, both as to numbers and the way in which they live. We know not whether your own situation is best for your race, but this is what has made the difference in our way of living. The pale-faced people are numerous and prosperous because they cultivate the earth, produce bread, and depend upon the products of the earth rather than wild game for subsistence. This is the chief reason of the difference; but there is another.

"Although we are now engaged in a great war between one another, we are not, as a race, so much disposed to fight and kill one another as our red brethren. You have asked for my advice. I really am not capable of advising you whether, in the providence of the Great Spirit, who is the great Father of us all, it is best for you to maintain the habits and customs of your race or adopt a new mode of life. I can only say that I can see no way in which your race is to become as numerous and prosperous as the white race except by living as they do, by the cultivation of the earth. It is the object of this government to be on terms of peace with you, and with all our red brethren. We constantly endeavor to be so. We make treaties with you, and will try to observe them; and if our children should sometimes behave badly and violate these treaties, it is against our wish. You know it is not always possible for any father to have his children do precisely as he wishes them to do. In regards to being sent back to your own country, we have an officer, the Commissioner of Indian Affairs, who will take charge of that matter and make the necessary arrangements."[1]

The interpreter had been working hard to translate in a sign language he hoped most of the chiefs could grasp and was relieved to observe nods of understanding from the delegation.

Lincoln stood and extended his hand to Lean Bear. He dutifully shook the hands of each of the other chiefs comprising the delegation. Each chief stood in turn to accept Lincoln's outreach. Bronzed-copper peace medals were handed out, and papers attesting to the friendship between the government and the tribes were signed. The other Cheyenne chiefs, War Bonnet and Stands in the Water, glanced at Lean Bear as they shook the president's hand. The Kiowa had the largest delegation, including Yellow Buffalo, Lone Wolf, Yellow Wolf, White Bull, and Little Heart. The handshaking concluded with the Arapahoe chiefs Spotted Wolf and Nevah, Comanche chiefs Ten Bears and Pricked Forehead, the lone Apache chief Poor Bear, and Caddo chief Jacob.

As each chief's name was announced, it appeared that Lincoln's curiosity had been aroused such that he might have wondered how each had received their peculiar names. The president nevertheless impressed the chiefs with the firmness of his handshake, a sign that exuded trust. Notably, the Kiowa squaws Etta and Coy were not introduced, as that would have been inappropriate per Indian custom. The treatment of women by both races was, in many ways, not all that different.

The delegation spent the next two weeks being shuttled around the various impressive government buildings and forts around Washington before heading off to fulfill their promise to P. T. Barnum in New York. The train ride from Washington was like a

---

1. Lincoln's Speech to the Indians, from Basler, Roy P. The Collected Works of Abraham Lincoln. The Abraham Lincoln Association, Springfield, Illinois, vol. 6, New Brunswick, N.J.: Rutgers Univ. Press, 1953.

prequel to Barnum's show in the big city, as crowds gathered at each station where the train was obliged to slow or even stop.

Regrettably, the Kiowa chief Yellow Wolf caught pneumonia and passed away on April 7th, casting a distinct pall over the adventure to the east. The remaining Kiowas were of a mind to leave early, but Barnum coaxed them to stay. They were nearing the planned departure date, and the showman sought to milk the Indians for every possible advantage.

Chief Lean Bear called a meeting of the delegation. They arranged to meet on a grassy knoll north of New York City, well out of earshot of Barnum and the government representatives.

Ever the showman, Barnum suggested that they were plotting to go on the warpath in New York City, but his joke was quickly rebuffed.

Lean Bear drew the chiefs close. "The pale face Barnum has invited us to stay longer. Two moons. He show us Boston and Philadelphia and place called Baltimore. He says he will give us great gifts to take back to our people."

The Kiowa chief Lone Wolf spoke up, "Our people worry about us. We must return soon."

Lean Bear's smile revealed a man comfortable with himself, one brimming with the confidence that comes with long experience in these matters. His way was always to promote peaceful settlement of issues. He figured the loss of the remaining four Kiowas would reduce the size of the delegation slightly but not diminish Barnum's overall plans. Besides, he had begun to crave the White man's gifts. "If brave Kiowa wish to leave…go." He wasn't able to prevent his facial expression from revealing his disappointment.

When the other chiefs revealed their desire to stay, the Kiowas reluctantly changed their minds.

Over the next two months, Barnum paraded the delegation in the major northeastern cities. As the commitment drew to a close, and the delegation anxiously looked forward to a departure of July 5th, the Commissioner of Indian Affairs stepped in for one last convincing display of the White man's military might. William Dole, a strong proponent of forging treaties with the Indians and moving them to reservations, heard of some sort of major incursion by the Confederate Army at a little farm town in south-central Pennsylvania. He enthusiastically seized the opportunity and shepherded the delegation by train to Baltimore and then in a caravan of four large carriages to Gettysburg. They arrived at the break of dawn on July 3rd.

Dole strode across the grassy knoll with the Indian delegation behind him in full regalia. He was understandably uneasy. As Commissioner for Indian Affairs, it was his duty to assuage the frustrations of the thirteen tribal chiefs and two squaws he'd lured to Washington with promises of peace for their people. He knew a costly war raged; there was hardly a place untouched by its writhing tentacles that seemed to suck the life from anything the insurrection touched. The Plains Indians were no exception. Dole heard that the major Rebel force that had arrived at Gettysburg was positioning for a decisive battle aimed at carrying the Rebel cause directly to the northeastern states. Chalk it up to a certain naïveté, but it was clear that he had no appreciation for the degree of distraction that his delegation of savages brought to an already tense situation.

General George Meade's eyes riveted like steel spikes onto those of the commissioner. His face reddened. "What the hell could you have been thinking, Dole?" He knew the chiefs could hear every word, but he didn't give a tinker's damn whether they understood English.

The commissioner was torn between standing tall as a show of strength for the delegation versus cowering under Meade's anger.

The general wasn't about to be distracted a moment longer. "See those trees over there on the knoll? That's Culp's Hill. Keep your damned savages out of sight behind those trees."

The general abruptly made a face, muttered something under his breath, and stalked off to attend to battle preparations. The Rebels had quite clearly been gathering forces all morning for some sort of assault and demanded his full attention.

Dole dutifully directed the delegation toward the trees on Culp's Hill. It afforded a vantage point from which the chiefs could barely view the battle that was to come. The delegation dutifully squatted in a line just in front of a gnarled old tree, its spreading limbs affording a modicum of shade.

General Meade reluctantly assigned a couple of soldiers to stand guard, both to ensure that no harm came to the government guests, and of greater concern, that they stay put. He didn't need a bunch of heathen Indians mucking up his defenses in the heat of battle.

The chiefs sat patiently. Dole had already begun to regret that he'd extended the savages' stay and come to this now godforsaken place. Culp's Hill was not an ideal vantage point to view the impending battle. Finally, in the early afternoon, the roar of Confederate cannon fire tore the pre-battle quietude apart. The Rebel yells soon followed as waves of butternut and gray swept toward Cemetery Ridge and into a devastating defensive barrage. Grape, canister, and musket fire riddled the Rebel ranks, yet they charged on.

It was as though the very earth was exploding as the din of battle reached the ears of the chiefs. Their eyes were transfixed by what little they could see of the battle as some stood, stretching tall, to take it in and communicating excitedly with hand signs in reaction to the conflagration unfolding before them. Given the considerably smaller scope of most Plains Indian battles, the sheer magnitude of the clash of humanity before them was overwhelming to their senses. It was not long, much to the nervous concern of the two soldiers guarding them, before the entire delegation was standing so as to better view the scene. More troubling still, they began to noticeably inch toward the battle.

Chief Lean Bear realized that he needed to relieve himself. He nudged War Bonnet standing beside him and pointed to his own breechcloth. With everyone focused on the melee before them, he broke from the delegation, eased over behind the gnarled old tree, pulled his breechcloth aside, and peed on a tree root.

"What the hell you doin' over here, ya damn savage?" One of the assigned guards had noticed the chief's departure and chased after him. The soldier was a corporal, and an older one at that. He spat a load of chewing tobacco juice from under his broad mustache. "Get yer sorry ass back with them other heathens!" he snarled as he pulled back the hammer on his musket. He'd done a bit of fighting out west and learned early on of the increasingly accepted advice that the only good Indian was a dead Indian. He had no concern with the niceties of diplomacy and fully no respect for any status afforded a Cheyenne chief. An Indian was an Indian.

Lean Bear had grown tired of this odyssey into the White man's great kingdom. His patience had grown paper-thin. The pale faces' big cities and curious crowds had long ago lost his interest, and the conflagration playing out on the fields of Gettysburg proved to him that the White man was no better than the red man. His eyes riveted in on the corporal. "Me no finish."

"Damn! An Injun what speaks like a White man!" The soldier offered up a derisive laugh but had the misfortune of losing his grip on the musket. It was an old firearm likely handed down within his family. The barrel was just a tad slick from the humidity. As he caught it, the stock hit the ground, the hammer released, struck the frizzen, and the musket accidentally discharged its payload into the sky. The sound of the shot was lost in the din of the battle.

Lean Bear reacted instinctively to what he perceived as an attack. His knife blade appeared in his hand, and he slashed savagely across the corporal's belly.

The soldier looked down at his stomach, his face contorted with pain. "Damn! I be bleedin'!" It was a serious cut, not a mortal wound, but the severity mattered none to him. His musket was now no better than a club. "You damned Injun'!" He gripped the barrel and began to raise it over his head.

The chief moved with catlike speed within inches of the corporal. He was too close for the soldier to club him, and his knife found the soldier's throat. A quick thrust and slice ended the fight. Lean Bear looked about. Apparently, no one had seen the brief altercation.

Lean Bear dragged the soldier's body behind the tree and out of direct line of sight. He figured it likely that the body wouldn't be discovered until after the battle. The chief took one last look around and was preparing to head back to the delegation when instinct overcame him. He stood over the fallen corporal and grasped the man's golden locks. A few deft slices of the knife, and Chief Lean Bear had himself a bluecoat scalp. He looked around cautiously once more, then stuffed the bloody scalp into his wampum bag. There was no point in drawing attention to a fresh scalp hanging from his waistband. He took a final look at the dead soldier, placed the corporal's kepi back on his head, gave a smile of triumph, turned, and walked confidently back to the delegation.

He sidled up to War Bonnet and caught the fellow Cheyenne's eye. Lean Bear permitted himself a satisfied smile as he glanced down at his wampum bag. A small blotch of fresh blood stained the lower portion of the bag.

War Bonnet's eyes quickly noted the telltale evidence of the chief's encounter. He couldn't contain a smile, sensing the same justice as Lean Bear.

The huge battle before the assembled chiefs raged on, the gray line at one point nearly breaking through the bluecoat defenses and causing some concern to the Indians. Through it all, the delegation stood as stoically as they could muster.

A lieutenant walked by, his bloodied arm hanging loosely by his side. He looked at the remaining soldier guarding the delegation. "Where the hell is Smith, soldier?" His eyes scanned the savages. "He run off again?"

Lean Bear could barely contain a triumphant smile.

The lieutenant didn't wait for an answer. "We'll find him later. Watch yourself." He stared hard at Commissioner Dole. "Damn politicians!" He strode off.

The battle finally came to an end with the Rebels in full retreat. Like the Indians so often were guilty of, General Meade didn't follow up on his advantage by pursuing and destroying the enemy. Dole was simply relieved to have survived unscathed and hoped to leave the scene unnoticed. The carriages were already being brought toward Culp's Hill.

General Meade caught sight of the carriages and instantly figured them as potential ambulances. "You there…Colonel!" he called out to Colonel Colvill, who'd most recently repelled the Rebel advance at "The Angle" on Cemetery Ridge. "Commandeer those damned carriages!"

The colonel was bone tired but wasn't about to challenge a direct order from the commanding general. He turned his horse toward Culp's Hill and was soon waving to get the attention of the approaching carriages. As the colonel rode in front of the Indian delegation, Commissioner Dole finally showed some spine. He waved a piece of paper at Colvill.

"You can't have them, Colonel!" He was nearly bowled over by the colonel's horse. "Got direct orders from President Lincoln!"

The recent heat of battle, coupled with Dole's resistance, was too much for Colvill. The Indian chiefs, in all their finery, threatened to put his mental state over the top. "I've got wounded men to tend to. Who the hell are you?" He looked over his shoulder and saw General Meade watching him. "Damn it, man! Give me at least two of those contraptions."

Dole rightly figured discretion was the better part of valor. His charges could be squeezed into two carriages for the ride back to Baltimore. "I'm Commissioner of Indian Affairs for the United States Government, Colonel. It would be my pleasure to part with two of my carriages to assist in recovering our valiant wounded soldiers." Dole swiftly directed the two lead carriages away from the delegation, while the chiefs piled into the remaining carriages. He had the abbreviated caravan headed out before General Meade could react.

Colvill caught Meade's resigned expression and led his newly acquired ambulances toward Cemetery Ridge. As he turned his horse away from Culp's Hill, the colonel's peripheral vision caught a pair of legs sticking out behind the largest of the stand of trees on the hill. He brought his mount around and cantered over to the tree. As he peered down, he couldn't miss the dead Union soldier lying behind it. He dismounted. Blood had streamed down the sides of the corporal's head. Suspicious, the colonel respectfully lifted the dead man's kepi and stepped back, aghast. The soldier's scalp was missing!

The Indian delegation had already lumbered from sight.

Colvill sprang into the saddle with renewed energy and rode hard toward General Meade. "General! General, sir! A word!" he hollered.

"At ease, Colonel. What the hell has you so all-fired upset? There's plenty enough of that to go round at this hour." Meade's horse nearly dumped him from the saddle as it took an unexpected sidestep to avoid a dead soldier. The general brought his mount back under control. "Out with it, Colonel."

The colonel caught his breath. "Scalped, sir! One of those heathen savages...they scalped one of our men!"

Anger flashed across Meade's face. Sweat was streaming down his cheeks, and his uniform was soaked. He scanned the field with its hundreds of bloody corpses and tried to block his ears from the moans and desperate screams of the wounded. The horrific odor of battle, of death, still lingered in the air. As though post-battle clean-up wasn't enough, a new challenge had now found its way into his consciousness. He sighed heavily, muttering a few curses under his breath.

"Write it up, Colonel...Colvill, is it? Make sure no one here sees that our man was scalped." Politics and its intrigues were not unknown to Meade. He'd have to take this up personally with President Lincoln.

Lean Bear nudged War Bonnet as their carriage lumbered its way toward Baltimore and the train that would soon be carrying them westward to their homelands. He turned back the flap on his wampum bag enough for his friend to peer inside at the ball of hair and flesh nestled inside.

War Bonnet nodded approvingly and offered up an uncharacteristic smile. He asked in the Cheyenne tongue, "Did you count coup?" War Bonnet was concerned that Lean Bear had exhibited bravery by touching the bluecoat, counting coup before killing him.

The chief winked and made a slashing motion with his hand. "Yes. Make good story at Council." The chief was adept at wrapping engaging stories around his combat prowess, and his surreptitious and fully unexpected engagement at Gettysburg would serve him well before the Council fire flames. Another feather would soon be added to the plumage of his already impressive headdress.

By now, their companions in the carriage had started to become aware of Lean Bear's accomplishment. Murmurs of approval found their way from chief to chief.

Soon enough, the stirrings reached Commissioner Dole. He reflexively turned toward Lean Bear with an inquisitive look.

The chief opened his wampum bag and extended it toward Dole.

The smell and blood stain at the bottom of the bag were enough to repel the commissioner. "What the hell have you done?!" he exclaimed rhetorically; the chief's accomplishment having been quite obvious. Dole shook his head, dismayed. He saw resignation from office in his future.

A broad smile creased Lean Bear's face, as though challenging the commissioner to do anything about it. The chiefs were tired—tired of the politicians, tired of the shows filled with curiosity seekers, tired of the pale faces showing off their military might, tired of seemingly endless days away from their people. The chief grew serious and shrugged. He finally strove to make light of the situation as he pointed to the commissioner's long dark hair, made a slicing motion, and held out the wampum bag. A murmur of approval emanated from the delegation, followed by light laughter that broke the tension.

A chill found its way up Dole's spine. He looked questioningly at the chief, trying to ascertain whether he might be serious.

Lean Bear caught the commissioner's eyes, smiled innocently, and mustered a bit of a twinkle. "We have problem?" he asked.

"Just hide that damned thing when we get on the train." He resignedly shook his head.

July 5th arrived in the nick of time, so far as the delegation and Indian Affairs Commission were concerned. Between Colonel Colvill not getting to his report until late in the evening and General Meade's concerns with other matters, the incident on Culp's Hill arrived at the White House far too late to do anything about it.

It had been a long day for Abraham Lincoln. He broke the seal of the leather pouch and drew out a sheaf of papers that included Meade's report of the third day at Gettysburg. Despite feeling utterly drained, the president dutifully skimmed through the report by candlelight. It pleased him that General Lee's forces had been repelled and sent into a full-blown retreat. He shook his head with frustration upon reading of Meade's plans to spend a couple of days regrouping his troops before pursuing General Lee's retreating Confederate Army. He mumbled under his breath about being unable to find a field general that was capable of pursuing and finishing off a retreating enemy.

Lincoln nearly didn't notice a piece of paper that yet remained in the pouch. Given what he'd just read, the report from a Colonel Colvill actually brought a wry smile to his lips. He thought on his words to Chief Lean Bear about children behaving badly and it not always being possible for any father to have his children do precisely as he wished them to do. It seemed the Indian delegation had indeed behaved badly. Still bemused by the irony, he shook his head. There was little to be done about it now.

Lean Bear's arrival in Denver was cause for considerable celebration, as more than a hundred Cheyenne had made the long trek from their most recent encampment in central Kansas. The other members of the delegation received similar greetings from their respective tribes as they raised the medallions Lincoln had gifted them.

Lean Bear was relieved to finally be mounted on his favorite pony. He led his assembled people aside so he could enjoy the reunion with his people out of sight of the Indian Affairs agents that had accompanied them on the train. His fellow Cheyenne chiefs, Stands in the Water and War Bonnet, rode on either side as Lean Bear triumphantly hoisted his prized scalp with its attached long blond hair. A great roar of approval went up as though the assembly was ignorant of the peace-keeping nature of their journey. They would be encamped many miles from Denver when the chief finally had the opportunity to recount the tale of his encounter with the bluecoat corporal.

After the sun had sunk below the horizon in a gaudy blaze of orange, Lean Bear stood before the great council fire and pantomimed his sneaking away from the delegation on Culp's Hill. He described stalking the bluecoat corporal, conveniently leaving out his purpose as having been to answer nature's call. He told of the bluecoat's shooting his musket and missing the chief thanks to his superior medicine. The chief paused theatrically before showing how he counted coup before slitting the soldier's throat and taking his scalp. He smiled deviously upon telling how the White soldiers were unaware of his mighty deed. The Cheyenne hooted and howled approval of Lean Bear's accomplishment.

Naturally, the story became embellished over time, as he told it every night until they reached the main village in central Kansas.

EPILOGUE

On May 16, 1864, a bit less than fifteen months after having met President Lincoln in Washington, Lean Bear, Black Kettle, War Bonnet, and others in the tribe were encamped near Ash Creek in central Kansas. The 1st Colorado Regiment under the command of Lieutenant George Eayre approached the encampment with its four hundred warriors. Despite a bloody fight having occurred a few weeks back involving aggressive Cheyenne Dog Soldiers at Fremont's Orchard, Chief Lean Bear was confident that the violence would not be linked to his peaceful tribe. He was certain that this would be a peaceful encounter, so he rode out alone to meet the soldiers and show his peaceful intentions. On his chest, the chief even displayed his peace medal that he had received on his trip to Washington, DC. In his hand, he held an official document signed by President Lincoln stating that he was peaceful and friendly with Whites.

Unbeknownst to Lean Bear, Eayre's troops were operating under orders from Colonel John Chivington to "kill Cheyennes whenever and wherever found." Chivington had necessarily knuckled to complaints made to Colorado Governor John Evans about the predations of Cheyenne Dog Soldiers. The 1st Colorado Regiment responded overenthusiastically to Chivington's orders, as they arrayed eighty-six men and two howitzers before Lean Bear's encampment. Eayre summarily ordered his men to shoot Lean Bear. The wounded chief fell from his horse, and then was shot multiple times by the soldiers as they rode past his body. The troops went on to attack the surprised Cheyenne in the encampment. Before too much damage could be wreaked, Black Kettle emerged to de-escalate the situation, and the troops retreated to Fort Larned. Thus, it was that government ignorance and treachery intersected with Indian trust and naïveté to prolong the conflict between the red man and White man across the American plains.

NICHOLAS DUNN: A REQUIEM
A FREE-VERSE ODE TO THE AUTHOR'S GREAT-GREAT-GRANDFATHER.

DREAM

Ah, Nicholas Dunn. Who'd have guessed the fine man you'd
come to be?
Born of the rolling hills and verdant magical forests of
County Kildare.
With fiery red hair, deep blue eyes, broad smile, and wild
starry dreams,
Transfixed, you watched as your Uncle Matt left to answer
freedom's call.
Drawn not just to the American land of plenty, no, he was
headed for Texas.
He'd left the Irish Potato Famine, the victims, the starving,
the struggles,
The over-bearing minions of the British oppressors of his
papist kinsmen,
To tie his hopes to General Taylor's soldiers in the war
against Mexico.
Grandfather Long Larry oft regaled you, fed your yearnings,
your mind
With embellished tales of what he'd heard from Matt, of a
new beginning

In a land of plenty. Vast prairies, rich dark soil, fruits aplenty,
   live oak mottes,
Cattle, horses, buffalo, deer, wild pigs, and more roamed
   'neath endless skies.
Opportunity beckoned, your wanderlust to be sated, 'twas
   now, 'twas 1850.
And so you bid your loved ones, your Irish home, goodbye,
   beannacht, slán. (Good-bye)

LIFE

Under your Uncle Peter's sheltering wing, off you sailed on
   the bounding main,
Landing at New Orleans and then on Corpus Christi's shores,
   gateway to your dreams.
From that day, the one when you stroked the muzzle of your
   very first longhorn bull,
Your Irish spirit fully captured, your heart, soul, and Texas
   became as one.
Alone you'd walk onto the vast night-sky prairie far from
   Corpus Christi's din,
The air so quiet you could hear the twinkling of the stars
   lighting up the night,
Silence broken only by the hoots of owls and howls of
   coyotes.
You rode the wild boundless range, spurs a-jingle, drove
   longhorns off to Abilene,
Fighting off savage Comanche, wild Apache, craven despera-
   does on the trail.
You learned to trade in cattle and horses, built a ranch, a
   twenty thousand-acre spread;
You withstood the dire challenges of family fought and lost in
   Civil War.
Dodging the yellow fever scourge that took its terrible toll on
   loved ones dear,
Sweet Andree Ann, your wife, the love of your life, nine
   godly blessings bore.

Most grew to adults, turning frontier into homes, *gràdh do na
h-uile.* (Love to all)

LEGACY

Your wild Irish spirit flows in the veins of many hundreds of
your blood.
Texans all, they join together in remembrances, to celebrate
your life.
You gave full of your bounty, donated precious land for
school and church;
The Dunn legacy conquered boundless frontier, built railroads, ranched coastal isles.
They forged lives on Texas soil, arid or green; grocers,
smithies, bankers, and teachers.
They drew the precious black gold from beneath the prairies,
grew cotton atop them.
Hearts for service to friend and stranger passed from generation to generation,
Your memory lives in yarns huddled round campfire embers
and dim lamplight.
Tales sharing the romance of the South Texas prairie and
dusty northward trails,
Stories of the battles fought, the loves that endured, and families that flourished.
As live oak and mesquite mottes reach for the skies and the
bluebonnets blossom,
As the sound of your memory wafts steady as a life breeze
'cross the wiregrass,
Your wild Irish dream, Nick Dunn, joined with Texas-sized
heart made life for us all.
Legacies linger, a requiem indeed, *Dia dúinn go léir.* (God
bless everyone)

PRAIRIE DOG

A TALE OF COURAGE MUSTERED
FROM DUTY

A WISPY RESIDUE of clouds hung in the sky, a welcome relief from last night's thunderstorm. Still, it was hot and muggy. Threatened to get even hotter. A groundhog poked up from his burrow and looked about. The critter nickered excitedly at the conflagration laid out before him and nervously ducked back inside. Odors of death and acrid stench of gunpowder wafted down across the field from Cemetery Ridge. If courage had an aroma, it was hanging over the battlefield this day.

Lieutenant Dandridge, gold-braid-bedecked dandy that he was, had strategically positioned Sergeant Colby McGraw in a tree just to the rear of the charging lines of ill-equipped butternut-clad rabble that passed for the Confederate Army. McGraw was a sharpshooter, but the smoke from the Federal cannon was so thick that targets were hazy at best. Twasn't like squirrel hunting back in Arkansas. Nope. He was supposed to sit sweating like a hard-ridden horse in that gnarly old tree and pick off Yankee officers, the ones with the fancy gold shoulder straps and setting high on their horses. He'd even brought his very own Sharps carbine to the fray. Stolen from a Yankee, McGraw found its 50-caliber cartridges and falling-block action served him well on his deadly missions.

The Yankee artillery had been merciless. Bodies...blood... limbs...carnage scattered wide across the field. McGraw had been unable to sit in that tree while comrades fell. Cemetery Ridge loomed ahead beyond Emmitsburg Road, and shrouded as it was in the fog of war, was barely visible. Now, he wished he had stayed in that very safe tree just south of Seminary Ridge. But no...he'd been unable to hold back. Now he was among his comrades, Johnny Rebs being slaughtered by grape and canister. Courage welled up within him. Courage, or was it insanity? Why should they die and he live?

McGraw had run to the fight. The pain that came with seeing his comrades die lurked deep in the recesses of his soul. It was excruciating. Burned like hell. He coughed a dry cough. "Damned hellhole," he muttered under his breath. *Thirst...water* roiled through his mind. Beads of sweat covered his forehead, and the rivulets running down his back caused his shirt to cling. Nothing seemed dry, save his throat. No ammunition, no bayonet for the Sharps. He'd charged but a hundred yards when the damnable cannonball took a piece of his hide. Twasn't much. Only grazed his leg, but he now found himself lurching and careening along desperately with his comrades in arms, moving away from the chaos of battle. The smoke stung his nostrils.

McGraw followed the poor souls staggering away from the slaughter. He half fell into a creek. He was so very thirsty. As he drank, a salty taste overwhelmed him. The water ran with blood. A pair of lifeless eyes stared at him from the water's edge. He shuddered, suppressed a gag, and spit the water from his mouth. Dry heaves shook his frame.

McGraw finally managed to stand. He hefted the heavy Sharps carbine over his shoulder and limped westward following the bloodstained trail of the retreating Confederate Army. He was angry at himself and especially at the circumstances that had brought him here. Now, he was done with it all...every bit of it. Duty? What was to be gained? States rights some said? Slavery abolished? The bluebellies had the resources to crush the Confederacy. It was only a matter of time, and it was not going to be his time. A horse would help. The wound across the side of his thigh was just serious enough to be a concern. Dang, but it burned! A couple of inches over, and he'd likely have lost the leg. It hurt real bad. The lieutenant said to have courage. Who the hell was he fooling?

McGraw watched as the thin ragtag line of retreating Rebels wended their way toward the heights of Blue Ridge Summit.

General Pickett had ordered the ill-fated charge of more than twelve thousand men. McGraw heard from stragglers that half had been wounded, captured, or would never see another day. Makeshift field hospitals became commonplace along a trail littered with amputated limbs and occasional graves. He shook his head ruefully. Lost cause indeed.

At last, off to his right, stood the answer to his prayers. From the tack, it had likely belonged to an officer. As he approached, the stallion flared his nostrils and flashed a wild-eyed gaze. Little wonder he was so skittish, as a boot hung heavily from the left stirrup with what remained of the rider. McGraw removed the offending appendage and lay calming strokes on the poor beast.

"What the hell you doing with that horse, Sergeant?"

Damned if it wasn't that peacock Lieutenant Dandridge with drawn saber. McGraw had failed to see the fool move toward him through the smoke-shrouded air to nearly within arm's reach. It was as though the young Rebel officer had appeared from nowhere. McGraw pressed his forehead against the saddle and tried to breathe.

"You can't have no horse. Only officers and cavalry have horses."

McGraw slowly turned his head and stared at him in stony silence.

"What are you looking at, you damned coward!" threatened the lieutenant.

A coward?! No. McGraw held more courage in his little finger than this dandified excuse for an officer could ever hope to muster.

The sergeant thought for a split second on the thousands of wounded, dead, and dying still littering the open field beneath Cemetery Ridge. Anger born of frustration filled him. McGraw's fist plowed deep into the lieutenant's midsection, doubling him over and dropping him to his knees to receive the *coup de grâce* across his jaw. The saber flew aside, clattering harmlessly on some rocks as the officer fell like a sack of potatoes.

McGraw looked down at his own poorly shod feet then stripped the highly polished black leather boots from the lieutenant. They turned out to be a perfect fit. With nary a moment's hesitation, the sergeant grabbed the stallion's reins, slipped a new boot into the stirrup, and easily swung into the saddle. The pain in his leg gave him a jolt, but he recovered quickly. The horse felt good under him. He hadn't sat one since before the war. He pressed his heels gently into the horse's sides and never looked back.

A determined McGraw made his way westward. He was committed to putting the horror of war as far behind him as possible. In the solitariness of his journey, he couldn't help but deal with his personal contradiction; that of a brave soul who had deserted his comrades and obligation to them. In a way, his desertion had taken more courage than simply running away in fear. His departure had been a principled, rational decision. It had more the trappings of a courageous act than of cowardice.

What with skirting so far as possible around military encampments and staying clear of the sounds of battle, it had taken him more than two months to find his way to Abilene, Texas. His growing up farming in Arkansas had embedded a love of the land within his very being. The land? It represented freedom. He fully expected to find that same freedom embodied in the vast openness of frontier prairies and hills. Thus far, he hadn't been disappointed. His journey across the northern reaches of Texas had impressed him with its vastness, with its big sky that downright overwhelmed the senses. Little wonder courageous pioneers journeyed from far and wide to find new opportunities here. McGraw was no exception.

Abilene thrived despite the war, or perhaps because of it. It was a hub for cattle drives. Yet it stood on the edge of an especially hostile portion of frontier still troubled by Comanche attacks. McGraw stabled his horse at the livery and made his way to the nearest saloon. As with many western towns, the local saloons were prime for learning about local goings on. He didn't reckon to be disappointed.

He ordered up a beer and looked around the saloon for a likely spot to park his trail-weary carcass. Over in a corner, an older bushy-mustached gent sat at a beat-up old oak table nursing a bottle of rot-gut whiskey. McGraw eased on over and cautiously grasped the chair. "Mind if I join you?" he asked.

The grizzled cowpoke looked up. "Sure. Set a spell," he said in a raspy voice punctuated with a faint grin. "Wait'n fer yuh." He laid fingers beside the brim of his beat-up old hat by nature of an affable greeting typical of cowboys on the range.

McGraw flashed back a quizzical look as he pulled the chair back from the table. He sat slowly to be sure the rickety contraption didn't collapse under him.

"Lookin' fer some drovers to move a fair-sized herd north," stated the trail-toughened cowboy. "Name's Walker," he added.

McGraw reckoned this was a man who sought men with enough confidence and moxie to ask to sit with him. "You know longhorns?" asked Walker.

"Ain't ever seen one, but I raised cows back in Arkansas. And I can ride just about any cayuse you put under me," McGraw responded.

Walker glanced at McGraw's boots. "Pretty fancy leathers yer wearin'. You a Reb or Yank?" he asked earnestly.

"Lost at Gettysburg. Retreated and kept retreating here to Abilene."

Walker smiled. "No matter. I pay $30 a month. Yuh git paid at the end of the drive."

Soon enough, McGraw was learning to drive beeves. Blessedly, he was a fast learner. He had to be, as he all-too-soon was driving a herd of longhorns northward.

The September sun poured out its wrath on the Texas Panhandle. Sweat trickled down McGraw's back. The wet, red bandana knotted around his neck did little to relieve the deadly September heat. In fact, it did virtually nothing. The only shade out here was the broad brim of his hat. It was his turn at drag, eating dust at the rear of the herd. He and his horse were caked nearly white.

McGraw had plenty of time to think back on his recent travails. He found himself haunted by the specter of his facing a war that seemed to grow ever more unjust and having found the courage to abandon the fray. Yet, his desertion hadn't mattered a hoot to Walker. In a perverse sense, rational thought had triumphed over any illusory sense of courage. The cannonball wound to his thigh had healed up well enough. Had he not cauterized it the first night out from Gettysburg, he might have lost the leg to infection. He recalled heating the saddle stirrup to nearly red-hot and applying it to the ugly gash before passing out. He'd likely screamed out. Fortunately, he'd journeyed far enough out of the hearing of fellow retreating Rebels. He was ever grateful that the Federals had been foolish enough to not pursue General Lee's army as it limped away to the Potomac River. He'd been fortunate on the second day to happen upon a poor farmer woman hanging clothes of about the right size to fit him. Except for his tack, boots, and the Sharps carbine, he had managed to fully rid himself of most vestiges of the Confederacy. He was officially a deserter, not that it mattered.

Prairie Dog—Dog for short or *Perro de la Pradera* in Spanish – had been the nickname the *vaqueros*, the Mexican cowboys, dubbed him owing to his penchant for occasionally falling off horses into the grasses, bushes, and prairie dog towns of the vast Texas grasslands. McGraw accommodated the name, but it stuck like a burr under his saddle. McGraw was no lightweight. He stood a tad better than six feet and weighed in at perhaps a couple of hundred well-muscled pounds. While an imposing figure in a saddle, he occasionally simply miscalculated, stopped too suddenly or turned too quickly, and wound up gracing the landscape. He'd even managed to fall on one of the furry prairie rodents, squashing the life from the poor little beast.

The drover life was a far cry from his growing up farming in Arkansas and surely far preferable to fighting a losing cause with the Confederate Army. He was challenged once about his service in the war, but a single punch from his angry fist ended the conversation.

As he looked out across the herd of longhorns stretching off into the distance and wrang the sweaty mud from his bandana, he caught motion in his peripheral vision. He'd never seen a Comanche before. It was only the third day of the drive, and he was about to be introduced.

The trail boss came galloping headlong toward him with rifle blazing. "Dammit, Dog! Start shootin'!" McGraw slid his Colt Army revolver from its holster, turned, and fired blindly just as a Comanche rode by close enough to feel the savage's hot breath. The attacker touched McGraw with a long stick.

Momentarily frozen, McGraw took in the fearsome black stripes painted across the warrior's face, coupled with his gruesome ear-shattering scream of triumph that seemed to epitomize the very essence of evil. It was as though Comanche horse and rider were one, as the attacker pivoted and began his deadly charge at McGraw with lance poised at shoulder level. The warrior's quite obvious intent was to drive the razor-sharp tip into the drover's chest.

Walker hollered, "Shoot him, dammit! The savage counted coup! Shoot!"

McGraw instinctively swung his gun around toward his foe, sort of aimed, and squeezed the trigger a second time. The bullet exploded from the muzzle and struck the Comanche full-on between the eyes. But there was no time for celebration, as he ducked the now errant lance, grabbed his Sharps as he slid from the saddle, and pulled his horse to earth. Using the cayuse as a shield, he could pick off targets at will. There were plenty to choose from; then, there were none. Quickly as the Comanche had appeared, they were gone.

Incredibly, the beeves had remained calm. Trail boss Walker began to account for his men. Other than the cookie taking a non-fatal arrow through his arm, no one had even been scratched. A quick inventory found four Comanche had gone to join the spirits of their forefathers.

McGraw finally looked down at the warrior he'd slain. The face with its lifeless eyes staring into space no longer appeared menacing. The savage's lance lay beside his body, its scalp trophies dangling in the prairie dust as worthless reminders of courage mixed with sheer savagery.

The trail boss rode up and placed his hand on McGraw's shoulder. "Nice shootin', Dog." He looked off in the direction the Comanche had retreated. "Folks talk about Comanche courage in battle, Dog. The savages are ferocious fighters...nasty as all hell."

McGraw offered a tight-lipped grimace. Seemed like just a few weeks back, he was blowing bluebelly officers from their saddles. Now? He sat on his horse watching the Comanches off in the distance as they paused on a ridge to raise lances and shout empty threats. He reckoned they would eventually fall to the onslaught of bigger armies with greater resources just as his rebellious Rebel compatriots were finding.

The trail boss had been pushing the drive hard, but now decided to ease up, letting the longhorns graze a bit to fatten up before the long push north to gold-mining territory. Soon, they'd reached the Canadian River and were drawing but a few miles south of the old trading post at Adobe Walls in the northern reaches of the Texas Panhandle.

Walker called McGraw over to him. "Dog, take Slim, Pug, and Gabby with yuh and see what's left up north at Adobe Walls." Walker had gained confidence in McGraw and reckoned he could spare his drovers in shifts to afford them a bit of relaxation at the remains of the trading post as well as to see whether the place might yet have commercial potential. The post had been closed by Kit Carson back in 1848, thanks in part to Jicarilla Apache hostilities. It was resupplied a year after Carson's visit, but it was said that its founder, William Bent, had finally blown the place up with gunpowder in frustration after hostiles had stolen or killed much of his stock.

There was no reason for the trail boss to think there could be the least bit of trouble, given the remoteness of the Adobe Walls ruins. "Rumor has it that some trade goods are cached among the rubble. See what's there, Dog," advised Walker as an aside to McGraw. He smiled at that unlikely eventuality. "No telling how much survived Bent blowing the place to bits." The trail boss reckoned that in a couple of days, the cattle drive would be passing Adobe Walls and then on through the rough terrain beyond the Santa Fe Trail toward Bent's Fort up on Colorado's Arkansas River. It made sense to scout ahead.

McGraw and his band of drovers wasted no time heading for the old post. It sure beat eating trail dust. Cookie packed them some grub, so they'd be fixed for a couple of days.

What could be seen and heard of Adobe Walls as McGraw and his companions approached was shrouded in an eerie quiet, as though not a soul breathed or might ever have breathed at the isolated post. A couple of vultures floated high above on thermal currents. McGraw saw the three wagons first, as they stood a lonely vigil just outside the rubble of the walls. Horses and oxen were nowhere to be seen. The wagons didn't look like the sort merchants used. The drovers cautiously rode closer. Closer inspection revealed that the wagons held the remains of household belongings and appeared to have been ransacked. Where were they from? How long had they been there? They were a long ride south of the Cimarron Cutoff from the Santa Fe Trail. What had driven them so far off course?

The cowboys dismounted while being ever-watchful of their surroundings. Only the squeaking of saddle leather, jingling of spurs, and occasional snorting and nickering of a horse broke the stillness. McGraw put a finger to his lips and cautioned his companions to slip their spurs into saddlebags. There was no telling what lay within the ruins. McGraw silently led the way with his Colt drawn and ready to fire. He nearly tripped over the body staked out in the shadows just inside the entrance. He gagged a moment at the corpse's missing scalp and the horror of the mutilation inflicted upon it. McGraw had heard that the Comanche were especially well known for their mastery of torture. He stepped around the hapless victim and walked into what appeared to be a courtyard framed out by the rubble of what remained of Adobe Walls. The drover behind him vomited his guts out.

A cautious McGraw stepped from the shadows, let his eyes adjust to the sunlight, and began to carefully scan his surroundings. He stopped in mid-scan. A solitary post stood before him. A woman half naked and covered in blood hung by her wrists. McGraw looked about and moved toward her. Incredibly, she was breathing. More accurately, she was gasping, taking in short, shallow breaths. McGraw's knife instantly found his hand. With his arm around her shoulders, he cut the suffering woman down.

McGraw held the woman as he took another cautionary scan of the ruins. He reckoned this indeed was Comanche work. They had finished wreaking their havoc and moved on. He wondered whether they might be the same band that attacked their trail drive just a couple of days back. In the vastness of the Texas Panhandle, any such question was unanswerable. War parties from various tribes roved the plains at will, taking revenge on the predations of the bluecoats when they weren't fighting among themselves.

He lay the woman gently at the base of the wooden post. His mind roiled, trying to grasp how one human could do this to another? He thought he had left the answer to that question on the gore-filled fields of Gettysburg. He shook his head at recollecting that horror. From the extent of the woman's wounds, he reckoned that the savages had left her for dead. They were almost right. He paused, as his eyes searched the ruins for some sort of shelter.

"Slim, fetch a bedroll. Let's get her inside what's left of that hut over there." He pointed to the remains of an old adobe structure with half a roof and some of its walls intact.

He looked down at the unconscious woman's peaceful expression, even as she still struggled to breathe. Her closed eyes gave no hint as to how much life yet survived within, nor what she had endured. But for a deep cut across her belly, most of her wounds appeared superficial, so far as McGraw could tell. If she survived, it would be the wounds to her mind that would take longest to heal… if ever. He gently lifted her and carried her limp form into the shelter of what remained of the adobe hut.

"Light a lamp or candle, Pug. Damn, but it stinks in here." Within the hut's shadows, he found a table that bore the scars of Bent's attempt to destroy the post.

Pug found a candle and struck a match. As the candle flame flickered to life, another gruesome sight was revealed. The bodies of three small children, a couple of men, and another woman were lying where they'd died defending the post. The victims likely hadn't been dead more than a day or so, but the pungent aromas of the beginnings of the moldering process filled the hut despite the dry Panhandle heat. Arrows and lance wounds had finished them all. Scalps had been lifted, even from the women and children. There was no way of knowing whether captives had been taken.

McGraw lay the woman on the blanket that Slim had spread across the table. He found himself taking charge. Maybe it was from his days not so long ago as sergeant, but he felt led to take command and no one was protesting.

"Pug, draw some water. Slim, you and Gabby haul these bodies out, grab shovels, and get to digging graves."

He turned back to the woman. She'd lost blood, but still breathed. He grabbed a dusty shirt he found on a nearby shelf, shook it out, and covered her nakedness as best he could. McGraw wasn't a praying man, but he closed his eyes and muttered a few words to the heavens. When his eyes reopened, he now noticed her beauty, the peace in her face as she lay totally vulnerable and clinging to life. He lifted the shirt to examine the wound across her belly. He shuddered. How could those heathens have done this?

"What are you going to do, just stare at her all day, Dog?" Pug had slipped in beside him with a leaky bucket of water and some spare bandanas that he'd dug from the drovers' saddlebags. Pug's chiding snapped McGraw from his momentary trance.

McGraw handed the drover a wet bandana. "Start at her feet, Pug. Be real gentle like." He scanned the shelves.

"Watcha needin', Dog?"

"Bottle of whiskey and a needle and thread." He lifted his own bloodied bandana from the gaping wound across the woman's belly. "Got to fix this, or she's a goner."

Pug pointed with his water-soaked and now bloodied bandana to a sheltered corner of the hut, scurried over, and grabbed a well-preserved whiskey jug. He popped the cork, took a whiff, and gave a satisfied smile. "She gonna drink it?" he asked, hoping there'd be some left for himself.

McGraw shook his head. "Got to clean the wound, Pug. Can't have it gettin' infected none. Must close it and stop the bleedin', or she'll die fer sure."

McGraw began to pull out drawers from the remains of what might have been a serviceable desk as he searched for needle and thread. Nothing. Of a sudden, his eyes widened, and he headed for his horse. He began rummaging through his saddlebags. "Ah…here we go," he muttered to himself, as he headed back to the woman. No self-respecting cowpoke would fail to include a needle and thread in his possibles bag.

McGraw threaded the needle and began stitching the wound together as gently as possible. The surgery, if you could legitimately call it that, seemed to take forever. The bleeding seemed to have stopped.

Slim walked in from burying the remains of the victims. "Anyone want to say a few words—?" He pulled up short, just as McGraw finished the impromptu surgery. Slim wretched involuntarily. "Damn, Dog." He half-stumbled as he backed out with a hand over his mouth.

McGraw glanced at Slim and wondered how the drover might have fared amid the gore and mayhem of Gettysburg? Soon enough,

189

McGraw was helping Pug clean her up. She seemed to be resting peacefully.

The woman's near-nakedness before the leering eyes of the drovers distressed McGraw. He left the hut to make a search of the wagons, finally finding a trunk with women's clothes. He rummaged through, found a blue gingham skirt and a blouse, and headed back to the adobe shelter.

"Whatcha gonna do?" asked Pug.

McGraw looked down at the woman as though trying to decide where to begin. "We're going to get her properly dressed," he answered. "And don't you be gawking no more, Pug." The cowboy's jaw had dropped as McGraw stripped off the bloodied remains of the woman's dress and fully revealed her nakedness. "Help me get these clothes on her, dammit."

They laid her now-clothed body out on a nearby pallet with a blanket for a pillow. McGraw kneeled beside her. "Pour some water into that tin cup," he said, tenderly raising the woman's head.

Pug smiled. "You gonna check her for leaks, Dog?"

McGraw's icy glare put an end to Pug's lame attempt at levity.

"Purty one, ain't she, Dog?"

McGraw put the cup to her lips, tilted the cup, and stroked her throat to get her to swallow. Pug was right. She was pretty. The fullness of her lips gave off a sultriness despite the circumstances. But she wasn't swallowing. He pried her mouth open.

"Oh, my God, Pug. The devils tried to cut her tongue out." He examined it as best he could. "It's mostly still there. I think it'll heal," he muttered.

McGraw stared at her. She was alive, but would she live? Whoever she was, the trauma had been appallingly cruel. She'd surely have more than physical scars.

Pug slipped the remains of a barely serviceable chair behind McGraw, enabling him to sit.

"Thanks, Pug." He pinched the bridge of his nose between thumb and forefinger as though trying to figure what might be done to ease their situation at Adobe Walls. Finally, he looked up at Pug. "Pug, get Slim and Gabby in here."

Slim came running but hesitated at the door, peeking in hesitantly lest he endure another gruesome surgery. "Yes, Dog?"

"I'm askin' you and Gabby to ride back to Mr. Walker and let him know what happened here," he said. "And fetch cookie." He knew that the trail cook had some medicines that might be helpful. "Tell him to bring medicine."

Slim and Gabby didn't need any coaxing. This place was far too creepy.

Pug was another matter. "Think I should go with them, Dog?"

"Nice try, Pug." McGraw flashed one of those looks that caused the drover to want to melt into the dust. Who was in charge had become ever clearer. "Don't know what we're facing here. Maybe them Comanche will come back."

Pug's eyes flitted between McGraw and the forms of Slim and Gabby already riding off into the distance. He was going to have to suck up his fears and muster some courage.

McGraw broke the spell. "Let's set a defense in case them heathens return," he said with a grim smile. He began picking up pieces of adobe rubble and stacking them around their position.

Pug hesitated, then joined in. "You done this sorta thing afore, Dog?"

McGraw didn't respond. They made short work of reinforcing the barrier. With a crude defensive wall now surrounding them, he cautiously walked over to his horse and drew the Sharps from its scabbard. He then attached what appeared to be a long metal tube.

"What the hell is that?" Pug's jaw dropped, but he quickly collected himself. He did recall what a telescopic sight was. "Whoa. You never did tell us what you did back east."

"Nope." McGraw ignored the question and slipped over beside the woman. "Pug, you take first watch. If any of them savages show up, just nudge me. Don't be sayin' a word."

Pug nodded. "One thing, Dog. I ne'er asked, but you ever been tight with a woman?"

McGraw said nary a word but laid his Bowie knife and Colt within easy reach on the edge of the pallet. He held the Sharps securely across his lap. Satisfied, he drank in a long look at the wounded woman. Her eyelids fluttered a time or two, but there was no other life sign. *Tight with a woman,* he thought. He'd never given it much mind. If there was praying to be done, now was the time.

Night fell, and but for the illumination from moon and stars, it was a challenge to see more than a couple of feet beyond the shadows. McGraw hadn't nodded off for but an hour, when Pug touched his arm. The look in the cowboy's eyes said everything. He held up three fingers.

Colby McGraw shook off sleep cobwebs. He placed a finger beside his lips as a sign of silence and motioned Pug to watch the makeshift doorway. McGraw's hand gripped the Colt revolver. As the drover set his position, a new threat emerged. Above the muffled voices of the intruders, McGraw heard the telltale rattle.

Pug heard it, too. He was a few steps away and helpless to react without making a din.

The snake had slithered its way to the end of the pallet near the woman's feet. There it sat, angry, coiled, and rattling up a storm. McGraw knew from having nearly landed on one a few days back that this was what Mr. Walker had called a prairie rattlesnake. No matter its species, it had to be dealt with quickly, quietly, and—most importantly—effectively. His hand slowly grasped the Bowie knife. As the snake began its attack, McGraw slashed upward, his razor-sharp blade catching the rattler in mid-strike. The near-headless creature writhed a moment in the dirt until the drover's boot ground it into the adobe dust. He glanced at the sleeping woman. She hadn't stirred.

Pug had no time to admire McGraw's handiwork. There was barely time to catch a breath before a deafening blast boomed from the drover's Colt. A Comanche warrior fell through the makeshift doorway. Yelps and the sound of retreating hoofbeats followed seconds later. Pug glanced at McGraw and shrugged admiringly. The drover was indeed deadly accurate and confirmed in Pug's mind what McGraw's role in the war had been.

A groan emanated from the pallet nestled in the dark shadows. The woman was coming to, roused by the gunfire. Her eyelids fluttered open, revealing an abject fear lurking deep from within her very soul.

McGraw slowly reached over and gently placed his hand on her arm as though offering reassurance, but she recoiled in horror, pulling back to the far side of the pallet. She grimaced in pain from the raw wound across her belly, as her fear-laden eyes darted from McGraw to Pug and back.

"We're friends, ma'am. You're safe." He strove to speak softly yet confidently to her but to little avail. She closed her eyes and faded back into the makeshift bed. McGraw shook his head in dismay at her fright, then turned to Pug. "Likely the savages don't know who we are or how many. They ain't comin' back until daylight," he said with false confidence. He looked down at the dead warrior. "Let's drag him oughta here, Pug."

The sun had barely peeked over the eastern horizon, when the two Adobe Walls defenders found themselves greeted by the mounted silhouettes of a half dozen whooping and yelping Comanche. They were keeping what they deemed to be a safe distance but seemed considerably disturbed at what hung outside the main entrance to the ruins. In a ghastly attempt to offer bad medicine, McGraw had placed the Comanche savage's head atop a post. It was bad medicine for the hostiles. It was a hideous act, but so was the torture and scalping of the victims at Adobe Walls.

In the span of but a minute and with unerring aim, McGraw's Sharps carbine unhorsed two Comanche. This medicine was too great, as the remaining four offered a less-than-confident war whoop and galloped off.

McGraw had just taken a breath aimed at relaxing, when he heard a weak gasping sound from behind him.

"Looks like she's comin' 'round agin, Dog," said Pug.

McGraw eased over to the pallet. He dared not touch her again, given her earlier reaction. He tried to offer a comforting smile. Growing up farming in the hot Arkansas sun punctuated by a habit of settling squabbles with violence, months of marches and battles for a less-than-noble cause, and now miles of driving beeves across the scorching prairies of the Texas Panhandle had left their imprints on Colby McGraw's face in the form of scars and lines. He looked older than his twenty-four years, as though he had already lived a lifetime. Yet, now the eyes looking up at him from the cluster of blankets offered nary a hint of the revulsion or fear they'd shown before. McGraw began to feel encouraged. She just might pull through.

McGraw motioned to Pug. "Keep an eye out. Maybe Mr. Walker will get here soon with the cookie," he said hopefully. He turned to the woman. Far as he could tell, she'd been oblivious to both the rattlesnake and the latest Comanche attack.

She was struggling to open her eyes, to bring them into focus.

"Do you have a name?" he gently asked.

She looked about. A hint of panic born of fear held fast in her eyes. Her fingers trembled.

McGraw could never hope to imagine the sheer terror she must have endured.

Her swollen tongue, coupled with suffering from the trauma of the attack, made words difficult to form. "Becka," she whispered through parched lips.

McGraw smiled as tenderly as he could. "Me, Colby...Colby McGraw." He reached into his possibles bag, felt around, and came out with a tin of bear grease. Popping the lid, he swiped a bit with his finger and gently applied some to her lips.

Becka drew back at his touch, but then relaxed just a little as she appreciated the soothing effect of the balm. She nodded almost imperceptibly and tried to smile, raising her arm perhaps an inch as though to gesture at him before it fell back limply.

McGraw continued. "We are driving cattle north and happened by," he said, praying she was comprehending him. He was dying to know what had happened here at Adobe Walls. The attack by Comanche had been obvious, but how and why the wagons had journeyed to this godforsaken shamble of a post not so much. How much of the horror might she recall? He'd talked with survivors of battles like Shiloh and Antietam, many not even remembering they'd been in a fight.

Becka closed her eyes as though in deep thought. Of a sudden, they opened wide, casting an expression more of panicky desperation than fear. But her wild gaze quickly settled on McGraw, and she quieted. Her hand grasped his with some newfound strength. "No e-eave," she said pleadingly.

"I'm not goin' anywhere, Becka." He said it so easily as to surprise himself with his own compassionate assurance. He suddenly found himself growing reflective. So many times on the trail and surely during nights, he'd weighed his wartime role fighting Yankees and now as a drover taking on the much-feared Comanche. He was good with a rifle. It was said by those putting together legendary tall tales that McGraw likely could shoot the wings off a mosquito at "a hunnert yards." The morality of his former job with the Rebels weighed heavily. Was picking off officers or gunners or savages killing or murder? Was there a difference? None of them had a prayer of fighting back, of avoiding his lethal purposes delivered at a distance. They'd simply been targets. Nothing personal. Was that courageous? On the other hand, a Comanche warrior charging full-on, aiming to kill you with his lance…well, killing for self-protection seemed to rise above sitting in a tree or on some knoll, putting bullets through unsuspecting victims. He had tried oh-so-vainly to settle the difference in his mind. He sighed, brought himself back to the here and now, and turned back to Becka. "How'd you get here?"

"Y-y-y-ost."

It took him a moment to realize her tongue wouldn't let her make an "L" sound. "Lost? You fall behind?"

She nodded. Her part of the wagon train had apparently been waylaid and tried to catch up but had taken a wrong turn. It was easy on the vastness of the prairie. "You had three wagons. How many people?"

The thought clearly brought pain to her. She raised both hands. "En."

McGraw closed his eyes. He prayed she could handle his next words. "We buried seven," he said in a near whisper. There was really no way to shield her from the horror.

Despite her weakness, her hand went to her mouth, stifling a gasp. Her eyes glazed over, and she lapsed into a hazy stupor of physical and emotional pain.

McGraw hung his head and sighed. The Comanche had indeed taken captives; likely children. He tried to sense what must have been Becka's deep anguish. She had survived, but what of those other two? Were they her children?

Pug stuck his head inside the hovel. "Here come our boys, Dog!"

McGraw's relief was palpable. He stood, looked down at Becka to be sure she lay at peace, and strode out into the midday sun to greet the trail boss who had dismounted along with Slim, Gabby, and Alphonso the cookie. "You're a sight for sore eyes, Mr. Walker," McGraw said.

Having ridden past two dead Comanche warriors on the ride in and now seeing the warrior's head impaled on the post, a properly impressed Walker instantly became very curious. "The Comanche attack again?" he questioned what seemed obvious.

McGraw smiled. "They might have considered it," he deadpanned.

Walker smiled a tad and shook his head ever so slightly at McGraw's understatement. "Comanche call it *sinupu*; big medicine. Yuh likely scared 'em off, Dog."

McGraw shrugged. "We have one survivor…a woman. Name's Becka. Cookie needs to look her over. She's hurt bad. Might have been a couple folks escaped or captured. Likely children. Don't know yet."

Walker motioned the cookie to go inside. "See what yuh can do, Alphonso."

"They got separated from a wagon train, then lost," McGraw continued. He went on to describe the Comanche threat they had defended against.

Alphonso emerged but a few moments later. "*Quién es cirujano?*" He smiled. "Who sewed her up?"

McGraw blushed. "Had a needle and thread."

A grim expression found its way across Alphonso's face. "They cut out…" His words trailed off.

McGraw's jaw dropped. Those heather bastards. "Oh, my God," he rasped.

"You saved her life, Dog," assured Alphonso, trying to be sympathetic to McGraw's pain.

Walker placed his hand on McGraw's shoulder. Reality necessarily set in. "We got a herd to take north, McGraw. Can't be lingerin' here," he said, looking Dog squarely in the eyes, "If yuh wanna hang here a bit and catch up with us later, I understand. Won't cost yuh pay."

McGraw thought on that. "Thanks, Mr. Walker. Maybe I can get her back to her wagon train. Might be family or folks she knows."

"We'll head out in the morning before sunrise. I'll leave you some food just in case yuh have to spend a few days here," Walker stated flatly. Then his gaze softened. "Yer one brave cowboy, McGraw."

McGraw simply smiled. A hint of a blush colored his already sunburned neck.

Alphonso did what he could to doctor Becka. He remained amazed at McGraw's handiwork. "She no travel for maybe three, maybe four days," he told McGraw. "*Mujer muy bonita, pero muy triste. Y trájico.*"

McGraw nodded. Indeed, pretty and sad surely described the young woman. Tragic went without saying.

The drovers departed just before sunrise. A single shard of light now pierced the space surrounding the crumbling adobe walls of the makeshift shelter. Walker's parting words had been, "Good luck, Dog. Yer a courageous soul."

Pug reluctantly said his goodbyes. The call to courage conflicted with his feeling of being odd man out with Dog and the woman. By Pug's reckoning, the Comanche had already been beaten back and were faced with decidedly bad medicine. McGraw would likely be safe.

With the drovers gone, McGraw now found himself alone but for the woman who'd fallen to his care. He'd willingly accepted the duty. If there was any courage within him to be mustered, now was the time. He felt a trickle of sweat inch down his back and swiped his forehead with his bandana. Dang, but it was going to be a scorcher.

Shortly after the departure of the drovers, Becka awakened. It was a struggle, but she managed to prop her head and shoulders up against the rolled blanket that served as a pillow. She looked intently at McGraw as he entered the hut.

McGraw felt her gaze. He reckoned that his strong presence had apparently begun to hold a sense of security for her. He could see her eyes fully take him in as he strode toward her.

By now, McGraw had pretty much shaken off the dust of the cattle drive and appeared reasonably presentable. His blue shirt had the effect of setting off his crystal blue eyes. He had removed his chaps for now and tucked his pants into the by now well-worn but still serviceable boots. The Colt revolver shoved into his belt was ever present, and the Sharps carbine was always within easy reach. McGraw looked comfortingly at her. He absentmindedly rubbed his tough, but as she had found out, kind and gentle hands together. In a less desperate time, he figured that she might have wondered at the stories behind the craggy lines of his face that made him look older than his years.

"We need to get you home, Becka." He strove to sound earnestly hopeful. With any luck, he just might be able to do it.

Of a sudden, her expression turned sad. It was as though some memory had awakened within her. Tears formed in the corners of her eyes, her beautiful green eyes. Her lips came together to form a question that seemed to come from some inner depth of her soul, yet one to which she intuitively already knew the answer. "Buh-buh?" she offered through swollen lips.

McGraw sighed. He looked away a moment, as he fought back the urge to cry. "No baby. There's no baby, Becka," he said ever-so-softly.

Her countenance now held a certain resigned sadness. She had indeed sensed the answer before asking the question. She had felt the emptiness within her. She had needed confirmation, be it ever-so-hard to bear. Life had been ripped from her body and her soul. Her eyes darted about, as though seeking some safe place to settle. "Home?" Her trembling lips were punctuated with grief-laden eyes. No more tears, but so sad. No one, least of all Colby McGraw, could ever grasp the depth of her loss.

McGraw could only hope for resilience from her. She had survived thus far. "I will get you home, Becka," he said as reassuringly as possible. He hoped he had enough courage for the two of them.

A winsome smile managed to crease her lips as she looked up. "No Becka."

McGraw looked puzzled.

Her tongue was struggling to twist around another sound. "Er... ruh...Ruhbecka," she finally managed to say.

"Rebecca?"

She smiled almost imperceptibly and nodded just a bit. "Duh... Duh...Dunn."

"Rebecca Dunn," McGraw repeated. Now, he recalled the torn Bible buried with the man tortured at the entrance to Adobe Walls. The name on its title page had been Grayson Dunn. McGraw caught her gaze. "Grayson Dunn?" he asked gently. A glimmer of hope in her eyes was quickly dashed by the drover's anguished look of despair.

It was as if she'd once again known the truth of it before he answered. Rebecca reached up with her arms. "Cuh-Cuhby M-M-Gaw," she called out to him.

They found themselves embracing as tightly as her wounds would permit. It was hard to tell who felt more secure, more safe. They had, by fate, become two souls grasping at new life. He had been of a mind to take her north and meet up with the wagon train that had left her behind. He could still rejoin the trail drive. Then again, he'd had passing thoughts of building a ranch up near the Yellowstone or even the North Platte. He'd heard the country up there was bountiful in its majesty and beauty. "Rebecca Dunn," he whispered softly in her ear. He felt her press more urgently against him. McGraw's thoughts drifted within the quiet peace of their embrace, as there were yet challenges to be overcome.

"Cuhby brave," he heard her muffled whisper buried in the folds of his shirt.

Brave? Was he really? Is this what his courage had wrought? He had indeed persevered in withstanding dangers and shown the moral strength that grew from what had been duty. Could there yet be hope? Arkansas and Gettysburg were long behind him. Perhaps, just perhaps, there was hope for the future after all.

In the silent moment shared between them, they were oblivious to the surrounding world. A warm desert breeze wafted through the ruins.

A breeze? A hint of buffalo dung? Startled, McGraw pushed away from Rebecca and turned while simultaneously reaching for the Colt in his waistband.

McGraw came up shooting. A Comanche arrow pierced his thigh, but the warrior never saw it strike his target. Had McGraw not stood, the shaft would have ended the fight before a shot was fired.

Facing a second warrior, McGraw grabbed his Sharps carbine and clubbed the attacker senseless with but a single stroke. Three more Comanche tried to push into the makeshift shelter but reeled back aghast at the carnage McGraw had wrought. More blasts from the Colt shattered the air.

A prairie dog poked up his head, looked around, and then dove into the safety of his burrow as war-paint bedecked warriors galloped past.

The arrow in McGraw's leg hurt like hell. Grimacing, he gripped the shaft and pulled it free. He nearly passed out.

McGraw staggered back toward Rebecca. Blessedly, she had fainted and not borne witness to the fight. He freed a Comanche arrow embedded between the adobe blocks just above where she lay. She need never know of it. He sat protectively on the edge of the pallet and stared back at the two dead attackers. Courage? He reckoned that he'd mustered plenty, likely owing to his sense of duty. The Comanche had paid the ultimate price for theirs.

McGraw turned back to Rebecca. She slept. Could they begin a new life? Yes, the North Platte country sounded about right.

FRONTIER JUSTICE

What is frontier justice? Who defines it's bounds?
When is justice just? Where is it to be found?
Descended from Hammurabi's Code to Dead Sea scrolls.
What is law in the west? For whom does it's bell toll?
Can justice be found in America's western doins?
Justice? From gold's boomtowns to ghostly ruins;
From ancient kingdoms and the Bible we invest
To the prairies and mountains of our frontier west
Men of the west found justice enslaved to the law.
Punishment, vengeance were but broken jackstraws.

Where then is justice? What indeed is the justice?
Judgment, imprisonment, retribution caught in an abyss.
Cortez' Aztecs, Pizarro's Incas, de Vaca's frontier plains;
To southern cotton fields, tobacco barns, and slavers' chains;
Justice was a shallow game, a life default, a claim we tried.
As lawbreakers flourished, so frontier justice died.
Dare we dwell on justice for past and present sins?
Just how does the wheel of western justice spin?
Justice remains an elusive charade, be it of utopian ilk,
Divine or soulless, it lurks for the unwary to bilk.

Delivered by the gun or the hangman's noose,

Justice dealt to desperados ever on the loose.
Frontier justice where lawmen were few and far between;
Mobs of vigilantes delivered justice sight unseen.
Ambushers, cowards, await the unwary;
Their frontier justice delivered like the tooth fairy.
What then is justice? Who defines it's bounds?
When is frontier justice just? Where is it to be found?
Mired in muddy justice, the red pill or the blue pill we'll see;
God forgives. In the end, "the truth will set you free."

DEAD MEN TELL NO TALES

Jesse James, Billy the Kid, Butch Cassidy were a few;
Bad men to the bone, broke ev'ry law they knew.
They courted mayhem wherever it could be found,
The rough and tumble frontier was their playground.

Oh, the likes of John Wesley Hardin's or King Fisher's breed,
Raised all fire and brimstone by the devil's seed.
Bandits caught in evil's self-destructive snare,
Hatred, greed, lust, revenge; oh, such shallow fare.

Desperados wrought their havoc riding from town to town.
But folk were done; the villains must be brought down.
And so the law came riding across prairies wide,
Strong branch and noose became frontier justice's guide.

One by one the lawbreakers fell, and one by one they died,
Their feats told in pulp rags that young readers' eyed.
Writers forged their legends, overlooked all their fails;
But in the end, we know dead men tell no tales.

A LOOK AT NUECES JUSTICE: LIFE, LOVE, AND LAW ON THE STRIP

THE TUMBLEWEED SAGAS BOOK ONE

In the heart of the untamed Texas frontier lies the Nueces Strip.

It's 1856, and the once mighty Texas Rangers have been defunded, leaving a lawless land in their wake. But for Ranger Captain Luke Dunn, known to the Comanche as Ghost-Who-Rides, duty calls louder than any official mandate.

Luke's unyielding quest to bring justice to the lawbreakers of the Nueces Strip has propelled him into a deadly cycle where hunters have become the hunted. From Corpus Christi to Laredo, the land is rife with cattle thieves, ruthless murderers, and fierce Comanche warriors. And as young Elisa's heart burns with unspoken love for the stoic ranger and the vengeful Carlos Perez seeks retribution, infamy burns brighter than the Texas heat.

With a crime wave unleashed and everything converging in the small, turbulent town of Nuecestown, Texas, can Luke make a final stand for the justice he believes in—no matter the cost?

AVAILABLE NOW

ACKNOWLEDGMENTS

Authoring books simply doesn't happen in a vacuum. The author provides the creative talent and crafts the stories, but there's so much more that demands acknowledgment. So it is with *Tumbleweed Tumblings: Western Tales & Verses*. I've been blessed with many friends and family who have supported my writings. My wife Carolyn's reviews and encouragement were a huge help, along with very important tech support from our sons, Mike and Matt.

Other supporters have included Cara Miller, Jim May, Ernie Angell, Chris Haug, Alan Bruzee, and my dear cousins Johnny Dunn, Jim & Cindy Holmgreen, Eddie Thornton, Joseph Meaney, and Father Bob Dunn. Many more friends have contributed support at some level to the creation and publication of *Tumbleweed Tumblings*, be it encouragement, wild compliments, critiques, or advice.

Whom you hang with is a critically important element of an author's creative experience. I'm ever grateful to Lisa Cantwell for her efforts with Catoctin Voices poetry gatherings, for the Gettysburg poetry group, and to the Texas and the Pennsylvania poetry societies. The Western Writers of America has been a tremendous asset toward my crafting of impactful novels, alternate history, short stories, and historical fiction biographies. A group of writers known as the Gettysburg Writers Brigade actually inspired me to begin writing short stories. It started off as a diversion, but it eventually grabbed me. As to verse, I've been a poet since ninth grade.

My heart also goes out to my friend Murphy Givens, the retired *Corpus Christi Caller-Times* journalist who inspired and supported my creative efforts. Murphy passed away in late December 2020.

Naturally, I am majorly grateful to the wonderful folks at Wolfpack Publishing. The team they bring to publishing is first-rate in performing the myriad tasks that lead to successful book sales.

Most of my authoring has occurred in my office as decorated to channel my inner Texan, but my creative juices have often been inspired and imagination stoked in cafés and coffee houses across America. My favorites were Hester's Café & Coffee Bar in Corpus Christi, TX; Nueces Café in Robstown, TX; Java Ranch Espresso Bar & Café in Fredericksburg, TX; PAX Coffee & Goods in Kerrville, TX; Ragged Edge Coffee House and Bantam Coffee Roasters in Gettysburg, PA; 1889 Coffee House in Helena, MT; Dunn Brothers Coffee in Rapid City, SD; Postmasters Coffee & Bakery and Brio Coffeehouse in Waynesboro, PA; Birdie's Café and American Ice Co Café in Westminster, MD; Deja Brew Coffee House in New Oxford and Deja Brew at Miney Branch in Carroll Valley, PA; and Baltimore Coffee & Tea Co., Frederick Coffee Company & Café, and Dublin Roasters in Frederick, MD. I must admit to also frequenting a few Dunkin Donuts and Starbucks around our fine nation. The décors and easy-listening music in these fine establishments, combined with savory cups of coffee, tended to set me in the right creative frame of mind.

Last but not least, I'm especially thankful for the many folks who have read and enjoyed my books.

Thanks to all of you.

ABOUT THE AUTHOR

Multiple-award-winning author Mark Greathouse is a fifth-generation Texan devoted to history and writing western genre fiction. He has published fourteen western novels, an anthology, and a biography, as well as published western history articles in various magazines and newspapers. He received a 2025 Western Writers of America Spur Finalist Award for Short Fiction with "Prairie Dog" published in a local anthology. *Guns on the Guadalupe: Justice on the River*, published by Wolfpack Publishing, continues Greathouse's passion for weaving fiction in a historical setting. He crafts an engaging adventure, featuring an ensemble of captivating characters woven into compellingly complex subplots. Importantly, he has stayed true to the western story being America's morality story, as good triumphs over evil. Whether expressed in his epic western genre novels or adventure-laced biographies, he couples a soul-penetrating creative spirit with extensive historical research that attracts a broad spectrum of readers. Greathouse is a member of Western Writers of America and several poetry societies. He holds BA and MBA degrees. Greathouse lives in Southern Pennsylvania but travels west regularly to walk in the footsteps of his characters.

* 9 7 9 8 8 9 5 6 7 2 2 8 0 *